The Mage of Ghostra

FRANK DECARIO

authorHOUSE®

AuthorHouse™
1663 Liberty Drive
Bloomington, IN 47403
www.authorhouse.com
Phone: 833-262-8899

Published by AuthorHouse 12/14/2020

ISBN: 978-1-6655-1047-9 (sc)
ISBN: 978-1-6655-1049-3 (hc)
ISBN: 978-1-6655-1048-6 (e)

Library of Congress Control Number: 2020924610

Print information available on the last page.

1

Hɪɢʜ ᴀᴛᴏᴘ ᴀ ʜɪᴅᴅᴇɴ ᴍᴏᴜɴᴛᴀɪɴ lays the majestic temple of Ghostra standing tall against the backdrop of fluffy clouds. The Temple covers the entire top of the mountain with a large ornate dome in the center with two Golden Dragons on either side.

The temple as well as the mountain are Magically shielded and invisible to all.

Within the temple two men stand looking down on the natural cloud formation that surrounds the mountain. Talking with a serious look on their face. They discuss a matter of grave importance.

The first man Richard Graham a young man perhaps in is late thirty's, dressed in blue trousers, blue shirt with strange Markings, and a blue cape is explaining to Dade Morgan, a handsome man who appears to be Perhaps in his mid-forties dressed similarly to Richard Graham only in all gray, that the one they have been searching for is in danger.

"Look Dade" Richard explains, "I've just received word that the one we've been searching for the past four years is in serious trouble."

"Where is he" asks Dade, "we're not sure" says Mark, "but word has come that the Demon Asuroff has been sent to destroy him, if we lock in on the demon it will lead us to him, of course we'll have to get to him before Asuroff does"

"Well that sounds like a plan" says Dade," but we have to be Sure, I'll consult Aserran, if it's true I'll go and extract the subject myself just In case it turns out to be a trap".

"Why is it do you suppose that we haven't been able to find him all these years". Dade looks at him," he must have a Powerful Magical shield surrounding him, the questions are who was powerful enough to create the shield, and was it done to protect him, or to hide him from us".

Dade hastily exits the room, leaving Richard alone looking apprehensive about the situation.

The place is the West coast of the northern continent in an old abandoned factory where many homeless are staying for shelter. The building is old dilapidated and condemned, but still usable for those with nowhere else to go. In the large main room of what once housed a thriving Garment business, sitting in front of the third box on the left sits Michael Reynolds a young eighteen-year-old boy who has been on his own since his father was killed in an automobile accident when he was just fifteen, his Mother passed away when he was born during child birth and it had been just him and his father up until the accident.

He was sitting holding his skateboard looking up and out the broken windows watching the sun go down, wondering where little Evelyn Grant was. Evelyn was twelve Michael had found little Evie over a year earlier after she had run away from an abusive foster care home and now he looks after her like she was his little sister.

Mike was getting a little worried because he'd told her many times about not being out after sunset, and sunset was fast approaching. He got up and began to pace back and forth Imagining what he was going to say for this latest infraction of the rules, when from behind him came a familiar voice, it was Evie.

She could see he was upset so she said, as if nothing as wrong, "Hi Mike, looking for me"? Mike was noticeable upset but calmly said "Evie you know better than to stay out this late".

"But Mike, it's not dark yet and you said I should always be back by dark". "Don't get technical with me miss you know this isn't the best neighborhood and you shouldn't be wondering around on your own. When I'm working these odd jobs I can't look out for you so you need to stay close by so I don't have to worry when I can't find you."

Evie tried to lighten the situation "Sorry Mike, But I made some money too. See".

Evie had twenty dollars and some change that she handed to Mike. Michael looked at her for a moment, "Evie tell me you haven't been ripping

People off again". She said "Well I have to help out too don't I". "Evie if you get caught doing this they'll throw you so far into a foster care hole that you won't see the light of day until your twenty one. Please Evie we'll make out Ok I can feel it, you just need to trust me". "Ok Mikey what ever you say and I do trust you".

It's real nice outside Mikey can we go outside and sit for awhile and look at the stars. Sure Evie but I don't know if we'll see many stars through the smog, and we should get to sleep early cause I've got a long day tomorrow, Ted the guy I worked for last week will pay me fifty bucks to help him clean out some apartments he's fixing up.

After a half hour or so of smog watching Michael and Evie went inside and crawled into their two bedroom box for the night. Laying on his sleeping bag staring up at the cardboard box Michael wondered if his life would ever change for the better, he was a smart kid and knew he'd have to find a real job, he also knew that in order to get a good job he'd have to get some more schooling, but with little money and the authorities looking for Evie, getting the training he needed wasn't going to be easy, but he was determined to do it somehow, for Evie's sake if not for his own. He knew he'd be able to make out fine, but he was determined to provide a stable environment for her, this was no place for her, she needed more than a box in a broken down building, she needed a home and school and friends her own age. The people they knew here were shady to say the least and a bad influence on Evelyn. All she was learning here was how to rip people off and get in trouble instead of playing with dolls and friends. Mike closed his eyes and as thousands of thoughts flashed through his head he slowly drifted off to sleep.

The following morning they woke shortly after dawn and already you could tell it was going to be a beautiful day. Michael broke out the cereal and the pint of milk he picked up on the way back yesterday, without a refrigerator they can't keep it more than a day, he also fired up the portable one burner camping stove so they could have their coffee before the days start. After a quick breakfast Michael got his things together for the days work. As he was about to leave he turned to Evelyn and said "Evie promise me you won't go anywhere today", Oh come on Mikey, I don't want to hang around here all day". "Please Evie I've got a real strange feeling about today, Stay here today and tomorrow I promise I'll take off so you and I can go somewhere and just have some fun, maybe even go to the movies, Promise me". "OK but I'm holding you to your promise. "Alright Evie I'll see you later."

Michael rushed off not wanting to be late and miss out, fifty bucks for a few hours work ain't bad and they can sure use the money. Michael got to the meeting place and waited, Ted hadn't arrived yet so mike just looked around, he couldn't shake the strange feeling he had since he got up. Then he spotted Ted's Pickup coming down the street toward him, he watched as Ted pulled up to the sidewalk and exited the truck, as he approached.

"Michael" he said "hey kid, Ready for some heavy work?"

Michael wanting to appear eager said "Sure thing, looking forward to it". Than out of the corner of his eye he saw a strange figure coming toward them fast. As it got closer he realized that it was some kind of creature he'd never seen before "What the hell is that" he said as he began to back away. As Ted turned to see what Michael was talking about the creature lunged forward Striking Ted knocking him to the ground, Michael looked but Ted wasn't moving, so he turned and ran but the creature was to fast, it struck Michael in the back sending him flying forward as he fell to the ground he rolled over to get a look at what was attacking him, the creature was hideous it looked almost like one of the stone gargoyles that can be seen on some of the older building in town. Mikes heart was pounding so hard he could barely breath, his mind was racing as fast as his heart, he didn't know what to do.

The creature stopped running and came toward Michael and as he did his fingernails were getting longer like sharp razors which sent Michael into total panic, fear gripped him like a vise. Suddenly from behind him he heard a cracking sound like a whip, then a second whooshing sound and a bright ball shot past him striking the creature square in the chest, sending it back with great force about thirty feet, it was only because of a parked car it's momentum was stopped. The car looked like it was hit by a truck a huge dent in the side. The creature however only seemed stunned, it got back up shook off the effects, glanced in Mikes direction growled and ran off. Michael turned and there he saw Dade walking toward him.

Michael couldn't immediately talk or stand his whole body was shaking, After a moment he gained some composure and asked the stranger who just saved him " who are you", "My name is Dade", Still stuttering slightly " What was that thing, and how did you do that"? Dade Replied "everything will be explained, but not here we have to go". Mike was trying to gather his thoughts " Go, Go where" Dade didn't want to waste time so he said simple "someplace safe", after his ordeal Mike wasn't feeling very trusting " I know you just saved my life, but I don't even know you, and you want me to go somewhere with you". "Kid we need to go and we have to go now before it returns and brings some friends".

In the distance Ted starts to move, he's curled up and moaning in apparent pain. Mike turns and says "we have to help him". Dade Raises his arm and waves his wand and Ted stops moving. Mike looked shocked "What did you do to him". Don't worry Kid he'll sleep for awhile and wake up feeling good as new with no memory of what happened.

"OK Dade how did you do that". "look all your questions will be answered, but not now and not here, **We need to go**". Dade got closer to Michael and Raised his wand, there was a slight glow, a cracking sound, a flash and when Michael opened his eyes he found himself in Ghostra. All he could say is "WOW! Where are we now". Dade explained "this is Ghostra the temple at the top of the world, this is where you will discover who you truly are, and where you will realize your full potential". Michael looked at him totally confused, " What do you mean". First "what is your name?". "my name is Michael, Michael Reynolds". "Well Michael Reynolds I know it's difficult for you to grasp right now but you are a MAGE and we have been searching for you for some time. "A Mage what is that like a magician?" "no not quite a magician is a trickster, an illusionist, someone with no magical powers who uses illusion to give the appearance of magic for entertainment", a Mage uses true magic for the benefit of everyone". Michael looks at Dade as if he were nuts, "sorry but I think you got the wrong guy, I'm just a kid who lives in a box with" Suddenly Michael remembers "Oh my god Evie, I need to get to Evie". "Who is Evie Michael". "Evelyn, She's like my little sister I'm responsible for her. Dade looks at Michael, he sees how worried he is but also realizes the Dangers " You can't leave here until your magically ready to defend yourself, you would be in great danger back there plus you need to start your training as soon as possible". "Maybe Dade, but I can't leave her there, she won't be able to manage on her own, she needs me. Dade looked at Michael for a long moment then said "OK Michael close your eyes". Michael looked at Dade than did as he asked. "Now Michael Picture the place where Evelyn is, now picture her in your mind". Dade closed his eyes and with palms facing upward raised his arms. Suddenly there was the familiar cracking sound and Evelyn appeared before him.

Slightly disoriented with a terrified look on her face she screamed and started away from the man in front of her. Michael opened his eyes and smiled when he saw Evelyn, He called her name, she turned Saw Michael and ran to him throwing her arms around him. "Michael what happened I was just sitting in front of our place and then there was a bright flash and I was here, where are we and what is this place. "I'm not sure myself, but this is Dade he brought you here when I told him I wouldn't stay without you."

"Stay what do you mean stay, where are we? I'm scared Mike." Dade interrupted their conversation, "I'm sorry Evelyn But all I can say right now is that Michael is in danger and I brought you both here for protection." "Danger, what kind of danger." "Michael can explain to you later what happened in the meantime we need to get you both settled in. Evelyn if you'll just go with Elaina she'll show you to your room."

Evie looked to her right where Elaina approached, Elaina is a lovely young girl about the same age as Michael with long auburn hair dressed all in white, she seemed to glow as she neared. Dade introduced her "Elaina is a priestess here in the temple and she will see to your needs." "I don't want to leave Mike." "Michael will be along shortly his room will be next to yours."

Elaina stopped before the young girl and bowed slightly and said in a soft voice "if you'll please come with me Evelyn, I'll show you to your room". "Your very pretty" Evie said to her.

Elaina just smiled and blushed a little, Michael also thought she was very beautiful, Elaina looked toward Michael smiled and blushed even more, She bowed once again toward Michael. "This way Evelyn let's get you settled, I think you'll enjoy your stay here, Michael will join you in a little while, I think they need to talk." "OK, Elaina and you can just call me Evie."

After Elaina and Evie left the room Michael turned to Dade. "Look Dade I still have no Idea what is going on, why was that thing trying to kill me? In fact I don't even know what it was. You said I'm, what did you call it a wizard or something, which by the way I doubt, I've never done anything Magical. Please just explain what's going on before I go crazy."

Dade looks at Michael, wondering what the best way to explain it so someone with no previous knowledge could understand. " Ok Michael, I'll try to explain it in simple terms from the beginning. First you need to understand That real magic does exist, it's been around since the beginning of time. We don't know how and those that do don't talk about it." Mike interrupts "those who know, what do you mean." "Don't worry about that now, you'll learn soon enough, First there are many levels of magic. There are Witches and Worlocks, Shaman, Witch Doctors, Medicine Men Etc.

I hate to group them all together, they all have different Philosophies and intentions for their craft, but they are all similar in that they have no inborn magical abilities, they gain their magic through information passed down from those who came before, they focus their minds using potions, symbols and images, they cast their spells into the ether or universe and wait for their spells to manifest, sometime they do and sometimes the don't. that's why witches form covens it helps to have multiple minds focusing together. But That's also why some were killed during the insane witch trials. their magic is not instantaneous otherwise they would have just teleported away, although most of those who were killed were just innocent people and not actual witches. For the record it is quite impressive, it can take years of practice to learn to focus properly which is why their symbols and images are so important, it helps them focus their energy."

"Next you have Wizards, they can be men or women they're all just called Wizards, you also have the Sorcerer or Sorceress", Mike interrupts again, "you mean they arer the bad ones."

"No Michael, Wizards use the magic of light, and Sorcerers use Darker magic, but that doesn't mean their bad, Magic whether light or dark is only as good or evil as the one using it, There are different kinds of magic, but light magic can be used for evil just as dark magic can be used for good."

Michael Shakes his head, "Now I'm really confused". Dade Smiles, "Don't worry Michael You have a lot of training ahead, it will come to you, but Let's not get ahead of ourselves, The Mage is the final piece of the puzzle, They are the most powerful within the magical world, They bring the balance to the whole, without them there would be magical wars and conflicts and many including normal people would be hurt, They would be caught in the middle. There are twelve Mage throughout the world, never more than twelve." Michael looks puzzled, "why Twelve".

"We don't know for sure, but it has to do with the balance, everything requires a delicate balance.

"This is all hard to believe, but like you said I guess I'll understand soon enough, I Hope, but Dade what was that thing that attacked me?, and why did it attack?, and how did you know?".

"Well that was a Lesser Demon, Their strong but not very smart and they have no magical powers, we don't know who sent it but not everyone wants the Circle of Mage to be complete again, Some out there are not very nice they want power at any cost. You were born in July, 18 years ago right".

"How did you know that?"

"That is When the last Dragon Mage was killed, Probable just before or the day you were born, see what I mean about balance, we believe he let down his guard and was killed by someone he trusted, we don't know for sure, but we and the sisters of the temple have waited a long time for you. Anyway we got word that the Demon Asuroff was sent to attack you, so I found him with magic and followed him, and he led me to you".

"If you can do that why didn't you just use magic to find me".

"Well Michael that's enough for now, it's time for you to get settled in there will be plenty of time for all your questions for now get rested, soon you'll start your training".

"Will Elaina show me to my room".

"Yes she's on her way now, oh by the way the sisters of the Temple have the power to read your thoughts, so until you learn how to block your mind try not to think about anything you don't want them to know".

Michael blushed as he left he turned and walked away, as Elaina approached Mike tried not to look directly at her wondering if it was true that they really could read his thoughts. Elaina bowed again slightly.

"Follow me Michael you have to be properly welcomed before I can show you to your room this way please, oh and yes we can read your thoughts".

Michael blushed once again as he meekly followed Elaina. He was led to a large hall where about two dozen priestesses formed a large circle three rows deep, in the center is an altar of some kind. Elaina led Michael to the altar. There behind the altar was a hooded figure from head to toe in a green and white outfit. Michael couldn't tell if it was a man or woman until she spoke. Michael was instructed to sit in his seat in front of the altar facing out toward the congregation. Elaina went and took her place in the circle directly in front of Michael and he was glad because he was becoming a little apprehensive about the situation yet looking out at Elaina seemed to calm him. The Woman behind the altar began to speak "we welcome the newest Mage and pledge our lives and our hearts to guide and protect him and aid him in all his quests". The sisters all chanted their confirmation and oath. The figure then came around and handed Michael cup and asked him to drink. the liquid was pleasant tasting and fulfilling, he immediately felt as if he had eaten an entire meal. He then handed her back the cup. Then she returned to her place behind the altar where she opened the book and began reading it in a language Michael had never heard before as she read the sisters chanted in unison in the same unidentified language. The Chanting stopped and they began to sing in a soft melodious tone, it sounded almost like a church choir only softer and much more beautiful. Michael could feel his mind floating, drifting, he felt completely at peace. Then Michael opened his eyes he was in a strange place, perhaps another Temple it was brilliant white he thought that he had to be dreaming he knew that this was a real Place and all the sisters he could still hear them singing. He turned and then he saw, a vision and white robes just like the sisters of Ghostra wore, there was an ora around her that was glowing he couldn't tell if she was real. She was just floating, her feet were not touching the ground she stood in front of a golden altar strange as this was he still felt safe and at peace. Slowly the image began to fade as he heard the singing end he closed his eyes and when he opened them again he was in ghostra still sitting in front of the altar, Elaina was kneeling beside him holding his hand.

She asked, "are you all right Michael"

"Yes fine, I had some kind of vision or dream only one where you know you're dreaming is that normal"

"No Michael that's very unusual, but it's a good sign, let me take you to your room now you must be tired".

As she led him away the others seem to be praying. When they entered his room Michael was amazed the room was large with a huge bed, closets and a full open wall out to a balcony. From The balcony he could see clouds all around and in the distance below him were snow capped peaks. He turned to Elaina and asked how if they were so high up they weren't freezing. Elaina told him that the Temple was surrounded by special enchantments which not only protect all within but also provide a comfortable environment.

"I can feel your confusion that's only normal you can't be expected to grasp all of this right away".

"I know but I don't think I can do this. I mean Dade says that I'm a Mage but what if he's wrong I've never done anything Magical or special".

"No Michael he's not wrong l I can feel your power, it's there, you just have to learn how to use it. Take this morning you felt something wasn't right, you knew something was wrong"

"how did you know that"

"Michael the sisters of the Temple have been given many gifts not only the power to read thoughts. Just then the door opened and Evie came running in.

Evie could hardly contain herself. "Michael this places awesome, I never even dreamed of a place like this it sure beats living in a box, but Mike why are we here and how long are we going to stay".

"Please Evie, no more questions right now my brain is about to explode.

"Okay sorry Mike" just then another priestess came in with a tray of food and drink and set it on the table. Elaina turned to Michael, Dade said to have some food then relax a while before trying to get some rest, tomorrow is another day.

"How can I get any sleep now it may be getting dark wherever we are in the world but we only got up a few hours ago at home".

"Don't worry Michael when you lay down and close your eyes you'll get the rest you need. By the way this sister is called Durrel she will be taking care of your everyday needs, Elaina looked at Michael and smiled, not those needs Michael". Michael turned even redder than before but then the thought occurred to him.

"What about you Elaina, I thought you would be taking care of us".

"Yes Michael I'll always be here for you". She and Durrel left the room.

Evie turned to Mike, "she's really pretty Mike. Can I stay in here with you tonight".

"I thought you loved you're own room".

"I do but I'm not sure I want to stay here alone my first night, so can I stay here tonight Please".

"Sure Evie, that bed is big enough for six people bigger than the whole box we shared together just no snoring or you're out".

They both laughed. Then they sat and ate their meal, they talked for a while and then went to lay down. Elaina was right once they closed their eyes they drifted off into a restful sleep.

2

I T SEEMS AS IF THEY just fall asleep when Michael opened his eyes and saw that it was already morning, Evie was curled up at the far end of the bed with her head buried in the pillow. She was still fast asleep, Michael waited feeling more comfortable and refreshed than he had ever felt before. A true feeling of euphoria fell upon him when he heard a soft voice.

"Good morning Michael" he turned and there sitting in a chair next to the bed was Elaina.

"I brought breakfast for you and Evelyn but didn't have the heart to wake you since you both looked to be sleeping so peacefully".

He looked at Elaine and smiled. "I've never slept so soundly or woke so refreshed".

"It's the enchantments that surround the Temple they help and you really look like you needed a perfect night sleep." Michael got up still wearing the same cloths he wore the previous day since they had no time to bring anything with them.

"I really need to go back and get the rest of our things, I'm starting to get a little ripe."

"That won't be necessary Michael you can clean up through there and your cloths are already waiting for you".

Elaina was pointing to the two doors at the far end of the room. "Oh did they bring our things"

"not exactly Michael from now on you'll be wearing clothes of our Temple, Michael Ghostra is the Dragon Temple and you will be the Dragon Mage your clothing and colors will reflect that. The Dragon Temple has a long proud tradition and is respected throughout the magical world".

With that said, Elaina went through the closet door and a moment later she emerged with Michael's cloths. The pants were pitch black with a thin red stripe going down the outside on both legs shirt was deep red with gold writing with letters and symbols Michael could not understand, jet black cape were the finishing touch. Michael looked at the clothes then looked at Elaina and all he could say was "WOW". Elaina just smiled.

"Okay Michael you can eat get cleaned up and change and I'll be back in a little while, but Dade is here already and I'm sure you want to get started".

"Thank you Elaina". Elaina smiled bowed slightly and left. Michael looked at the table there were two bowls of cut up fruit and two glasses of all light violet liquid, he ate some of the fruit and drank some of the liquid which turned out to be the most delicious drink he had ever had, a few more pieces of fruit and off he went to get cleaned up. He went inside the other door Elaina had indicated, it seemed like a standard bathroom only more elegant than he had ever seen before at the other end of the room behind the shower doors Michael could already hear the water running, he wondered if Elaina had started the shower for him and left it running. As he opened the doors he was shocked to find a beautiful outdoor waterfall running into a large pool size tub. Michael removed his cloths mesmerized by the site he stepped into the water half expecting it to be very cold waterfall but found it warm and soothing.

"Wow I almost forgot were not in the real world anymore".

After his very relaxing bath he put on the cloths Elaina had provided and was amazed at how well they fit, it seems they thought of everything. Michael was still a little apprehensive about getting too comfortable as he still wasn't sure that they had the right person and figured they may soon be back to living in a box. When he exited the bathroom he saw that Evie was already at the table eating her breakfast, she looked up and said "morning Mike, don't you look cool" in between mouthfuls. He sat at the table with her she looked very happy here. He thought he had to give it a try for her sake even if he had to fake it for as long as possible. Michael got up and strolled over to the balcony looking out at the horizon, the sun was bright above the clouds surrounding the mountain below and a clear blue sky as far as he could see. Everything was so beautiful here. As Michael admired the view Dade arrived looked around and saw Michael on the balcony.

"Well now you look better. Today is going to be a great day are you ready to get started".

"Oh! Are you going to start training me today".

"Well I figured we would start with a little tour. There is a lot to see and I want to explain about your training in future. By the way Michael I will not be the one training you although I will help with your studies".

"Oh! I just figured you would be the Mage to train me". Date smiled, "I'm not a Mage Michael, I'm the master wizard of the gray order. Master wizard is the head of an order and almost as powerful as Mage. My order is assigned to you Michael, as with the sisters of the Dragon Temple we protect and help you maintain the balance within the magical world.

"Well okay but if you're not going to be training me to become a Mage who is".

"To help you release your power and be your guide in all things you will have to call upon your guardian spirit who will first help you find and use your magic, then help guide you to become a Mage that will use your power to guard and protect others".

"What is a guardian spirit and are you sure I even have one".

"Everyone has a guardian spirit Michael, who guides them and helps them make the right decisions if they choose to follow the subtle hints the spirits give them, the guardians try to help but the ignorant just don't listen. Normal people can't see or hear the spirits, but the spirits do leave them clues the people just need to recognize these clues and act on them".

"Well if I can't see or hear my guardian spirit how can the they teach me anything, wait a minute Dade you're not talking about guardian angels are you".

"They have been called that, they are not from this world"."Please tell me you're not talking about aliens from another planet".

Dade laughed, "no Michael I'm not talking about planet it's like another dimension, another realm, a realm we can't see normally, but they can make their presence known if they choose to. You can call upon your guardian spirit through invocations. It's going to take a little practice but once your spirit appears to you they will help guide you forever".

Evie walked over to them "Michael I'm going to go to my room now and get cleaned up then have a look around remember Michael we're going to do something later together". "Okay Evie I'll see you in a little while."

Michael and Dade talked as they walked through the halls of Ghostra, Mike was a bit overwhelmed by what he had been told. Dade walked to a large oak door and opened it.

"This Michael is the library." Michael saw many books and scrolls containing magical spells and enchantments.

"The door at the other end of the room is your personal library Michael. It contains books of magic in an ancient language that only you will be able to read and understand once your guardian spirit bestows that ability on you."

They continued down the hallway a little further down Dade approached another door.

"I think you'll find this interesting."

They went in and saw about a dozen priestesses in combat hand-to-hand and some with wooden knives and swords. They were awesome and quick, despite the age differences they all look like experts Michael could tell he took a couple of years of karate when he was younger before his dad was killed in the accident. Across the gym Michael saw Elaina practicing with another sister. She saw Michael watching and came over to him.

"Hello Michael care to practice a bit?"

She and the other sisters were no longer in their white robes but wore a workout outfit in the same black red and gold as his cloths.

"Nice outfits but I think you girls are a little too good for me."

"Well you'll need to practice with us starting tomorrow anyway, so you may as well show us what you've got."

She smiled and Michael smiled back. "Okay but I'm not sure I'll need to know physical combat if I know magic."

"of course magic will work for you for most situations, but you never know when manual combat will be the best response, besides it helps keep you in shape."

"Yes I can see that." Michael smiled and Elaina smiled and blushed a little bit. "Well at least it's you blushing this time."

Dade looked at Michael "go ahead Michael give it a go."

Michael removed his cape and shoes and stepped onto the mat. Elaina said "okay Michael, freestyle or do you prefer a weapon."

"Well you look extremely good at freestyle and I'm not looking to be embarrassed my first day but I am pretty good with the staff." Elaina grabbed two staffs and tossed one to Michael, they stood across from each other and bowed and took a fighting stance. Michael saw how well she handled herself while she was sparring but was still a little concerned that he might hurt her so he started off easily. Elaina was not so gentle she knocked his pole aside and struck him twice pushing him back. Michael a bit embarrassed quickly countered still trying not to use too much force but once again Elaina responded with great speed this time disarming Michael and flipping him to the ground. "I can sense that you're holding back Michael trust me you won't hurt me and your combat training is a vital part of your overall well-being. Please Michael in the future give it your all. Some creatures are actually immune to magic and hand-to-hand or weapon combat maybe your only defense. "Sorry next time nothing held back."

As they talked out of the corner of his eye Michael saw another person was dressed similar to Dade enter the room he walked to Dade and they whispered back and forth then Dade came over to them. "Elaina would you continue Michael's tour something is just come up I'll be back in a little while."

"Yes of course Dade." Michael could see that something was wrong Dade was clearly concerned. Dade and the other man quickly left. Michael turned to Elaina you could tell that she was also showing signs that something was wrong. "Elaina what is it what's wrong"? "Nothing Michael we should continue with your tour." "Look Elaina I don't have to read minds to tell something was going on. Everyone is telling me about how I'm going to be this powerful Mage and how I need to trust you and Dade but apparently no one trusts me enough to tell me what's happening."

"I'm sorry Michael, I just thought that if they didn't tell you it's only because he knows what you've been through the past couple of days and doesn't want to add more to that especially since there's nothing you can do right now." "I can understand what you're saying I still have to keep pinching myself to see if I'm dreaming. But I'll make you a deal I will not lie to you and won't hold back anything if you'll do the same, I need to know someone here won't lie to me even if they think it's for my own good, is it a deal." Elaina thought for a moment, "Deal Michael, first of all I normally wouldn't be able to read Dade's thoughts but with strong emotions thoughts can project out and we picked them up, I wasn't trying but they were very strong it appears Michael as if one of the wizard orders is under attack and their Mage and most of the order aren't there I'm sure they'll get word to them but in the meantime Dade has taken some of his order to assist them." "But who was attacking them?" "They don't know who or what it is but I'm sure they'll find out."

"Does this kind of thing happen a lot?" "No, at least not for centuries, come on Michael let's continue your tour as Dade suggested." They slowly walked down the marble hallway and were soon joined by Evie who was doing some exploring on her own. "Hi guys what are you up to?"

"Just giving Michael a guided tour of the Temple you need to know where everything is." "Great can I come along?"

"Sure it looks like this will be your home for a while too."

As they walked they talked about all sorts of things that had nothing to do with magic or the Temple or anything that's happening. They were all just getting to know each other. Elaina said "come this way Michael you need to see this." She opened the door.

"This is the library." Michael and Evie followed her inside, "Dade already pointed this room out to me Elaina but we didn't go into much detail", it was a very large room he could see shelf after shelf of books scrolls and parchments.

"Are all these books and things about magic?"

"Yes Michael mostly magic some magical history there are many forms of magic our library covers them all. It's quite extensive. Down at the end of the room those two doors one on the left will be your study room where you'll learn the different forms of magic that your guardian spirit finds most appropriate some of the books that are already in the study are in an ancient language that your guardian spirit will teach you, the door on the right is your spirit sanctuary where you will summon and speak to your guardian once the room has been sanctified no one else will be allowed to enter it."

Evie said, "WOW! Is a true Michael are you really going to be some kind of magician?"

Michael and Elaina looked at each other and smiled, Michael remembered what Dade had told him about magicians.

"I guess so Evie, that's what they keep telling me. I don't know I guess the reality of this place and what's happening is just starting to sink in."

Michael picked up a small book which had strange symbols on the cover and began to leaf through it he put the book back down when he suddenly felt energized like he just downed several energy drinks at once.

"What happened Michael?" Said Elaina, "I just got a very strange feeling from within you as if you had just had a surge within your mind."

"I don't know I suddenly felt very strong and wide-awake like I've never felt before." Michael's hand began to tingle he looked at his hand and saw a small flame that seemed to burst from his hand and sit in his palm everyone just looked at the flickering flame as it rested in the palm of his hand. Michael could feel its warmth but it did not burn him Michael closed his hand and the flame disappeared he looked at Elaina and Evie both still appeared surprised."

Michael asked, "what was that, is that normal?"

"I don't know Michael I've never heard of a Mage being able to produce magic until he had his guardian spirit help him unlock his power."

Evie said, "Wow Mikey, that was cool how did you do that? Can you do it again?"

"I don't know Evie, I don't even know how I did it the first time." Elaina still surprised said "I think we should just continue our tour we'll tell Dade what happened when he returns maybe he can explain it."

"Yeah" said Michael, "a good idea let's keep moving." They continued to tour as before they talked about nothing in particular but as much as he enjoyed their conversation he couldn't shake the thought of what had happened he felt he should try to get his mind on something else.

"So Elaina tell me how did you come to be a priestess here you were born here?"

"No Michael I was born in a small town, but I've been here since I was five. I was brought here by Paul Reed a wizard from the gray order when my family was killed I was the only survivor."

"I'm sorry I didn't mean to bring up bad memories"

"that's okay it was a long time ago." Evie said, "I'm sorry Elaina my parents are gone too."

"I know Evie which is why you might consider joining our order."

"Really you mean I could be one of you and can live here to."

"Yes of course. It's up to you but I'm sure the Matriss will ask you before long, you need to think it over first it's a lifelong commitment." They finally came full circle and found themselves back at Michael's room inside they found lunch was already waiting.

"I'll be going now Michael" said Elaina "I have chores and prayers but I can come back in a couple of hours if you like."

"That would be great I'll see you later then."

"Can I come with you Elaina? Asked Evie. "Okay, I'm sure everyone would like to meet you, is that okay with you Michael." "Sure it's okay with me."

Evie and Elaina left and Michael went to the table and poured some juice in a glass and carried it to the balcony where he sat in one of the cushioned chairs. A lot of things were running through his mind he was confused and was having a rough time organizing his thoughts. There was so much happening and so many unanswered questions. He could see that major things were happening but felt helpless. Everyone was saying you'll be a powerful Mage, that he just needs training so why was he just sitting here why didn't they let him get started, tell him what he had to do even the beauty of the sun and the clouds in the mountain peaks off in the distance couldn't shake the feeling that he needed to act to do something, anything but sit around. He decided to go back to the library and have a better look around. He wanted to check out his study area and sanctuary rooms maybe look at some of the books and scrolls he strolled down the hall, it was surprisingly quiet none of the sisters attending to things as they had before he guessed they were at prayers like Elaina said whatever it was they did during the day or evening. Then it dawned on him that he really had no idea what they did or why. He felt that since he would be working closely with them these are things you should know. Oh great he thought something else to add to my list of stuff I need to find out about. He reached the library and entered he still found it amazing that a place like this actually exists. He headed straight to the rooms at the far end. He entered the study there was a desk, a couple chairs a bookcase on either side of the room and on the wall behind the desk was a map of the world with different colored flickering dots he went over and touched one of the dots and the map ejected out into a dimensional globe of the Planet he walked around it and saw the dots were actual locations around the world he didn't even know what they meant but he was amazed by it, he touched it and it collapsed back to a map on the wall. "Wow! Now that's what I call cool." He picked up one of the books and opened it and saw that it was written in some strange symbols that he could not understand.

"This must be the language that Elaina told me about." He left the study and went to the other room but wasn't sure if he should enter or not.

"Oh what the heck" he said as he opened the door and went in. The room was dark there were no windows to let light in, by the door just to his right was a glowing ball about the size of a soccer ball it looked almost like one of those globes you see with purple electricity dancing around inside, he reached out to touch it and suddenly the lights turned on dimly. As his hand got closer the lights got brighter to where he could see the room clearly. In the center of the room was an altar with candles, on either side were two statues of Golden dragons just like the ones on the Temple dome. All the walls were covered with some strange symbols the same as those in the books in his study. On the back wall was a pedestal with two brackets and on the brackets were a wooden staff with a crystal on the end. On the ground were two circles with symbols evenly spaced around the outside. One circle surrounded the altar the other much smaller circle sits alone directly in front of the altar, as Michael approached the altar he began to feel strangely calm as though he has nothing to worry about. Michael put his hands on the altar and felt a strange surge of energy within him but different than before this was more calming and euphoric. He closed his eyes and began drifting he found himself in another Temple totally different from the Dragon Temple but still stunning to look at, but he couldn't dwell on the appearance there was a battle going on. There were dozens of creatures many like the ones that attacked him and some that looked even worse and about two dozen that seem to be casting spells there were five men dressed as wizards only their outfits were red. Then he saw Dade and six of his wizards they came into the battle area and immediately began blasting away. Everything seemed to be happening at twice normal speed. Michael couldn't tell if was actually happening that way or if his mind was seeing it at an accelerated pace it was dizzying. Fire lightning and energy waves flying back and forth but it was clear the wizards had quickly turned back the attack. The creatures fled and it was easy enough to see that the red wizards that were knocked to the ground were not seriously hurt. In a flash Michael found himself back at the altar shaking and a little disoriented he decided to return to his room when he exited the library he noticed that it was getting dark already. He couldn't understand when he got there it was midafternoon and thought he was only there maybe half an hour yet here it was getting dark. He wondered what happened to him and how long was he actually in there. He rushed back to his room, no one was there so he went back to the balcony sat and closed his eyes. What happened was it real or illusion, he wondered whether he should say anything or whether they would think he was losing it. Moments later Elaina and Evie entered the room.

"Michael where have you been," asked Elaina "we were looking all over for you is everything all right."

"Hey Mike" said Evie, we were getting worried"

"no I'm okay I was just exploring a little on my own"

Michael didn't feel quite right lying to them especially after the deal he made with Elaina and by the look on her face she wasn't buying his excuse anyway, but if he did decide to tell her he didn't want to do it in front of Evie he didn't want to worry her. Durrel brought dinner in and placed it on the table, Michael thanked her and she left. This time Elaina stayed and ate with them they ate and talked in the lighthearted conversation which helped to ease Michael's mind about the days mysteries.

"Michael asked, "well Evie what did you do today."

"Wow Mike, I saw the head of the place what is she called again."

Elaina replied "high priestess or mother superior or just Mattris is fine"

"yeah and she was great she showed me how they pray and work and train guess what Mike, it's all to help you ain't that cool."

"Yes Evie that sounds great"

Evelyn yawned and said, "well I'm kind of tired I'm going to go to bed in my room tonight. I want to show them I can take care of myself but if I have trouble sleeping can I still come here to sleep Mike."

"Sure you're welcome to come back if you can't sleep"

Evie yawned again and left. Michael smiled, she seemed really happy. Michael and Elaina brought their drinks out to the balcony and sat down. The night was calm the moon was just beginning to rise above the clouds off in the distance.

"Dade apparently didn't make it back today do you think he's all right" asked Michael.

"We haven't heard from him Michael, but I'm sure he's fine. Michael you were gone for hours Evelyn and I looked all over for you and couldn't find you anywhere I know you're safe here but we were getting really worried where did you go.

"I'm not sure if I should say anything you might think I'm nuts."

"I'll believe you Michael, besides we promise not to lie to each other remember you need someone to trust, well that works both ways."

"I know, and you're right but hear me out before you say anything."

Michael recounted his story to her where he had gone what he had done trying not to leave anything out. When he had finished Elaina looked at him from moment not knowing quite what to say trying to take it all in.

"Well what do you think maybe I shouldn't have gone in the sanctuary.

"No Michael, that's all right there is nothing wrong with that, eventually you'll be spending a lot of time there. What's hard to grasp is what you saw, your vision if it really happened that way is very unusual for anyone who is yet to release their powers."

"Elaina I have never had any kind of magic nothing at all, my whole life nothing strange like this is ever happened. Now I come here and things are happening every time I turn around. I'm getting worried and I'm kind of freaking out, because no one seems to know why or how I can do these things. Yet all everyone say's is I'm going to develop these powers eventually but it's only been a couple of days."

"Relax Michael, I'm not an expert on what to expect but this is not necessarily a bad thing. It's unusual to see your powers emerge so quickly especially before you been able to invoke your guardian spirit's help, but it could be a good thing I mean I've never seen the making of a mage, so I'll I only know what I've read or been told but I do know that you shouldn't worry there are a lot of people here to help and support you, and I'll be here for you anytime you need me."

"Thanks Elaina, what about Dade should I tell him what happened today."

"Yes of course, he knows more than I do he may have some explanation for you." With that Michael and Elaina just sat and relax a while not saying much just kind of enjoying the view and companionship, they could see the stars. Michael laughed, "Evie loves the stars where we were living we couldn't see them much and they never looked as brilliant as this. Behind them they heard a noise, they turned to see Dade come into the room and walk to where they were sitting.

"Well sorry I was gone all day but some things came up."

Michael said, "yes I know, Dade I really need to talk to you."

"Okay Michael what's on your mind."

"I'll leave the two of you to talk."

"No Elaina please stay, your my moral support."

Elaina nodded and smiled. Michael explained to Dade everything that happened today but hesitated when he got to the vision part, when he looked at Elaina she nodded her encouragement, so Michael continued to tell the rest. When he had finished Dade just looked at them for a moment then smiled.

"Well Michael that's amazing. You seem to be progressing faster than any of us could've imagined. The battle occurred just as you described it. The magic is within you Michael, it's always been there but dormant. Partly because you didn't believe, partly because you've never been exposed to it before, and partly because there hasn't been anyone to help you release it. This place is itself magical the library and especially your sanctuary contain great magic and apparently just being here is having an effect on you. This is an unexpected but welcome occurrence, it's nothing to be concerned with or fearful of, in fact it's excellent news and indicates that when you learn to control your abilities you will be a very powerful Mage.

"Thanks Dade, I feel more at ease now thanks to you and of course Elaina."

"Relax Michael, tomorrow you will actually begin your training, and I understand Evelyn will also begin training, but you don't need to worry about her she's not obligated in the beginning it sort of a trial. For the first year or two. See you tomorrow kids." With that Dade left.

Michael turned to Elaina, "a trial period, Did you have a trial period?"

"Yes of course, but I knew right away that I wanted to be part of the sisterhood."

"Did you know the last Mage."

"Not personally, but we all knew him."

"Then you didn't take care of him like you do for me."

"No Michael, no sister serves as companion for more than one mage."

"So is that what you are my companion?"

"Yes, so that you have someone to depend on, confide in, and someone to work with you and protect you with their life if necessary. I was chosen for you, of course you could ask for someone else if you wanted to.

"No, your perfect, I mean the perfect choice. Which one is the sister who serve the last Mage."

"She's dead, killed protecting the last Mage."

I don't want anyone, especially you to die for me, if it ever comes down to that." "But that's what we do Michael protect you just the way you protect everyone else it's what we train for and it's what were devoted to. We don't throw our lives away but we will do what we have to do. Just so you know these life-threatening occurrences don't happen very often. There are magical laws Michael and it's rare that someone breaks them."

"Laws what are they?"

"They're pretty simple, don't reveal our existence to normals, don't do harm to others specially normals, and help others when you can as long as it doesn't interfere with the natural order of things. There is a list of laws but it all just boils down to be a good and caring person."

"Wow to always be good sounds like a tall order."

"I wouldn't worry Michael, I think you've already got that part covered. Well I'll leave now and let you get some rest. See you tomorrow 7 AM sharp at the training arena for combat training."

"Okay Elaina I'll be there, good night."

Michael got ready and went to bed but sleep was not coming easily he couldn't get what happened today out of his head. He tried focusing on something more pleasant but kept returning to the events of the day. He tried clearing his mind completely but that didn't last long. It took a couple of hours of trying before he was able to fall asleep.

3

MORNING CAME QUICKLY, MICHAEL WOKE to a slight nudge in a friendly good morning Michael it was Durrel and he saw that she had already brought breakfast and laid out his clothes. They were not his mage clothes but looked more like workout clothes that you'd see in a normal gym although the colors were still the black red and gold.

"Good morning Durrel, how are you this morning?"

"Fine Michael, you have about an hour to eat and get ready Elaina wants you in the training center at seven sharp."

She smiled and left. Michael felt exceptionally good this morning, he felt remarkably energized. He ate quickly and headed straight for that amazing shower. Once in he wished he could stay in soaking it all day long, but didn't want to disappoint Elaina, he wanted to show he could be prompt. After getting dressed he went straight to the Training Center., Elaina was already waiting for him.

"Elaina said, good you're right on time are you ready to work up a sweat?"

"Absolutely! What do you have in mind."

"Combat training, it teaches us to fight and helps keep us in shape."

"Oh okay that's good to."

Michael looked across the floor to the far corner where he saw Evie Getting basic instructions from another sister.

"How is Evie doing?"

"Fine she seems to be having fun and she's picking up very well. So should we start with the basics?"

"I took martial arts for almost 2 years before my father's accident so I don't think I need the basics."

"Okay we'll just spar for a while so I can gauge your level and know where to focus our training. We'll start lightly hand-to-hand." They stepped on the mat bowed and began he would attack and she would defend and then they would switch Michael could tell she was going easy on him, from what he has seen previously. She was at a much higher level than he was, in fact he felt she was at a higher level than the black belt who taught him. One things for sure they definitely worked up a sweat. After two hours there combat training ended for the day Elaina took Evie and went to clean up and start their daily routine and Michael went back to his room to take another dip in the waterfall and change. When he came out he found that Dade had already arrived and was waiting at the table.

"Morning Michael how are you on this beautiful morning? Are you ready to begin your journey?

"I feel great Dade, but what journey are you talking about are we going somewhere?"

Dade smiled at the misunderstanding. "No Michael, I'm referring to your magical journey the journey that will transform you from what you are into all you can be."

"Wow Dade, you sound like an Army recruiter but I guess I'm as ready as I'll ever be."

"Good then let's go to the library and get started."

They walked to the library and talked along the way Michael was curious about the battle of the previous day. He asked Dade if that was a normal occurrence or if Elaina was right and that it was a very unusual occurrence.

"Michael you need to understand there are other realms that exist just like the guardian spirits have a realm so do dark beings demons, devils, and all sorts of magical dark creatures. We help to keep these dark creatures from entering our world. But in the past 5 years there has been a power building behind these dark creatures, who or what it is we haven't been able to discover. We even believe that 18 years ago it may have been behind the murder of your predecessor. Those creatures that attacked the red order were not a powerful group they consisted of minor demons and a few grebin which or dark minions with some magical ability. We believe that knowing the red order had only a few wizards there at the time they were testing defenses. They had to know that force could not overcome the order even though there were a lot in number they were very short on power. The real problem is that they were able to enter our world. With some help from the more powerful beings you'll get an occasional Demon or other creature through a temporary rift or dimensional portal to create some chaos which accounts for most of the myths of the world about creature sightings. But the openings can't be sustained very long. It's been centuries since anyone has created a portal large enough to get so many creatures through at one time and apparently was held open long enough for the attack and for them to return to their dimension. So Michael when you do finally make contact with your guardian spirit, you need to try and find out the who and why of what's been happening lately because we've been unable to find out despite our best efforts."

"Would a guardian know that?"

"They know many things but they're not always willing to share information something about knowledge were not supposed to have for our own good. We gave up trying to figure out what they consider our own good or why. I know it's a lot to heap on your shoulders when this is all so new to you but it's terribly important."

"Of course Dade I'll do what I can."

When they got to the library Dade headed straight the bookshelves on the far left side and took a book and a scroll off-the-shelf then returned to Michael. The book had a symbol on the leather bound cover the scroll was rolled up parchment paper they then went to the study.

Michael these are the first two documents for you to study they are written in an old language so they may read a little odd but you'll be able to understand them and should spend at least two hours a day reading and following the instructions and practicing what they teach. The most advanced books are here on your study shelves but you won't be able to read them until you contacted your guardian spirit."

"How do I do that?"

"That's the second part. Each day you will enter your sanctuary and attempt to summon the spirit." Dade went to the desk and took a small folded parchment from the top drawer.

"This is the invocation you will recite for at least one hour each day." Michael took the paper from Dade and looked at it. The parchment was written in a strange language that Michael had never seen before.

"How can I read this?"

"It's okay to read it in our language Michael the translation is on the back."

Michael turned it over and read "spirits of our fathers I bid you join me in this place of knowledge and share with me your wisdom and guide me in my future journeys."

"You need to repeat this at the altar for one hour each day until your guardian appears to you and give you further guidance."

"What you mean every day won't they appear right away."

"No not till they feel your ready, I'll stop by and check your progress each day and stay a while to talk if you have questions about your studies."

"Okay Dade whatever you say but I wish this would just happen already."

"We would like that to Michael but one thing we found, you can't rush the guardians they have their own timetable and agenda. Dade left Michael in the library. Michael went straight to the sanctuary he walked to the altar lit the candles and began the incantation over and over for one hour. Nothing happened so he brought the book and parchment Dade had given him back to his room to study and left the paper with the incantation on the altar in the sanctuary. Day after day after his combat training with Elaina which was the highlight of his day he would study and practice for two hours returned to his sanctuary for one hour to perform his incantation as instructed. Dade would come by usually late afternoon to discuss the day's activities but Michael was clearly becoming discouraged since nothing was happening and his guardian spirit had failed to appear to him. He made his disappointment known to Dade.

"Michael I know it can be frustrating but you can't start getting lazy with your incantation don't just say the words you have to feel them."

"I'm trying Dade but it's been almost 3 months how long does it usually take?"

"It could take quite a while, there is no set time they have to feel your ready and we don't know what they use as a gauge."

That evening Elaina stopped by as she sometimes would she went and sat with Michael on the balcony.

"How are you doing Michael."

"Okay I guess, I'm just beginning to get a little discouraged."

"I know Michael, Dade told me he asked if I could help cheer you up."

"You do, just by being here"

Elaina smiled, then for a while they just sat looking out at the stars. Finally Michael turned to Elaina.

"Elaina do you think I may be doing something wrong. I mean after being here a couple of days unexplainable things happened remember the fire and the vision, but then after I actually started training when you would think more things would happen nothing at all. I mean something for a little encouragement would be nice."

"I've never been through this process before Michael, but from what I've been told except what happened those first couple of days what's happening is normal. You just have to keep going and don't give up, I know what will happen in time."

"I won't give up on it as long as you and the others don't give up on me."

"Never Michael, never."

She reached out and took his hand in hers he gripped her tightly and smiled and they just sat quietly for the rest of the evening. The next day started out much the same as every other breakfast followed by combat training, followed by studies, followed by his time in the sanctuary. But today Michael had another one of his strange feelings that he just couldn't shake. Whether it was a good thing or bad he couldn't tell. His guardian spirit still hadn't appeared or given any sign that it Ever would. So Michael decided to see if Elaina was busy he stopped by the training center and looked in and there was Elaina giving Evie some help with her training which Michael thought was nice of her since Evie had her own instructor but was having trouble with some of her moves. He didn't want to disturb them so we headed back to the library. He figured he get his book and take it back to his room to study a little more. When he got there he started for the study when he heard a loud noise coming from outside so he went to see what was going on. When he got to the hallway the sisters were scrambling down the hall as they passed him one yelled to him Michael stay in the library were under attack. When Michael heard that he ran after them just as he turned the corner he saw about a dozen of them including Elaina had formed a line across the hall some had swords some staffs Elaina saw him coming.

"Michael go back we may not be able to hold them off until the wizards arrive."

"No I'm not leaving all of you to fight while I run."

"Michael you're probably the one there after something powerful must be with them they got past our protective spells."

"Well if it's me there after here I am and I'm going down fighting I'm not running."

Before anyone could say anything else they saw the enemy a dark hooded figure stood at the end of the hall he waved his arm and cast a lightning bolt down the hall toward them. The mother superior who stood in front of the line holding a golden staff with a crystal on the top raised the staff and deflected the lightning. The dark figure raised his arm and demons turned the corner and more came over the balcony at the far end of the hall from behind the figure. They must of been 100 running down the hallway the sisters though outnumbered got into a fighting stance and raised their weapons. Suddenly Michael saw a woman to his left she was the same woman he had seen the first night during his welcoming in the great Hall. Michael looked around and everything except him seem to be moving in slow motion. When he had seen her before she said nothing she just floated there this time she came toward him and said Michael, with a smile. She touched him on his shoulder and he began to tingle through his whole body he saw Elaina looked back at him with a strange look on her face he then began shaking and without further warning there was an explosion that came from Michael a wave of energy out in all directions it flew past the sisters with no effect but when it hit the attacking creatures it was like they were hit with a bomb they were thrown back with tremendous force. The blast pushed them out of the Temple where they felt downward to their fate. The sisters look toward Michael stunned at what they had just seen, Michael just fell to his knees and then backwards to the ground where he passed out.

4

MICHAEL WAS DRIFTING THROUGH SPACE nothing beneath his feet everything was dark but he was not afraid in fact he felt very peaceful occasional flickers of light seem to help this calm than the light of a candle appeared in front of him and the flame seemed to grow he was being pulled toward it but still there was no fear. The flame enveloped him as if passing through a bright doorway as he exited the other side he saw a familiar sight it was the room he had seen when he first arrived during his welcoming ceremony when he first saw the beautiful woman in his vision. "Hello Michael" he heard the voice come from the altar and then she appeared.

"You're my guardian angel aren't you?"

"Yes Michael and I've been watching you your whole life."

"Why didn't you show yourself before this."

"We don't show ourselves to anyone, we don't even appear to mage until they are ready, but you Michael your mind has come to me for the second time, that has never happened before no human has been able to come here. We're not sure how you did this but it is a rare thing indeed."

"You mean this place is real, not a dream?"

"No Michael not a dream it's quite real, tomorrow in your worlds time I will meet with you in your private place and we will begin your journey to enlightenment, for now Michael you must rest. But a word of caution your power has been released and your control over that power is minimal so be careful not to harm anyone, till tomorrow Michael."

Once again everything went dark. Michael woke in his room Elaina and Evelyn were sitting next to the bed and Dade was at the far end of the room talking to another wizard. When Elaina saw him open his eyes she took his hand.

"How are you feeling Michael, Are you all right?"

"I guess so, what happened is everyone okay?"

Evelyn spoke "everyone's find Mikey thanks to you, you really beat the crap out of those things."

Dade finished his conversation with the other wizard and came to his side as the other wizard left the room.

"Welcome back Michael."

"What you mean back."

"Well you've been unconscious since yesterday."

"Yesterday what time is it"

"about five in the afternoon, when we arrived yesterday we heard what happened I don't know how you did it but it was very impressive.

"I didn't do it, she did it. She touched me and my whole body seemed to explode everything seemed to move in slow motion."

Elaina said, "I saw you Michael your whole body began to glow and then the energy went out in all directions I could feel the warmth of the wave as it passed us."

"She Michael, was it your guardian spirit."

"Yes and it seems as though that was the second time I had seen her. The first was during the welcoming ceremony when I went into some kind of trance.

"Well Michael" said Dade, "that's strange but it looks as if your guardian spirit has finally revealed herself to you. That's enough for now get some rest I'll be back tomorrow. We are beefing up protections around the Temple although I don't think they'll try that again."

Dade left and Elaina said maybe we should leave also so Michael can rest.

"No, please stay, I think I've had enough rest."

"Did you want something to eat Mike." Asked Evie.

"Sure Evie that's a good idea I'm not real hungry but I should eat something.

They sat around the table and talked. Mike had a bit to eat. Michael felt he shouldn't tell them what happened while he was unconscious at least until he checked with his guardian angel, if she actually appeared again he wasn't sure that he didn't just dream the whole thing. As the evening got on Evie began to get tired.

"I need to go Mikey, I need to get started early tomorrow."

She walked over to Michael and threw her arms around him.

I'm glad you're okay Mike I was really worried about you."

"Thanks Evie, I'll see you tomorrow."

"Maybe I should go too." Said Elaina

"couldn't you stay just a little longer?"

"Of course Michael's I'll stay as long as you like, but remember we got to train too, if you feel up to it."

"I know, let's just sit a while and relax."

So they went out to the balcony and sat just enjoying the calm evening.

The Following morning Michael was up early, he didn't sleep very well anyway since his mind kept running over everything that happened overwhelming his thoughts. He remembered what his guardian told him about his powers being released. With no one around this would be a perfect time to see if it was true or whether the whole thing was just a dream. So he went into the bathroom and locked the door. He opened the curtain to the pool and waterfall he thought for a moment and remembered a spell he read in his studies a lightning bolt spell similar to the one the dark figure used during the attack. He raised his arm in the waterfall and muttered the spell under his breath suddenly electricity was everywhere all around him arcing and crackling and a moment later subsided Michael looked all around and said "whoa that didn't go quite as planned". At least it worked, well almost. He thought to himself at least I know it wasn't a dream. I think I should hold off till I learned some control. Michael felt a lot better knowing he had actually contacted the guardian or at least she had contacted him and that she was ready to start his training. Michael got ready for his combat training he was finally feeling pretty good about the way things were going but didn't want to get too comfortable, seems every time he did, something went wrong and he didn't want to jinx it. When Durrell arrived with his breakfast he was already sitting at the table enjoying the morning.

"Good morning Durell how are you today."

"Find Michael, you're up bright and early this morning."

"Yes I think I slept enough yesterday." After she left he had a quick bite and headed for the training center where Evie was already working out and Elaina and another sister were waiting for him.

"Good morning Michael." Said Elaina

"good morning, what sort of training are we doing today?"

"This is sister Sarah she is the master of the sword."

With that she tossed Michael wooden sword and Sarah began

instructing them in the finer point of sword fighting. After a little more than an hour they ended their session and Michael headed back to his room to get cleaned up and changed. He was excited and a little nervous about getting to the library and starting his lessons he went straight to the study to prepare, He picked up the book he had been studying took a deep breath and went to the sanctuary he went to the altar looked around and began the in invocation. That's when he heard her voice.

"That's no longer necessary Michael, you just need to call and I'll be here." Michael noticed that she had appeared over the circle next to the altar.

"It's good to see you now I know I'm not nuts."

She floated there several inches off the ground. "I don't know what to call you, what is your name" he asked.

"No one has spoken my name in a thousand years, but it is Cassondra."

"Cassondra, that's a beautiful name"

as she floated there Michael realized that she had the appearance of a ghostly figure not quite solid but not completely apparition either. He had 1000 questions but thought it best at least for now to keep them to himself until he had spent more time together.

"Well Cassondra where do we start"

"I see your eager, that's good. But before we get to any serious training you need to learn to control your power, but learning complete control is going to take some time so you need to practice faithfully whenever you have spare time. To start with I need you to picture a flame a candle or lantern there in front of you." Michael closed his eyes but Cassondra interrupted.

"You can start with your eyes closed but eventually you'll need to be able to picture it with them open in the beginning you'll probably only see it for a few seconds but after a while you should be able to focus your mind on it completely." Michael saw what she meant he would picture the candle and then it was gone his mine wondered somewhere else. He opened his eyes.

"I can't do it, my mind keeps drifting even with my eyes closed how will I ever do it with them open.

"I told you Michael this will not happen overnight, mental training takes time, but let me show you what total control will be like." Cassondra then became solid and stepped onto the floor, she walked over to Michael

"Cassondra you're here, you are solid I didn't know you could do that.

"Yes Michael we can take solid human form when we need to, we don't because then others can see us as well." She walked behind him and placed her hands on either side of his head just touching his temples Michael got a surge of energy and many feelings erupted within them he felt good but couldn't describe exactly what it was like if he tried. Cassondra must have realized what was happening and quickly tried to focus his mind on the task at hand

"All right Michael once again picture the candle."

Michael did as she requested and found that he could now focus completely on the candle

"Okay now Michael move closer to the candle, the flame is getting closer, it's getting bigger, the flame has no heat only light, The flame is all you can see now, the light envelops you so there is nothing but light now you pass through the other side and you are here again." She removes her hands and returns to the circle and once again takes her ghostly form. Michael stands there not quite knowing what to say. Finally he say's

"WOW! That was awesome and what happened when you touched me I never felt anything like that before.

"Sorry Michael, but when we project into the minds of those were responsible for, especially in human form we release a flood of emotions in them. It was not intentional but you do have a good heart Michael that's why the feeling was so pleasurable and it will take a while for those feelings to pass, that's enough for today but you should begin practicing just what we did whenever you can.

"I will Cassondra thank you."

She smiled at him and disappeared as silently as she arrived. Michael practiced for about an hour longer then headed back to his room on the way he practiced some simple spells. He took a coin from his pocket held it in his hand and made it start to spin like a top until it flew off and bounced against the wall. Focus, focus he kept saying to himself. When he got back to his room Elaina was there sitting on the balcony. She got up and came to him and said. "How was your training Michael" he put his arms around her and kissed her right on the lips. She wrapped her arms around him and kissed him back but just for a second when she realized what she was doing she pushed away from him and said in a surprised manner "Michael." Michael looked at her and the look of shock came over his face. He began to stutter grasping for word

"Elaina I'm so sorry I don't know what happened, yes I do, it's her fault she said my emotions would be out of whack for a while, I'm sorry, I'm really sorry." Elaina regained her composure. "It's okay Michael I understand, relax there's no harm done." But Michael was still very upset

"I didn't mean to do that Elaina I'm sorry.

"Calm down Michael it's all right, come and sit down, take a deep breath.

"Okay Elaina, I'm alright now." As much as he was trying to act as if he was okay, he still felt embarrassed about what happened Elaina can sense how he felt and thought it best that she leave so he could relax

"Well if your sure you're okay Michael I'll be leaving, but I'll meet you tomorrow morning for combat training all right.

"Sure Elaina I'll see you there."

Elaina got up and left but as she approached the door a smile came over her face as she remembered their kiss.

5

THE NEXT MORNING DURRELL ARRIVED at 6 AM with breakfast as usual, and notice Michael was still in bed. She approached to wake him but saw that he was already awake.

"It's 6 o'clock Michael you should get ready Elaina will be in the training center shortly." Michael looked at her and said "yes Durell, I'm not feeling very well this morning, I think maybe I should skip the lesson today. Could you tell her that for me." She looked at him for moment and then said "sure Michael I'll let her know." After she left he got up and began pacing back and forth he was still embarrassed and didn't know if he could face Elaina right now. He didn't feel like eating so he went to take a quick bath. When he finished Dade was already there sitting at the table.

"Hello Michael, I hear you're not feeling very well today."

"I'm fine, I just can't face Elaina after what happened last night. I'm sure you heard you seem to hear everything."

"Yes I've heard and Elaina isn't upset she realizes it wasn't your fault that you weren't in control. She also knows that you've been wanting to do that for weeks but were too much of a gentleman to do anything about it until you lost control, through no fault of your own."

"Oh thank you Dade, I feel so much better now, you're telling me she knows that I've wanted to kiss her. Great how can I face her now?"

"Well Michael I've told you they can read your thoughts and feelings so just deal with it. Elaina is your partner your companion and your friend unless of course you decide to choose someone else." Michael snapped back quickly "No! I don't want anyone else."

"Good then if were through worrying about small problems let's get down to some serious business. The mage Council has decided to convene a meeting in two weeks to meet their newest member, so you'll need to get over whatever insecurities you have because of what happened and prepare the best we can in the time we have." Michael thought for a moment

"Do you think I'll be able to master being a mage in two weeks."

"Master being a mage in two weeks Michael, you'll be lucky if you master some control, it will probably take you many years to become a master mage maybe more."

"many years, I'll be an old man if I live that long."

"Michael magic has its advantages it keeps us healthy and prolongs our life. I'm nearly seventy years old Michael."

"What, are you serious". "Yes very serious, but no more questions right now Michael. I think Elaine is waiting for you."

"Okay, thanks Dade" Michael changed into his combat uniform and went to the training center. When he got there Elaina was waiting. She looked up and said, "you're late".

"I know, I had some soul-searching to do so that I could get my priorities in order." He walked over and gave her a quick hug and said "let's get started". She tossed him a staff and they began practice as if nothing had happened. The training went well, Elaina would show Michael some new moves and reinforce what he has already learned, and the fighting helped relieve some of the built up pressure. Elaina was going easy on him so he would think he was progressing faster than expected. Michael knew it but said nothing. He appreciated the fact that she was trying to boost his confidence. After the session Michael went back to his room to clean up and get ready to go to the sanctuary. He was not quite as excited as he was the previous day. In fact he was a little hesitant after what happened. Michael reached the sanctuary and called for Cassondra she appeared without hesitation.

"Hello Michael, have you settled in your mind about the kiss."

"Yes thank you, hey wait a minute is everyone except me know everything that goes on around here."

"Michael I'm always with you. I know everything about you and only want what's best for you."

"Thanks but you might of warned me about what could happen."

"I did, you just underestimated the power of your emotions."

"I sure did, but all was okay now." Cassondra waved her hand and on the altar in front of Michael appeared many strange yet familiar looking symbols.

"These are the symbols of language you will be learning. I will teach you the pronunciation and you will practice each day until you can read and pronounce and understand flawlessly."

"This is the language in the books in my study isn't it"

"yes it is, very good Michael. This is an ancient language from a time before humans had a language"

"you mean it's your language the language of the Angels?"

"No Michael, no human knows where this language came from."

"Maybe no human, but you know don't you."

"Yes, but that Michael is information we cannot share even with a Mage. Learning the language is all that's important so that you can read and understand the ancient texts. Now Michael for the next hour you will practice your focus just as we did yesterday, then we will begin our studies together."

The day went well, after his focus exercises he and Cassondra began going over the symbols and pronunciations. Cassondra taught him some simple spells and enchantments and told him to practice them carefully since he was still not in full control of his powers. In between his lessons Michael confided many things to her, his feelings for Elaina, his apprehension about being a Mage, his fear of letting everyone down. She consoled him and explained as much to assure him of his power and his importance to his friends and the world. When Michael left at the end of the day he was feeling much better about his situation and himself. When Michael arrived at his room Elaina and Evelyn were there waiting for him. Evie ran over and hugged him.

"Hi Mike she said, how did your lessons go."

"Great Evie I'm learning a lot."

Elaina said, "hello Michael, I thought I'd bring the chaperone tonight."

They laughed and then sat down to dinner. When they were done they all went and relaxed on the balcony. There was only a quarter moon out tonight but it still seemed to light up the night. Michael found these relaxing nights on the balcony with Elaina and sometimes Evie helped him wind down after a long day. The next few weeks went by quickly with the usual combat training in the morning and studies in practice with Cassondra the rest of the day. He was even beginning to grasp the ancient language and starting to read the books and scrolls in his study. Cassondra was very pleased with the control Michael was beginning to gain over his magic. One afternoon while going through one of his ancient texts he saw spell that caught his attention it said simply combat. He thought it was a strange name since many of the spells he studied were combat type spells. He wondered what made this spell so special. So he decided to stop and translate this spell and see just what it was. To his surprise he found that the spell was not some kind of attack or defense spell but was actually a spell that would take someone with some physical fighting knowledge and give them extreme fighting capability. Michael was puzzled why would a mage need a spell to make him a combat expert when he has magic and others with him who have combat experience. Then he thought maybe it's not for the mage but for those who serve him those trained in combat could become experts. Then he thought what if he did use it on himself wouldn't Elaina be surprised. She'd never know it was a spell. Michael laughed and hurried to the sanctuary, he went to the altar open the book and with all the feeling he could muster perform the spell. He waited but there was no flash no lightning no indication at all that the spell had worked. Oh well he thought I guess we'll see tomorrow if it worked or not. He thought of the surprised look on Elaina's face if it worked. Michael stayed late in the study he didn't want Elaina to read his mind and spoil the surprise. She told Michael she doesn't read anyone unless there is good reason or when someone is very emotional which make it difficult not to read, since strong emotion broadcasts everywhere. Following morning was much the same. He ate a little something and headed to the arena on the way he was having second thoughts about springing his surprise on Elaina. If he showed himself to be an expert that may cancel future lessons since Elaina might feel there no longer needed and he liked his morning workouts and his morning time with Elaina. Upon reaching the arena he saw everyone practicing. "Good morning Elaina I thought we get an early start. I have a lot of work to do today and don't want to work as late as last night, I missed our relaxing downtime before bed"

"okay Michael we'll do some hand-to-hand to start."

When they started Michael felt his heightened ability and speed but held back so no one would notice. After the days work out she complemented him on his vast improvement. Michael just thanked her and said he's been practicing. After he left the arena he was feeling a little upset with himself for deceiving her. He felt like he had cheated on a test. That sure didn't go the way he had originally planned it. But he was intrigued that by using magic he was able to give someone an ability that they didn't originally possess. He wondered if there were other abilities that could be passed on through magic. Michael put the thought aside so he could hurry to clean up and get to the sanctuary he felt that he needed all the practice he could get before his meeting with the mage Council. When he arrived at the sanctuary and called Cassondra she came right away. The first thing she said was "nice the way you deceived Elaina"

Michael shook his head and said, "you know what I did"

"of course I know, I know everything that happens to and around you Michael."

"Well I didn't intend to deceive her, I wanted to play a joke on her then tell her what I discovered but I chickened out at the last minute, I'll tell her when the time is right."

Well that's up to you of course but I am glad to see that you're discovering and using new spells on your own, and very effectively your focus has improved greatly and more quickly than expected. In fact Michael we can now begin to move to more advanced training" after a full day of training Michael returned to his room tired and looking forward to a relaxing evening. Elaina as usual was waiting and greeted him as he sat for a quick bite. After dinner they went and relaxed on the balcony which was usually Michael's favorite part of the evening but tonight he was wrestling with whether or not to tell Elaina about his secret which he didn't tell her before. If he didn't he would be violating her trust and if he did she might be mad that he didn't tell her before, but a deal is a deal so he decided it's best to come out with it and take his punishment if necessary.

"Elaina I need to tell you something"

"what is it Michael" now but just as he was about to tell her Evie walked in and Michael was not going to look like a fool in front of someone else.

"Not in front of Evie, we'll talk later." He whispered to Elaina as Evie approached.

"Hi guys, what are you up to" asked Evie"

"just relaxing" said Michael "pull up the chair" he was a little disappointed and at the same time a little relieved. They sat back and relaxed the rest of the evening. The next two weeks were very exciting for him each day after his combat training, which he was still holding back on, he and Cassondra were training with some pretty advanced magic. She had never seen anyone learn so quickly and she was surprised at the yet untapped power within him. He was learning devastating attack spells and powerful defensive spells. He was enjoying his time with Cassondra almost as much as his time with Elaina. He felt the friendship and kinship with his new friends that he hadn't felt in a long time. Now he and even Evie have people who care as much for them is for each other. Then one day which started out like always with a quick breakfast and heading off to the combat arena. When he arrived Elaina was talking to the Mattriss and several of the elder sisters. Michael didn't approach them because he didn't want to appear to be ease dropping so he went to the mat to prepare for his training session with Elaina. After a few minutes they came to him they bowed slightly and Michael return the courtesy. The Mattress spoke,

"Michael we've been evaluating your progress which is been very impressive and have decided that Elaina skills have taken you as far as she can. So the more experience sisters, specialists in their own particular skills will continue your daily training." Michael responded sharply

"Elaina is my instructor I feel she has done a fine job and has much more to teach me."

We agree Elaina has done a fine job but we feel she has reached the current limit of her skill. Michael Elaina is your permanent companion and protector unless you choose another but for your combat training we must do what's best for you especially with your first meeting of the Mage Council just a week away, your instructors must be our choice." Michael thought for a moment then said, "Elaina has already taught me more than I could learn from any of the others and I've seen how amazing they are at their art."

"That is unlikely Michael but we would never doubt the abilities of our Mage. So would you be up for contest so we may determine your skill level."

"Of course, and if I'm wrong and don't measure up to your standard I will naturally do as you suggest."

"Wonderful and let us gauge your skills, you will fight hand-to-hand, with sword, and with staff, in each case you will face our resident expert in each class. Elaina prepare him we begin in five minutes." Elaina got the padded gloves, wooden sword, and staff and brought them to Michael." Michael you can't seriously expect to defeat them. They're the best and they won't go easy on you, this is a test."

Michael thought to himself, now is the time when I see how well that combat spell worked I can't hold back.

"Don't worry Elaina, I'm not training with anyone but you"

"Michael I don't think you understand I'll continue as to your partner, your aid."

"I understand completely."

"Time to begin" said mother superior "hand-to-hand first" they stepped onto the mat's gave the customary bow to each other and began. She came hard at Michael in order to demonstrate the limits of his abilities, but Michael moved like lightning, Countering every attack with amazing skill in initiating blistering attacks of his own, being sure to stop just short of contact after all he didn't want to hurt his friends. Everyone looked on in utter amazement. But no one was more amazed or confused than Elaina. She had never seen Michael fight with such skill or prowess. The results with sword and staff were just as impressive in the end he had defeated them all. They all ran up to him and hugged and congratulated him. The Mattress came to him and said "you have proven your superior skills you can of course continue training with Elaina, she has trained you well" she turned to Elaina "whatever your teaching Elaina please continue you have both exceeded our expectations" she bowed to them and left with the others. Elaina turned to Michael with an angry look on her face.

"How Michael, how could you possibly do what you just did, I can't believe you pretended from the beginning that you are a novice all the time you are an expert."

"I was a novice when I came here Elaina but something happened, I don't think we should talk here with others around. Can we discuss it tonight, I'll tell you everything that's happened."

"Okay Michael but I want the whole truth"

"I promise I'll explain everything later" Michael rushed off to talk to Cassondra. He entered the sanctuary and called her, once again she came right away.

"Congratulations Michael on your victory."

"Yeah but I cheated I use the magic."

"What's the difference Michael, you're a Mage you are magic, you have enhanced your ability so that the ability is yours. The sisters aren't concerned with how you got the ability their just glad you're doing so well. This is not a contest to them they care about you and would do anything for you." "Elaine is mad at me" "well she thinks you;ve been lying to her the whole time, she cares very much for you and feels you betrayed her trust. Just tell her the truth she'll understand. We'll forget the training for today, you'll need time to practice your humbling speech, she smiled and disappeared. Michael went back to his room got cleaned up and spent the rest of the day deciding how to explain what happened to Elaina. When Elaina arrived looking pretty upset she walked up to Michael, "you've been lying to me all this time you're an expert in combat and led me to believe you are a novice, why Michael?"

"That's not what happened Elaina. When I came here I was a novice."

"That's impossible, there's no way you could get that good that fast"

she stopped short as though an idea just popped into her head "Magic, you used magic didn't you?"

Michael began to explain, he told her about the book he found containing the combat spell and use it on himself so he can amaze her with his newfound ability. He told her how he chickened out at the last minute"

"but why Michael I would've been happy for you not angry, you should know that."

"Yeah but I thought if you knew we would stop training each morning I really liked training and being with you."

"Michael we would still need to train in order to stay in peak condition, it's as much about exercise as it is about training besides now you can teach me some moves."

"I won't have to I'm going to give you the ability too."

"I don't know Michael is that possible can we do that?"

You're supposed to have my back if necessary not in training but in the real world, shouldn't you be as good as possible to help protect us both."

"Well yes I guess so"

Michael told her to move back and he performed the combat spell just as he did before. She looked at him "did it work"

"I don't know try it attack me". Elaina attacked Michael but nothing was different it hadn't worked. "What happened Michael"

"I don't know but I will find out tomorrow I'll talk to the guardian and see if I missed something don't worry I'll get it to work."

They went out to the balcony as usual, but Michael couldn't enjoy the evening he was too busy wondering what had gone wrong. The next day Michael and Elaina had the training time together although it was mostly exercise and having fun. Once it was over Michael went straight to the sanctuary. Naturally the first thing he asked Cassondra was what happened with his spell.

"I did it just as I had here but it didn't work".

"That Michael is because it is a protected spell, it can only be performed on consecrated ground. Some spells such as those that give people special abilities are protected spells so that they are not abused. They can only work on consecrated ground when performed by a mage."

"Why? That doesn't make any sense".

"Really Michael, how would it be if an evil wizard created an army of experts at combat and had them attack a wizarding order, how many would have to be killed to drive them back. Or what if they created two armies and had them kill each other."

"Okay okay I get the point so what you're saying is I need to bring Elaina here."

"No Michael, Elaina can't enter here, no one can without an exceptionally good reason."

"Look she won't see you, you don't even have to show up."

"It's not that Michael, this room is sort of a special place almost between dimensions if anyone else tries to enter they won't get past the barrier they may even be hurt but there is another consecrated room in the temple."

"What? Where is it and why didn't anyone tell me."

"They don't know it exists Michael."

"Well why didn't you tell me?"

"Because you didn't need it before, clearly Michael you are progressing more quickly than anyone expected and your moving well beyond normal wizarding abilities. Your Becoming a true Mage Michael and I'm very proud of you." Your other sanctuary is in your study. I've put it's location into your mind…

"Thanks Cassondra I couldn't have done any of this without you. Wow! I've got to go find Elaina."

6

MICHAEL SEARCHED THE TEMPLE AND found her in the chapel for prayers he waited in the doorway trying to get her attention. When she finally saw him she immediately look to the altar and noticed that the Mattriss had also noticed him. Mother superior looked from Michael to Elaina and smiled and nodded her approval. Elaina got up and quietly went to Michael.

"What is it Michael?" "Come with me Elaina."

He took her straight to the library and told her why this spell didn't work. He explained that she couldn't get into the sanctuary but also told her there was another room that was consecrated and led her to his study. He went to the picture next to the mirror and tilted to the left heard the latch lift and a door pop open slightly. Elaina was shocked "Michael I don't think anyone had any idea this was here."

Elaina went to enter but was stopped by an invisible barrier.

"Michael I can't get in." "Take my hand Elaina."

She did as he asked and they walked in together. As they entered the room lit up. The entire back wall was a huge Dragon sculpture embellished in the mages black red and gold colors. The other walls were covered in ancient symbols and writings, in the center was an altar just like the one in the sanctuary and on the floor were two circles one surrounding the altar the other to the side both with ancient markings around them.

"Wow Michael this is amazing, what's that?"

Michael looked where she was pointing and hanging in the back corner of the room was some kind of uniform.

"Looks like more clothes" said Michael.

"Michael those aren't just clothes, that's ancient battle armor, I've read about it I've never seen it before, like I said this is amazing." Michael had

Elaina stand inside the smaller circle while he went to the altar he opened the book took a couple of deep breaths and read the spell once again. He saw light close around her which quickly went away he wondered if that happened to him and he just didn't notice.

"Did it work Michael?" "Yes I believe it did. Let's try it."

Sure enough, Elaina moved like a cat with the speed and skill of an expert.

"That's the most amazing feeling I've ever had during sparring. It's like I became the wind."

She ran up and threw her arms around him. "Thank you Michael,."

Then she realized what she had done and backed away.

"That's okay Elaina, now your a true protector, an expert."

They looked around the room for a little while longer and found the cabinet built into the wall that they hadn't noticed earlier. Inside were some ancient relics and some stones and crystals. They each mentioned guesses as to how old they might be. After a little while they decided to go back to Michael's room and have some dinner and relax. When they were done eating they went to their usual place on the balcony. Elaina moved her lounge chair right next to Michael's he looked at her and waved his hand over their glasses. Elaina asked what he had done.

"I changed the juice into a fine wine." "Wine, I've never had wine before, I mean I know what it is but I've never had any." She took a sip.

"Oh! I like it."

They sat for a while relaxing and sipping their wine. When they heard a voice from behind them, it was Dade.

"Well you two sitting there relaxing, hard day."

He walked over and picked up a glass and sniffed. "Wine and a good one at that but don't get too comfortable remember your meeting with the Council is in a few days which brings me to why I'm here. I think you should take two of my wizards with you for added protection, they plus Elaina should give you a good edge if the need arises. We don't expect any trouble but better safe than sorry. Come and meet the two I've selected, with your approval of course. First this young lady is Thalia she had been studying for five years and she's very good for her age. Then we have Lucas he's only been studying for two years but he is anxious to help and to meet you. Thalia is all about business and kind of anti-social. Luke on the other hand is a social butterfly, in fact he can be annoying sometimes he questions everything. Now if you want I can give you older more experienced wizards, but I felt you would be more comfortable with those around your own age, the choice is yours."

"No that's fine Dade I respect your judgment and you're right I will feel more comfortable with younger wizards in case I do something stupid they may not notice."

Michael walked up to Thalia, she nodded to him and said simply "Mage"

"hello Thalia you don't need to call me Mage just Michael will do."

Thalia looked at him and nodded once again. Then Michael approached Lucas who started talking almost immediately.

"Dragon Mage it is a real honor to work with you sir, is it all right if I call you Michael too, this is an amazing opportunity sir." Michael interrupted

"Lucas stop and breathe." Then Dade said "Luke that's enough you and Thalia can go. Tomorrow we will discuss the details of your mission." Thalia nodded again turned to Lucas and said, "come on geek before you make a bigger fool of yourself." With that there was a flash and they were gone.

"Well Dade, they're a lively pair."

"Don't worry Michael they'll be fine you will keep them in line. Okay Michael I'll leave you two to finish your wine in peace, but I'll be back tomorrow with your escort to go over the details of your trip."

Michael and Elaina went back out to the balcony to relax a little while before finally retiring. The following morning Dade arrived bright and early along with Thalia and Lucas. When Elaina arrived they sat at the table as Dade explained to Michael what to expect. He then went over with the others just what their role would be in how they should behave. Then he went over their placement exactly where they should be at all times.

"Elaina you will stay by Michael's side at all times. Thalia you and Luke will be behind him several yards back during the meeting and closer the rest of the time. Michael was puzzled, "are you expecting trouble Dade."

"No not really Michael, you should be well protected while there but after the attack here I'm not taking any chances." After the meeting broke up Dade sent the others out to the balcony to relax while he spoke to Michael.

"Michael it's tradition for the Dragon Mage to lead the Council since you're just getting started they may wait for you to take over that post or they may ask you now, whether you accept it now or later is up to you but I'm letting you know so it doesn't come as a surprise if they do."

"Why the Dragon Mage?"

"Because the Dragon Mage is usually the most powerful of all the mage, mostly because of the power within him and because of his knowledge. We have the most extensive library and only the Dragon Mage has the ancient books and manuscripts that are in your study. They contain powerful magic. Not to change the subject but I've arranged to have Luke and Thalia stay here so you can get acquainted and trained together for the meeting that way you'll all know what to expect from each other. I'll see you again before you leave."

Dade left the room and Michael and Elaina joined Thalia and Lucas at the table Elaina poured them all some juice while they talked well mostly Lucas talked. Michael never saw someone who could rattle on about nothing the way Lucas could. He found it very amusing. Then Michael noticed Thalia's wand

"wow nice wand may I see it."

Thalia looked at him as though debating whether it would be alright, finally she handed it to Michael. The wand was a dark wood with a beautifully engraved handle and smooth front end with a crystal embedded in the tip and a gold rear tip "it has a gold core to help channel energy." Said Thalia

"this is amazing workmanship where would you get something like this."

"No Michael every wizard has to make their own wand during their first year of training."

"This is really nice Thalia, Elaina isn't this something?"

"Yes Michael it's great, but we should get going to the training center for our workout."

"I think we can skip it for today to get acquainted with our guests what Dade said and tomorrow we'll all train together."

"Okay Michael, but I still have things to do so I have to get going and I'll see you later okay."

"Sure Elaina, I'll see you later."

As she left the room you can see the slight tinge of jealousy on her face. Michael handed Thalia back her wand. Lucas pulled out his wand.

"Want to see my wand Michael." "Sure Luke let's see it." It was a simple tapered piece of wood with a crystal tip not nearly as intricate as Thalia's.

"That's real nice Luke."

Then Lucas went on about how he made it, when he made it, what wood he used, where he got the crystal and on and on. Thalia just shook her head. A short while later Durell came to show Luke and Thalia to their rooms. After they left Michael headed to the sanctuary. Over the next few days the routine was the same. They would all meet for combat training, Thalia and Lucas were very surprised at how good Michael and Elaina were. Michael would just say that Elaina was a good teacher. After combat training Elaina would go off with the sisters for chores and prayers, Luke would go back to his room to study and Thalia you would stay and continue training. Like Dade said she was all about business. Michael would go and get cleaned up and head off to train with Cassondra.

On the final day before the Council meeting Cassondra arrived with a long leather pouch. She became solid again and stepped barefoot onto the floor. She walked to Michael without so much as a word and handed the package to him. Michael opened it and inside found a sword with a beautiful jeweled handle. He drew it from it's sheath. The blade was a glimmering gold color with writing on it.

"Wow! What is this" Michael asked.

"That Michael is dragon's breath the sword of the first Dragon Mage. It hasn't been seen out of the sanctuary in more than 1500 years."

"Why" he asked

"because none of the Dragon Mage since have been accepted by the sword, they were unable to release its power."

"How do you know if it will except me".

"I don't, only the sword can feel if you're worthy to wield it. The ancient writing on the blade the language you've been learning read it, translate it.

Michael looked at the glimmering blade and read. "uLa nuance, we are the power." The blade immediately burst into flame.

"Touch the blade Michael the flame will not harm you."

Michael did as she requested, he gently ran his hand down the blade his eyes were wide open in amazement.

"Now Michael, point the blade at the shield on the wall and think attack."

As Michael did so the flame leaped from the sword like a flamethrower hitting the shield dead center.

"If that shield had been anywhere but in the sanctuary Michael it would've been destroyed completely. The sword has excepted you Michael is yours now, it will serve you and only you for as long as you live, use it wisely to dispense justice. Now tell the sword to rest."

Michael said "brega" and the flame extinguished.

"There is a powerful evil rising Michael, even we can't see who or what is behind it but it is growing and it appears to be moving more aggressively now that the mage Council is complete once again. That is why all the attacks lately, they're moving more openly. Trust none but those closest to you don't even trust the other mage completely even though they all want to achieve the same goal, peace and balance each has their own agenda and feelings about how to accomplish this and each is sure their way is the right way. Despite our guidance and help they've strayed from the original path and it seems each generation of mage are diminished. Their power is not what it once was but you Michael seem to possess all the power of the ancient Mage. We don't understand this but are hopeful you will be the one to restore order."

"I'll be careful, thank you Cassondra."

7

ICHAEL TOOK THE LONG WAY back to his room. He had a lot on his mind he thought of what Cassondra had said and about the meeting tomorrow. When he got back to his room Lucas, Talia and Elaina will already there. They sat together and ate and talked for quite a while Lucas was the first to leave he said he had to leave the temple to attend some business but would be back first thing in the morning. They all felt a little relieved that they would have some silence after Lucas left. They even joked about it. Thalia went to her room shortly after while Michael and Elaina went to the balcony to relax for the rest of the evening. The next morning Michael woke early feeling very nervous so he figured he would bathe in the warm water under the waterfall. Elaina was the first to arrive and saw that Michael was not there. She wondered if he had gone to the sanctuary for last-minute guidance. She knocked on the bathroom door and called his name but there was no answer. She entered but didn't see him until she moved the bath curtain aside and saw him bathing. She immediately turned around her back to him.

"Michael, I'm sorry I didn't know you were there."

That's okay Elaina, why don't you join me the water is great."

"Michael you know I couldn't do that" but she smiled as she said it."

"I'll wait for you outside Michael."

"Okay Elaina I'll be right out but you don't know what you're missing."

Michael got dressed and entered the main room.

"Hi Elaina, it was a great bath."

"I couldn't get into the bathing pool with a naked man not even our Mage."

"Tell me Elaina am I never to know love."

"Well Michael, we are in a sentimental mood today aren't we."

"Sure, it helps keep my mind occupied so I'm not so nervous."

"Okay Michael in that case I forgive you."

Just then Thalia entered the room in what look like full battle gear. Michael asked if anyone had seen Lucas but no one had.

"Well we have to leave in one hour with or without him."

Dade arrived with last-minute instructions and to ensure them that there was nothing to be nervous about. Elaina left to get ready and said she'd be back shortly Michael added a belt and his sword to his waist no one was as yet aware that he possessed the dragon's breath. He and Thalia sat at the table for a late breakfast. Before they were done Lucas arrived in his normal wizard apparel.

"Hey Luke we were beginning to wonder if you would get here on time how are you?"

"I'm fine was his only response Michael thought that was very unusual for Lucas but felt they were probably all little nervous except for Thalia nothing seem to bother her. Elaina returned and she too was in full combat gear.

Michael said, "hey guys were not going to war."

Dade said, "it's normal Michael for aides to be in combat dress."

The time had finally come, the four of them gathered together. Dade said to Michael, "I'll teleport you there once you've teleported to the location it will be ingrained in your mind and magic and you'll be able to teleport yourself to and from whenever you like." Dade raised his wand muttered a phrase and with a flash and they were gone. They immediately reappeared inside a lighted cave high in the Arctic. 20 yards away stood 11 individuals some wizards some sorcerers dressed in full combat gear. They approached Michael and bowed the blue wizards spoke "Dragon Mage we are here to escort you to the Council chamber, this way sir."

Michael and the others followed them to a large round room with decorative armor and weapons and flags of different colors, in the middle of the room was a large oval table around which the other 11 Mage stood awaiting Michael's arrival. The honor guard that led them to the Council chamber broke up and each went to stand behind their respective Mage. From the far end of the table a Mage came to greet Michael followed by his aid the blue wizard.

"Hello Michael, my name is Richard the ice Mage, temporary leader of the Council and this is my aide Morgan."

"Hello Richard, Morgan, since you know who I am let me introduce Elaina, Lucas and Thalia each bowed in turn "Please Michael have a seat we're about to get started.

Richard returned to his seat and Michael took the vacant seat at the table. Richard stood, "first Michael we are all equal here, magic does it work within the Council chamber which is why we transport outside and walk in being equal means any Mage has the right to speak when they have something to say. Now for introductions."

From the other side of the table a Mage dressed in tan and white stood.

"Why is it that Michael arrives with three aides is he expecting a battle and looking for an advantage."

Richard turned to the Mage and said that Dade had told him he was sending extra protection due to the recent attempted attack on the Temple.

"He has a priestess with no magic for protection, what kind of protection is that." He said with a laugh.

"Michael got angry, he stood up placed his hands on the table looked the mage straight in the eye and said "she is my friend and companion and where I go, she goes."

The mage looked into Michael's eyes and then sat back down. Seeing that Michael had the situation in hand Richard continued once again, "now maybe we can get to introductions, the rather loud mage you are just speaking to Michael is Henry the lightning mage, to his right is David the mountain mage, then Ryan the stone mage, Paul the dark mage, Edward the water mage, Julian the fire mage, Raymond the desert mage, Gregory the forest mage." Each of them stood and nodded as their name was called except of course for Henry. Richard then called the meeting to order they discussed what they were able to find out about the growing darkness and recent attacks. They were each asked to use all their resources to get a handle on the problem. They were clearly worried about what was happening. Then Richard made a proposal "finally, the Dragon mage has always lead the Council and I think Michael should assume his position as our leader." Michael was about to speak when Henry once again jumped up.

"I disagree, Michael is inexperienced and I don't believe he can properly lead the Council at this time."

The others began a heated discussion among themselves Ryan jumped up I second Richard's motion"

Michael stood up and everyone became silent to hear what he had to say. "Thank you Richard, Dade said we might come to this point and I've thought about what I should do. I hate to agree with Henry, but many things are happening right now which require a more experienced leadership than I feel I can provide. I'm truly honored but I think for now Richard should continue to lead the Council."

Richard stood and nodded toward Michael "as you wish Michael. If there's no other business meeting is adjourned refreshments are on the far table." Michael didn't want anything to eat but did have a glass of juice. Elaina stood close by his side while Thalia and Luke hung back out of the way watching. Michael was talking to some of the other mage getting to know them just socializing a bit when he noticed Raymond the desert mage approach Luke whisper something to him and walked away. Luke suddenly got an angry look on his face definitely not normal for Luke. A moment later Luke drew his sword yelled death in a loud voice and started to attack. Thalia turned and saw Luke charging toward Michael she drew her sword and slashed Luke across the chest and Luke dropped hard. When she realized what she had done she dropped to her knees beside him he was bleeding and unconscious. Michael turned toward Raymond and said "what did you do to him."

What are you talking about, I did nothing" was his reply.

Michael was angry. "You whispered something to him what was it."

"I only asked if he wanted some refreshments."

"I can sense your lying" said Elaina.

Raymond drew his sword "how dare you call me a liar you insignificant nothing." Elaina quickly had her sword out she knew his magic wouldn't work in the Council chamber, Michael looked at Thalia and Luke. Luke was lying on the floor and she was holding his hand and calling his name "Luke I'm sorry I had no choice she said."

Michael realized there was no time to waste with this mage right now, so he drew his sword and said "ula nunce" in the Dragon sword burst into action. Raymond was moving toward Elaina stopped dead in his tracks. Everyone else stared in amazement. From off to the side Richard said "dragon's breath, the sword of the Dragon mage it hasn't been seen in centuries."

Raymond said "that's impossible magic can't work here."

Richard said, "dragon's breath carries his own magic and responds only to the Dragon mage."

Michael turned to Raymond "if we had time I let you go Elaina would cut you to pieces." He then said "brega" and the sword extinguished. He and Elaina ran to Luke. Thalia said "Michael he's dying."

Michael said "not yet Thalia" he picked up Luke and told Thalia and Elaina to grab his shoulder. They did as he asked but Elaina said "Michael we need to leave the chamber to teleport." Michael looked at her and mumbled an ancient phrase and in a flash they were gone. Morgan turned to Richard "that's not possible" he said. Richard looked at him "well I guess it is, Morgan. Michael just may be the mage we been looking for to help bring order back to the Council. In the meantime keep an eye on Raymond, if Michael's right we may have a problem." Second after leaving the Council chamber Michael and the others arrived in Luke's room in Ghostra. Almost immediately the sisters came running in and started working on Luke.

"Please Michael you and the others should leave we'll take it from here" said Sister Beth the lead healer. "Can I help with magic" asked Michael "no Michael perhaps later the rest of you can help him recover more quickly but this injury requires natural healing."

Michael shook his head and turned to leave with Elaina and Thalia. "Michael I need to stay with him," said Thalia

"no Thalia, we need to let them work they know what they're doing."

"But it's my fault, I did this to him."

"No it's not your fault, I felt something was wrong with him this morning but thought he was just nervous like I was I should've said something then, but whatever it was I think the Mage Raymond said something to set him off and if so that means he was in on what happened.

"If your right Michael I swear I'll kill him."

"Stand in line, I've got first dibs."

Thalia smiled, sort of forced smile. Elaina went over to her hugged her and said "come with me Thalia we'll get you cleaned up you've got blood on your hands and clothes. You want to get cleaned up to Michael."

Michael headed to his room pondering whether he was right about Raymond and if so why would a mage do that. He reached his room before he could bathe or change Dade arrived. "Michael how was Lucas." The sisters are working on him now they'll let us know when there's any news. Thalia is taking it pretty hard, she really must care about him."

"She does, but not the way you think. She lookes at Luke like a little brother. When Thalia first came to us she had a hard time she trusted no one not even me. She trained hard and was very good but always had a trust problem never getting close to anyone. We didn't know why so when Luke came to us we made her responsible for him. It was my idea and it worked. She became close to him and started to open up. She stopped being a loner and became a welcome part of the order. She had a rough childhood. She lost her kid brother to illness, she was abandoned and Luke seemed to fill that void in her life. If he doesn't make it she'll be devastated."

"Wow Dade I had no idea."

"I got a report of what happened at the meeting they say you have dragon's breath may I see it." Michael handed Dade the Dragon sword. Dade looked it over "it's beautiful" he said and handed it back to Michael.

"I also heard that you teleported out of the Council chambers I don't know how you did it, but I'll bet that scared the hell out of them."

"I don't know either, I only knew I had to get Luke out of there as fast as possible."

"Well Michael, you may have saved his life. We'll talk more later I've got to see Thalia try to ease the guilt she must be feeling."

Dade left and Michael got cleaned up and changed. After a long soak he sat at the table feeling like the weight of the world was on his shoulders. He was worried about Luke, he was worried about Thalia and everyone seemed to be relying on him. He didn't know if he could live up to everyone's expectations but he knew that he had to try. A short while later sister Beth came into the room and Michael held his breath. "How is Luke?" Michael asked.

"He's fine Michael, a week or so and he will be as good as new. We gave him some herbs so that he can rest he should sleep till morning, right now he needs his rest."

"Thank you sister" said Michael "has anyone told Thalia yet"

"Not yet, we felt you should tell her."

Michael nodded and headed for Thalia's room when he got there she was on the bed crying. As soon as she saw Michael she wiped her eyes and jumped to attention you can see the fear in her she knew Michael had news. He walked over to her and said "Luke is going to be okay" immediately her posture eased and tears once again filled her eyes. "Thank you Michael" she said as she put her arms around him something he hadn't expected from her "you saved his life Michael."

"The sisters saved his life Thalia I had nothing to do with it."

"I thank the sisters with all my heart Michael but you did the impossible, you got Luke here in time the way he was bleeding if we had to get out of the magical barrier he would've been gone before we got here I know that so do you. Can I see him?"

"They have him sedated, he needs his rest, but I don't think it will hurt for you to sit with him for a while."

"Thank you Michael" she said, and then headed for the door.

Michael went to the sanctuary he needed to see Cassondra he had many questions that he felt only she could answer. When he got there he called Cassondra and she appeared.

"Well Michael how did you make out."

"You mean you don't know already."

"Michael we don't pierce protective barriers without an invitation that would be rude."

"It was a real mess, I think someone put a spell on Luke which caused him to attack us, Thalia had to stop him and now he's in the infirmary, and another thing I don't trust all of the other Mage. There's something going on and I thought you may be able to help me sorted it out."

"Your instincts are good Michael, we believe that two of the Mage may be conspiring against the others. Henry the lightning Mage and Raymond the desert Mage have stop seeking guidance from their guardians and have been disappearing into a secret room that is protected by very powerful magic we believe their speaking and planning with dark forces."

"Do you mean that cloaked figure that shows up whenever there's trouble."

"That cloaked figure Michael, whoever or whatever it is shows that it possesses powerful magic. But we believe that it's doing the dirty work for an even more powerful being. It looks as if they're trying to break the balance in create wars again turning Mage against Mage in order to take over. If that happens Michael the world will change dramatically and not for the better. Millions of innocent people could be killed not to mention the devastation of the magical world."

"Dade mentioned there were once magical wars, what actually happened."

"2000 years ago there were no Mage Michael and the magical world had no guidance. Wars waged over the quest for power, and people were caught in the middle. Human and animal sacrifice became common. That's when most of the magical myths and legends were born, it was a terrible time for everyone. We did what we could to protect the people. It got so bad that we debated whether we should come through the barrier and destroy all magic but if we did that the world would have no protection from the dark realm. So we would be forced to stay there and keep the monsters and demons and other dark creatures from destroying everything. Then out of nowhere the first Dragon Mage appeared. We don't know where he came from but he was the most powerful magical being we had ever encountered. He knew of our existence and summoned one of us to this place. The sanctuary within the temple that had not existed before. He told us that he would bring peace and order to the magical world and protect the people. He commanded a pair of Black Dragons and was able to summon an army of warriors out of the elements air, water, fire and Earth and force all the magical factions to stop their fighting. He then broke them into 12 magical orders he put the most powerful order under his direct control and brought forth 11 other Mage. We're not sure if he created them somehow from the wizards of the circle he created or brought them from where he came. We're not even sure if he came from an unknown realm or if he was just a wizard who somehow magnified his powers. He never shared his story with us, but he was good on his word he brought peace and protection to the world. Over time the wizarding orders formed loyalties to their mage, these loyalties eventually became mutual dependence on each other and the original Dragon Mage vanished as quickly as he had appeared and was replaced by his successor."

Michael said, "wow that's some story and no one knows where he came from or where he went."

"No Michael it's a mystery even to us we think maybe he just went into seclusion with the priestess he fell in love with and they live their lives together."

"You mean like the priestesses who lived in the temple now."

Yes, they are part of the same order. When the Dragon Mage fell in love with the priestess Lorana whose own temple had been destroyed in the wars, he brought their entire order to live in the temple and they've been an important part of the Temple ever since, and they have fought for and died for their Mage countless times."

"Then it's okay for a Mage to fall in love."

"The responsibilities of a Mage always have to have priority, but no one expects a mage to sacrifice love Michael, love is an important and powerful force and after all you are still human."

"One more question, whatever happened to the Black Dragons."

"That too is a mystery Michael perhaps he took them with him or send them back where he had gotten them."

"Thank you Cassondra, I don't know what I would do without your help."

It was already dark when Michael got back to his room Elaina and Thalia were there already waiting for him.

"Hello Michael," they said almost simultaneously. "It was getting late we were beginning to worry, how are your lessons," asked Elaina.

"There were no magical lessons but I learned a lot today, how is Luke"

Thalia said "he looks much better now, he got back most of his color but they're letting him sleep until tomorrow to help regain his strength."

"That's good, I can use a glass of wine how about you two." Elaina said, "yes, I found the wine very relaxing the other night."

"How about you Thalia."

"I don't know Michael, I've never had wine before but if it'll help me relax, is it any good."

Michael waved his hand over their glasses. "With the stress we've been under this may just become one of my favorite spells," Michael joked.

Thalia picked up a glass smelled and then tasted it. "Oh! I like this."

They spent the rest of the evening just relaxing after what seemed like a very long day.

8

THE NEXT MORNING MICHAEL GOT up early and hurried to the infirmary to see how Luke was doing. Thalia and Elaina were already there. Luke was awake and they were talking.

Michael said "how are you doing Luke."

"I'm a little sore but otherwise I'm okay, Thalia was telling me what happened but I don't remember any of it. I don't even remember coming here yesterday.

"Yeah, we think you are under the spell of some kind."

"Thalia told me you saved my life, thank you Michael."

"Hey were a team we need to take care of each other."

Just then Dade came into the room with two other wizard's. They approached the bed and Dade looked down at Luke and said "well you don't look any the worse for ware."

"Hi Dade I'm fine." The other wizard's said hello to Luke and Thalia and nodded to Michael.

"Michael this is Paul and Marcus we are on our way to the blue orders homebase. We got word there is going to be another attack there today."

"The information, is it reliable," asked Michael

"the source has proven reliable in the past, Richard the Mage and his order will meet us there."

Michael said, "I'm coming with you."

"Are you sure that's a good idea."

"No but I'm coming anyway, it's about time I start helping out."

Elaina jumped up "you're not going anywhere without me Michael."

Michael turned towards Elaina and saw the determined look at your eyes and knew there was no sense arguing. "Wouldn't dream of it Elaina but stay close."

Thalia looked at the others "what about me" she asked.

"You stay here and look after Luke and the others just in case. The Temple is much better protected now but if there is a problem send us a message and protect the sisters in the temple until we arrive". Thalia nodded her okay.

They teleported out and arrived at the headquarters of the blue order. Everyone greeted each other. Michael got a lot of "glad to finally meet you". Moments later Richard and his aide arrived. He saw Michael and shook hands "good to see you again Michael, how is Lucas?"

"He's doing well Richard, almost talking is much as usual" Everyone laughed. Michael looked around, the large room they were in and several tunnels exiting. in the room itself was adorned with all the maps and ancient armor "okay, how do we handle this" Michael asked. Richard said, "we can split up into small groups each taking a hallway and signal the rest when your area comes under attack the others will come leaving a guard behind just in case."

Dade said, the rest of our order is standing by if we need them."

One blue wizard stayed behind while everyone else form small groups and headed out. Michael Elaina and Marcus took one hallway and walked about 100 yards in past a couple of dozen rooms Marcus said, "these are probably sleeping areas, can't tell for sure with the doors closed but that's what it looks like."

They came to the end of the hall to what appears to be a lounge area with a big picture window. Outside looked like an ice cave.

Michael said, "well I guess we wait here."

Marcus said, "even if they don't come in here we can see what's moving through the cave and can warn the others."

They waited about an hour but nothing happened Michael asked Elaina "are you sensing anything at all."

"No Michael, nothing."

A short while later Elaina said "Michael I feel something, but it doesn't feel evil."

Suddenly Michael saw Cassondra, but none of the others can see her. She spoke to Michael "Michael the attack is beginning but not here, it's a human civilian target you must follow me."

Michael yelled to Marcus "the attack is on a civilian target tell the others and have them follow my trail I'll leave a clear path." Michael took

Elaina by the hand and ran towards Cassondra who transported them to the area of the attack. There were many demons and dozens of other creatures Michael had never seen before. Michael started firing energy waves and lightning bolts knocking some creatures back and incinerating others Elaina had drawn her sword and was slashing down demons. There were a couple of dozen creatures that looked almost zombielike. Suddenly one of them produced a fireball and threw it at Elaina. Michael reacted quickly and cast an invisible shield around Elaina the fireball hit the shield but could not penetrate. Then Michael drew his sword and said "ula nunce" and the Dragon sword ignited as if sensing the battle. The flame swirled around the blade like a flaming tornado. The flame became white-hot. Michael waited for the civilians fleeing the creature's until they were in the clear then pointing the sword toward 20 advancing creatures and with a thought the flame shot forward 30 yards and as Michael move the sword the flame followed like a huge flamethrower incinerating everything in its path. Behind Michael and Elaina were multiple sounds as more than two dozen wizards appeared but the remaining creatures were already in retreat. Michael spotted the cloaked figure on the hill overlooking the area but the figure transported away before Michael or the others could act. Michael saw a small demon to his left trying to escape he raised his sword and said "in Trotta" and dragon's breath shot a fire web trapping the creature. Dade and the others ran up, he looked the area over. "Good job Michael" the others came over and looked at his sword. "That's the Dragon sword we heard about isn't it."

"Great job Michael." Richard came over with a big smile on his face "you didn't leave any for us," and they all laughed.

"What is this place."

Dade said, it's a nuclear power plant. They were obviously planning on creating a major catastrophe. We need to remove the memory of what these workers saw and take this creature back for interrogation."

Richard nodded to his wizards and they went to deal with the civilians. Michael went to Elaina "are you okay."

"Yes Michael, thanks to your shield."

Dade talked to Richard for a moment then walked over to Michael. "Richard and his wizards will clean up here, Paul and Marcus will take care of the captured Demon. We can go home."

Michael shook his head and he Elaina and Dade teleported back to the temple. When they arrived Dade asked Michael, "how did you know where the attack was happening."

"My guardian appeared to me and said to follow, that the attack was already in progress."

"Your guardian, I've never heard of one appearing to a Mage outside the sanctuary and certainly not out of the Temple."

"You mean they're normally not able to or allowed to."

"Well Michael they can do pretty much whatever they like, but I've just never heard of it happening before."

"Maybe it's because of their target. Nuclear power plant could cost thousands of deaths, horrible deaths from the radiation poisoning."

"You're right Michael this is very troubling they've elevated this to a whole new level. Now they're targeting normals and not small attacks either. I'll be back later Michael I need to check on the information we got."

After Dade left Michael and Elaina went to check on Luke and Thalia. When they got there Thalia was still at Luke's bedside, when she saw them she said "hey guys, how did it go? Was there actually in attack."

"Yes, but not where they thought."

"Really, where was it."

"It was at a nuclear power plant."

"Oh no, what happened."

"A couple of civilians were killed, but we stopped the attack before they reach the power plant."

"I should've been there with you" said Thalia.

"There's nothing more you could have done we had more than enough help. We just got there a little late, because we didn't know until the attack was already started. How are you doing Luke, you look a lot better."

"I'm okay Michael, ready to get back to work."

"No rush, we need everyone at 100%."

Thalia said, "if they're killing normals Michael what are we going to do."

"I don't know Thalia, but we need to come up with a plan. Right now I need to go to the sanctuary."

9

MICHAEL HURRIED TO THE SANCTUARY and called Cassondra, she knew he was coming.

"We stopped the attack but innocent people were killed."

"I know Michael, I saw."

"You knew the attack was coming, why didn't you do something."

"I'm sorry Michael but we're forbidden from directly using our powers in your world."

"I don't understand, I don't suppose I'll ever understand completely, you have the power but won't help, why?"

"In our spirit form were unable to use our powers in your world it's our most forbidden law. We can only watch and guide, and to take on human form is also forbidden and punishable. It is a way of keeping our powers in check so that it's not misused."

"Misused, I thought all of you were good."

"Even among guardians there have been those who thought their powers made them better than humans and they use their powers for evil and conquest."

"What happened?"

"It depended on how serious their infraction was some were cast out stripped of their powers and sent to live among humans. the more serious were cast into the underworld where they became damned souls."

"You mean the devils."

"There are many devils Michael they go by many names. The most powerful of them were once guardians cast out of our realm. They are the kings of the underworld but they were kept in check so that they are also unable to use their powers in the human world."

"It seems Cassondra that the more I know more questions I have."

"I'm sorry Michael, but I've told you all that I can, even more than I should have."

"Elaina was almost injured today one of the zombie looking creatures shot a fireball at her. If I hadn't seen it and put a shield around her she had been hit."

As your aide with no magic abilities she remains vulnerable, and with the current conflict there is a strong possibility sooner or later she could be injured or killed. You need to understand that."

"What can I do to protect her?"

Cassondra looked at Michael but didn't respond. Michael felt she was holding something back, he asked again. "Cassondra, is there a way to protect her."

She then looked him square in the eye "no Michael, she will have to protect herself."

Michael felt she was trying to tell him something without actually coming out with it, probably the rules getting in the way again.

"I can't let anything happen to her.

"Michael you can't enter a battle and focus on protecting her. She'll have to protect herself." She said it slowly and deliberately.

He felt again that she was hinting at something but couldn't figure out what it was.

"That's enough talk for today, you should go to your study and read the ancient texts you know enough to understand them well now."

"One more question Cassondra what were those creatures, the ones with magic."

"They are Minars, they are foul creatures that were created long ago by necromancers, they were evil wizard's brought back to life at the moment of death to serve the necromancers and the Devils of the underworld realm that gave the necromancers their power."

"Where are these necromancers now."

"They don't exist any longer they were defeated and killed centuries ago."

Michael said, "thank you Cassondra," As he turned and left the room. Michael went to the study and selected a book from the shelf and began flipping pages his mind wasn't really on studying he saw spell to allow him to cross to other realms and thought that's pretty cool but didn't find it useful. And there was a spell called lightning blast, that could be useful so he studied it for a while so that he could memorize it. He then came across a spell of invisibility, this was more like it he thought. Maybe he could use it to protect Elaina. Michael studied and practiced the spell making small objects disappear and reappear. He had already decided not to bring Elaina along when he knew they would be facing danger. But if danger found them unexpectedly he now had a means of protecting her after a few hours he decided to leave and check on Luke. When he got to the infirmary Thalia and Dade were there cheering luke up. Luke saw him first "hi Michael where have you been?"

"Studying Luke, how are you?"

"Find! I'm ready to go."

"That's great Luke, glad to hear it."

Dade took Michael aside "I have some things to talk to you about Michael."

They walked out to the hall. Dade looked around to make sure no one else was listening.

"We've gotten some information from the demon you captured, he said they have a base here on the planet connected to a passage that leads to a portal to the underworld realm. He doesn't know where the base is, he was teleported to and from it, but we believe it's in a desert from his description of the outside of the cave. They're staying in a large underground cavern. Our wizards as well as others from the red and blue order or searching for signs."

"That's good news Dade please keep me up-to-date on what they find."

"Of course Michael, one other thing, Richard would like to meet with you one-on-one to discuss the situation."

"Fine, tell them I'll meet with him tomorrow morning, I'll bring Thalia with me."

Dade looked at Michael, "your not bringing Elaina."

"No not this time, she was almost hurt maybe killed in that last battle, without magic she's vulnerable to magical attack."

"She's here to watch your back Michael, not the other way around. She won't understand being left out."

"Dade I can't let anything happen to her."

"She's not exactly defenseless Michael, she's well trained and like it or not she is your aid and she won't like you leaving her behind."

"I know but just this time, I'm working on something that may help."

"Okay Michael I'll explain it to her tomorrow after you've gone."

"Thanks Dade I really want her by my side but not until I can protect her."

Dade left and Michael return to Luke's room. They sat and talked for a while. Elaina felt something was going on especially since Michael was blocking his thoughts from her. After a bit Michael suggested that they let Luke get some rest and go and relax in his room. Michael and Elaina started for the door Michael turned and said.

"Coming Thalia."

Thalia looked over at them, "I'll be along shortly just going to sit with Luke a few more minutes."

When Michael and Elaina arrived at his room she asked him what was wrong.

"Nothing's wrong why do you ask."

"Michael you're blocking your mind, we promised not to lie to each other."

"Okay Elaina, Richard wants a meeting at his place tomorrow and I'm taking Thalia with me. I'd like you to stay here and look after Luke."

"Luke is almost completely better he doesn't need me you do. I'm your aide or do you want to change that."

"No Elaina I don't want to change that, I want you by my side always, but this once please do as I ask."

"Fine Michael, you are my Mage and I will do as you ask. Now if you'll excuse me I have things to do."

With that she quickly exited the room. Michael tried to call to her but she kept going. He was feeling pretty bad but thought he was doing the right thing for her. A few minutes later Evie came into the room.

"Hi Mike, what happened I just saw Elaina going down the hall and she was crying."

Michael realized that was why she didn't look back she didn't want him to see she was crying, now he really felt terrible.

"I have a meeting tomorrow and told her to stay here. I'm taking a wizard with me but it's for her own protection."

"I've learned a lot since we've been here Michael in doing that to her is a real slap in the face, you don't understand it's her honor to be with you and don't tell her I told you but she has deep feelings for you leaving her behind is an insult."

"I don't want to hurt her, I have feelings for her to and I'm afraid she'll get hurt."

"Better that than feeling rejected by you and trust me that's what it feels like to her you need to make this right."

"Thanks Evie" he kissed her on the cheek. "I'll take care of it."

Michael went to Elaina's room he had never been there before. He knocked but there was no immediate answer. He knocked again a bit louder and called her name. He could hear shuffling around and footsteps and then her voice telling him to come in. He looked around the room it was about a third the size of his room and not decorating quite as fancy but nice and comfortable. Elaina was not there but from the other room which Michael assumed was the bathroom he heard her say that she'll be right out. Michael looked at the bed it was messed. She had been lying on it when he arrived probably crying. He walked to the bathroom door he knocked and said, "are you decent, can I come in? I need to talk to you."

From the other side of the door she said, "you've made yourself very clear the first time."

"I'm sorry Elaina I was wrong."

Very slowly the door opened, when Michael saw her he realized she had actually been crying.

"You're a Mage and you're admitting you were wrong."

"Why, a Mage can be wrong we're also people."

"I guess they can but they don't like to admit it. Probably concerned about protecting their image."

"Well I'm admitting it I was wrong and you were right we're a team, partners and it's not right to keep you here even if my reason was valid. I was afraid of losing you. I care very much for you, but I can't keep you from being who you are, I can't protect you by pushing you away. So where I go, you go, together always."

Elaina smiled, she walked up to Michael put her arms around him and kissed him "thank you Michael" she said.

He hugged her and looked past her into the bathroom. There was no pool and waterfall just a normal tub, nice but nothing out of the ordinary.

"Do you have a bathing suit?" He asked.

"What," Elaina looked at him strangely for this crazy change of subject.

"What are you talking about."

"Swimsuit for swimming or bathing."

"I don't know what you talking about Michael but we don't do much swimming here."

"Oh! Okay it was just a thought. Well, come on Elaina let's take a walk, we have things to discuss for our meeting tomorrow."

They walked to Michael's room talking along the way. When they arrived Michael said casually "oh yeah by the way let me show you something" he led her to the bathroom.

"Michael why are we in your bathroom I've seen it before remember."

Michael walked over to the curtain with a tub would normally be and opened it. Elaina's face lit up.

"Michael, it's beautiful, last time I was here I didn't get a chance to really appreciate just how beautiful it really was. Wow! This is amazing has this always been here."

"I don't know, it was here when I got here. I thought everyone's bath was similar until I saw your bathroom."

"We don't have anything like this".

"Well you can use it whenever you like, the waterfall is very relaxing and the water is always warm."

"Thank you Michael, I really like that."

"Come on Elaina let's go sit on the balcony we'll have a glass of wine and relax a bit, another big day for us tomorrow."

The next morning Michael woke early only to find Elaina sitting next to his bed.

"About time you woke up sleepyhead."

"How long have you been sitting there?"

"I've been here a while and breakfast is already on the table like you said it's a big day today."

"Well instead of sitting there you could have woke me up."

"No we don't want a grumpy Mage with not enough sleep taking care of business."

"Grumpy, when have I ever been grumpy."

Elaina didn't answer his question, she simply said, "forget it let's eat."

They quickly ate a light breakfast. Then Michael went to get ready. Elaina was already dressed in her don't mess with me I'm ready for a fight uniform. When Michael emerged from the bathroom Elaina asked, "are we going to bring Thalia with us."

"No I don't think we need a wizard today, we're just going to see Richard and he's okay."

Soon Dade arrived and saw Michael and Elaina ready to go.

"Elaina, I thought you were taking Thalia with you Michael."

"I thought about it, Elaina is my aide and should go with me."

"Good" said Dade "now Michael, Richards palace is under tons of ice in the Arctic I had intended to accompany you but have important matters to attend too, please give my regards to Richard and tell him I'll be in touch."

"Okay I will, where ready when you are."

Dade waived his wand and in an instant Michael and Elaina arrived at Richards Palace. The hall they were in look like a crystal sculpture. Richard and his aide Morgan waiting to greet them.

"Hello Michael glad to see you," said Richard.

"Good to see you too, what's happening."

"Not much right now must be the lull before the storm. Dade briefed me about the information they got from the prisoner. If it's true will be able to strike a major victory and maybe even find out who's behind this. On another subject Michael you remember Raymond and Henry from the Council meeting don't you."

"Oh yeah, how can I forget them." You could sense the anger in his voice.

"Well Michael since the meeting we been keeping an eye on them and questioning some of the wizard and their order and we suspect there could be a problem with them."

"Yes Richard I know, they've even stopped consulting with their guardians."

"What, how could you know that I'm sure that's not something the guardians would share."

"I got it from a very reliable source."

"The only source that could know that is another Guardian and that's not something they would normally share either. If it's where you got the information you must have a very unique relationship with your guardian."

Michael didn't answer for fear of getting Cassondra in some kind of trouble she did after all give him the information in confidence.

"Michael I also called you here in hopes of convincing you to assume your place as head of the Council. I know you don't feel your ready but I'm sure you can help unify the Council and help keep others from seeking power with the growing evil."

"But what makes you think they'll follow me I'm still young and inexperienced."

"You're the Dragon Mage and the Dragon mage has always been head of the Council. They have always been the most powerful of all the Mage, and what you did in the meeting both intimidated and impressed them all. A few of them even tried teleporting after you did and couldn't."

"Alright Richard, if you think it will help, but I need you and Dade to help me with understanding the Council and what's expected. After all I've only attended one meeting and it was rather short."

"Agreed, we'll help anyway we can and I'm sure Dade will too. We'll set another meeting in one week. In the meantime we'll keep looking for the enemy stronghold."

Michael and Richard sat and discussed matters. Michael asked Elaina to sit but she instead just stood at his side as did Richards aide. After a short while Michael and Elaina said their goodbyes and left. Upon arriving back at Ghostra he asked Elaina why she didn't sit and relax. She explained that when away from the Temple she stands by his side at all times, it's the way things are done, it's respect.

"Elaina you know I don't go for all the superiority stuff. I know you respect me and I'm sure you know I respect you."

"Yes Michael I know, but to the others their aides are just that aides and they would see it as a sign of disrespect and would look down upon it and you, and I can't allow that."

"Well I guess we'll have to do something about that," said Michael.

"What am I going to do with you Michael."

"I guess you have to keep a close eye on me from now on."

Elaina just smiled and walked off. Michael went to his room. He seemed very pleased with himself. As he went to hang up his cloak he realized that his sword was missing. He started looking around wondering if he might've put it somewhere else, but it was nowhere to be found. He sent a mental message to Dade just saying that he needed to see him as soon as possible. He then rushed off to Elaina's room and knocked at the door. When she answered she could see something was wrong.

"Michael what is it, what's wrong."

"Elaina, my sword, Dragon's Breath it's missing."

"What! Are you sure, did you look everywhere."

"Yes, I always keep it in the closet with my dress robes, but when it wasn't there I searched the whole room. I'm sure it was there this morning."

Together they started from Michael's room, Just then Dade came down the hall.

"What is it Michael, I got your message."

Michael explained to him what happened.

"This is bad Michael, very bad. No one from here would take the sword and with the new defenses up no one except trusted individuals could get in, at least not without us knowing it. Maybe you should check with your guardian they would have a way of knowing things."

"That's a good idea Dade, I'll head their right away."

He ran to the library and entered the sanctuary. When he called her name, Cassondra came in and saw that Michael was distressed.

"What's wrong Michael."

"My sword is missing, it was there this morning when I returned it was gone."

Cassondra closed her eyes and turned her head from left to right.

"You're right Michael, it's not anywhere in the palace which is very strange. I should've sensed if anyone that the sword doesn't recognize were to take it. Whoever has it will not be able to use it but maybe they don't intend to. Maybe they just want to keep you from using it. We will look for it and let you know what we find. I'll go now Michael and alert the others."

After Cassondra left Michael stood there for quite a while thinking about what his next move should be. He was concerned about the sword but also knew that sooner or later they would discover the enemy stronghold and a major battle, perhaps the final battle would take place. He thought we could finally stop these attacks on civilian targets and bring the fight directly to them. He also knew that when that time came he had to be ready which meant going back to his study and continue practicing and studying as much as he could. Michael was committed to studying the ancient books and scrolls for at least four hours a day, more whenever time permitted each evening he and Elaina would return to the balcony to relax and sip fruit juice or wine, sometimes Evie would join them. Evie was becoming a fine young lady. She really liked being here, her self-confidence was building and she was well-liked and Michael had never seen her happier. The week passed quickly and the day of the Council meeting arrived. Michael was still hesitant about taking over the Council but he gave his word. Michael got ready early. Elaina also arrived at his room early. They ate a light breakfast before Dade arrived.

"Hi Dade, what are you doing here, come to give last-minute advice."

"No Michael, Richard said this meeting was important and he requested the head of each of the magical orders to come as well."

"Oh that's good, I'll feel better with you there."

Just then Thalia came into the room.

"Hello everyone. Dade, Lucas returned to the order as you requested and I'm ready to accompany you to the meeting."

"Dade is it okay if we show up with this many people."

"Yes Michael, Elaina and Thalia are still your security and I'm going because I was asked to."

Dade reached under his cloak, "here Michael we had this replica of the Dragon sword made. Naturally it doesn't have the power of dragon's breath but no one will be able to tell the difference."

"It's beautiful, it looks just like the real one"

"well shall we go." Said Dade they all gathered together and in an instant were gone. They then reappeared in an area outside the protective barrier and walked to the Council chambers.

When they arrived most of the Mage were already there. Michael turned to Dade "Raymond and Henry aren't here not that I'm really surprised."

"You're right their not but Raymond's master wizard is over there the one in the white cloak. Come on I'll introduce you and maybe we can find out what's going on with them, meanwhile keep an eye out for anyone who looks surprised that you have your sword."

Dade nodded to Thalia then drifted into the crowd. He must've given her instructions earlier thought Michael. Elaina stayed right at Michael side they walked over to the lone wizard standing away from the others. Dade introduced them

"Michael this is Miles Norton master wizard of the white order, Miles this is Michael Reynolds the Dragon Mage."

"Hello Michael it's good to finally meet you but I don't know if you want to talk with me, the others seem to think I'm only here to spy on them since our mage Raymond went rogue."

Michael muttered to spell to himself so no one would realize, an aura of green light encircled Miles head an aura that no one but Michael could see. Green meant he was telling the truth.

"Tell me Miles what happened to Raymond" asked Michael.

"I don't know, none of us know, he's been acting strange, talking crazy for months. Talking about the Council outliving its usefulness, talking about a mage more powerful than any of the others who was going to take over everything and if we don't join him we will be destroyed like the Council and the other orders that refused to join him. A few of my wizards are still loyal to Raymond but most of us refused and set up barriers to keep him and the others out of our stronghold."

"You're welcome to move in with us for the time being" said Dade. "If this new mage or whatever he might be is as powerful as he claims your barriers may not hold."

"Thanks Dade I'll tell the others when I get back. Will bring only those that we know we can trust."

"Good and when I get back I'll make sure everything is ready."

Then Richard called the meeting to order. The last of the mage had arrived except of course for Raymond and Henry who no one was really expecting anyway. Each of the mage took his place at the table the master wizard's were also asked to sit at the table next to their mage. Their aides all stood close by. Richard stood to address the Council.

"You have been called together today for two reasons. First Michael has agreed to take over leadership of the Council. I will stay on as his assistant until he becomes familiar with our workings but as of today he is the new head of the Council, are there any objections?"

The water mage stood and said "I have no objection I think Michael will make a fine head of the Council. But I'm wondering with everything that's going on right now if this is the best time for him to take over given his youth and inexperience."

Richard responded, "I believe this the perfect time to send a message to the enemy that we back the power of the Dragon mage and we will not falter from our goal of protecting our planet. As for his inexperience both Dade and myself are here to advise and assist him not to mention the fact that the Dragon mage has always had a stronger bond with the guardians than the rest of us. Now if no one else has anything to add."

Richard hesitated to see if anyone else had anything to say.

"Good we'll set a time for the official ceremony but as of now Michael is the head of the Council. Now as for the second reason for our meeting. It is an update on our progress on finding the enemy stronghold.

Richard began with the update, breaking it down as to what's been done so far and where the search was headed. Suddenly Michael heard a voice as if someone were standing behind him he turned but saw no one. That's when he realized the voice was in his head.

"Hello Michael, we need to meet."

"Who are you," Michael thought.

"I'm the one you've been looking for, the one who is going to rule this world, and I've decided that I'd like you at my side."

"I have no interest in being at your side and you're not going to rule anything."

"Well Michael meeting with me is the only way to bring a peaceful end to this conflict and protect your new friends."

"Why should I trust you."

"Because we have much in common Michael. I'll set it up and let you know when and where."

Then the voice was gone. Dade looked at Michael and said, "is something wrong."

Michael looked toward Dade debating whether or not to tell him what just happened, but decided now was not the time. "No Dade everything's fine."

Elaina also noticed something was wrong but knew now was not the time or place to ask. After the meeting everyone stayed for a while for refreshments which Michael thought was amusing. After this big meeting talking about a war and now everyone just hanging around drinking juice like a bunch of kids at a high school dance. One by one the other mage would come up and congratulate him and assure him if he needed any help with anything he could count on them. Michael politely thanked them and listen to their thoughts on what could be done and although some had good ideas he couldn't get his mind off the voice he heard and whether or not he should accept the offer to meet. When they returned to Ghostra Dade took his leave and Michael and Elaina went to his room where dinner was already waiting. They were quiet as they ate. Michael was deep in thought. Elaina knew something was going on but figured Michael would tell her what was bothering him. Dinner ended and they went to sit on the balcony looking out at the stars. Michael still hadn't confided in her so Elaina decided it was time to find out.

"Michael what's going on."

"What are you talking about."

"There's something going on that you're not telling me. You've been distracted all day. The meeting today you weren't paying much attention to what Richard had to say and I felt something your mind was occupied as though you were talking silently to yourself and ever since then you've been thinking about something. You hardly ate and totally ignored me like I wasn't even here."

"I'm sorry Elaina but I got a lot on my mind."

"Yes it started at the meeting and you're hiding something even though you promised not to keep things from me."

Michael looked at her not sure whether or not to say anything, he did promise and she only wants to protect him, he really doesn't want to break her trust. They sat quietly for a few moments then Michael said.

"He contacted me the one behind this whole uprising. He wants to meet with me he wants me to come alone to a location he will send to me."

"No Michael! You can't trust him he's trying to order you into a trap."

"He said we have a lot in common and we could end this conflict. No one else would get hurt."

"Michael you can't go meet him alone that's just what he wants if anything happens to you the Council will fall apart that's what he wants."

"I've thought about that I haven't decided to go yet I'm still thinking about it. If there's a chance to end this, I just don't know."

"Michael you've got nothing in common he's a monster."

"Well at least I know your opinion. Tomorrow I'll check with Cassondra maybe she knows something about this person. Let's not discuss this anymore tonight my brain is going to fry if I keep thinking about it."

10

T HE NEXT DAY STARTED THE same as usual Michael got up early. Got dressed and had some breakfast and went off to spar with Elaina. After an hours brisk workout, Evie joined them and they had a little fun. When it was over Michael returned to his room and spent the next few minutes soaking under the soothing waterfall. After dressing into his mage clothing he headed to see Cassondra, he had much to discuss with her on his way to the library a voice entered his mind.

"Michael, you must come and meet with me now."

"Just like that I'm supposed to drop everything and run to meet with you."

"We can end this conflict Michael no one else needs to get hurt I just need for you to hear my side of the story. There's a lot you don't know."

"I need to let someone know I'm going."

"If you do that others will follow and we will not be able to talk freely."

Michael hesitated then said "Okay where"

Michael saw the place in his mind where he had to go and teleported just as Evie turned the corner and saw him teleport, she thought it was odd that he would go anywhere without Elaina or Dade. She quickly went to find Elaina to find out if everything was okay. Elaina was still in the training room working out when Evie asked Elaina if anything was wrong and what she had seen. Elaina knew right away what happened.

"Evie get help and find Dade, tell him Michael may be walking into danger and he should try to locate them. I'm going to the library see if I can get the guardian to help even if she kills me for violating the sanctuary. Go quickly Evie."

Evie ran off to get help while Elaina ran to the library. She went to the door of the sanctuary and hesitated she remembered that there was a story of someone who is not a Dragon mage entering the sanctuary and never being seen again. But Michael was in danger so Elaina entered the sanctuary (she was not prevented from entering) and went to the altar.

"Guardian" she said, "guardian please Michael may be in trouble."

Cassondra appeared before her. Elaina quickly dropped to one knee her head down looking toward the floor. With her voice trembling Elaina said, "please guardian I meant no disrespect in entering the sanctuary but I believe Michael may be in danger."

Cassondra looked down at her. "Rise Elaina tell me what happened."

Elaina began to explain what she knew and what she feared. Meanwhile Michael had already arrived at the designated location. He looked around but saw nothing. And suddenly about 30 yards away he saw a figure appeared over a small hill he wasn't a devil or demon or monster of any kind, in fact he appeared to be normal.

"Hello Michael my name is the baylor and I've waited a long time to meet you, which by the way is not your true name."

"What you talking about my father was Anthony Reynolds are you trying to say he wasn't my father."

"No Michael, he was your father but his real name was not Anthony Reynolds it was Alomar Rayhn."

"You don't know what your talking about."

"Well I didn't expect that you would believe it, but that's not important right now what is important is that you and I together are more powerful than all the other mage combined and if we work together we can rule this world."

"Is that why you called me here I thought you said we could end the conflict. Bring peace."

"We can end it with minimal casualties. Of course some examples of power would have to be made people of this world think their armies and technology can protect them but they don't stand a chance against our magic or the dark armies we can summon."

"You're crazy, power-hungry we are here to protect the world not rule it, and protect it we will against anyone or anything you can bring out of any dark places. You don't have to do this, there is a place for you here and you can have everything you need or want while helping the world and the people."

"All right Michael, even though our families have been at odds for over 2000 years I thought we could work together rule together I see now that's not possible."

He turned as if to walk away then suddenly turned again and fired and energy bolt at Michael. Michael was quick to respond he blocked the attack and retaliated with spells of his own the battle ensued with spells being fired back and forth till one spell penetrated Michael's defenses knocking him to the ground. Although hit slightly he sprang back up and continue firing he was feeling overwhelmed by the onslaught as Baylor is using spells Michael was not familiar with. Then Baylor waved his hand and two dozen creatures appeared about 100 yards away some of them also casting spells. Michael knew he couldn't withstand this attack much longer and couldn't lower his defenses in order to teleport away. Suddenly Michael heard a sound behind him when he turned he saw Elaina teleport in and quickly drew swords taking out the creature that was about to attack Michael from behind.

Michael shouted, "Elaina what are you doing here."

"My duty Michael."

Than Elaina ran toward Michael and Baylor shot and energy bolt which struck Elaina dead on throwing her backward to the ground.

Michael shouted, "no Elaina no."

He ran to her took her body into his arms and through an energy shield around them he knew it wouldn't last long with Baylor continuing his attack but he had to protect her for as long as he could. The evil minions continued to close on his position and Michael could see they were being led by two devils. Elaina appeared lifeless she had no pulse or heartbeat Michael felt this was the end, at least they would die together. Suddenly Elaine opened her eyes looked at Michael and said "fight Michael don't give up fight."

She leapt to her feet and fired a shock wave of energy at the oncoming beings sending him flying like rag dolls. THis energy was quickly followed by a wave of fire which sent the creature scattering in terror. Michael still in shock began a counter attack on Baylor who blocked his initial attack but when he saw Elaina turned her attention toward him he knew he couldn't take her and Michael at the same time so he quickly waved his hand and open the portal of some kind and escaped. Michael watched as the portal quickly close behind them. Michael was trying to come to grips with what just happened he turned to Elaina still confused.

"Elaina what happened? How did you do that?"

She turned to him "Michael I'm not Elaina I'm Cassondra. Elaina is badly hurt I need to stay in her body for a time while she heals. She was almost gone so I took over to keep her alive and help you. If I leave now she will die."

Michael went over to her and put his arms around her. "Thank you Cassondra I couldn't bear to lose her."

"I know Michael, but no one else can know it's actually me if my kind found out I could be in a lot of trouble I've violated our prime rule."

"I won't say a word about it Cassondra I promise."

Suddenly several flashes came from behind. Michael turned and quickly prepared to attack until he saw that it was Dade with a dozen wizards from the gray order. Dade looked around, "what happened are you too alright."

"Yes Dade we're all right, Baylor is the name of the one leading the uprising. He asked me to come and meet with him under the pretense of ending the conflict when in fact what he wanted was for me to join him and work together, when I refused he attacked and summoned some of his underworld followers to take me. With Baylor and his minions both attacking he might of succeeded if Elayna hadn't arrived she took on his servants with her sword while I fought Baylor. Dade looked at them and simply said "well it looks like you two make a great team."

"We do," said Michael. "But we can no longer underestimate Baylor he is very powerful and seems to know spells that I have not yet discovered in the library. "if he's human how could he have gone undetected all this time?"

"I don't know Michael if he was cloaked like you were he might've gone undetected but to get as powerful as you say he would have had to practice a lot and have a trainer to show him how to use his power. Those things should have been detected. No cloak would conceal that use of magic it is a real mystery."

"Well Dade if you don't mind you and the others make sure we didn't overlook anything that may give us a clue as to who he is and where he's hiding. Elaina and I need to get some rest and lick our wounds."

"Sure thing Michael we'll check out the area and I'll talk to you tomorrow."

With that Michael took Elaina by the hand and teleported them to his room in Ghostra when they arrived Michael looked around to make sure no one was there then he turned to Cassondra "how is Elaina"

"she's hurt badly Michael but I think she'll be all right it'll just take a while for her to completely heal. In the meantime I'll stay in her body to help her heal and protect her."

"I don't know how to thank you."

"there Is no need Michael but you need to stop worrying about her and focus on finding and defeating Baylor. Without him this uprising from the underworld will collapse they don't have the power to fight the mage themselves but if Baylor should get a foothold or turn any more of the Mage this world could be in a lot of trouble and you will be unable to take them by yourself I felt his power and he just too powerful."

"You and I drove him away today Cassondra. Together we overpowered him if we combine our power we should be able to defeat them."

"I don't know that even our combined power would be enough. Remember he can summon any number of creatures which would divide our attack on two fronts. He ran today because he couldn't defeat us both. But I don't know that we could have defeated him either. I just don't know, besides I can't keep using my power or the other guardians will sense it and would pull me out of Elaina which would probably kill her. Not to mention what would happen to me."

"I won't let them hurt you Cassondra."

"You wouldn't have much to say about it Michael but I appreciate the thought."

"I won't let them hurt you I promise."

Cassondra just looked at him, she knew he meant what he said but she also knew he couldn't stand up to the guardians so she just smiled.

After having a bite to eat Michael said "come on Elaina and I will usually sit and relax on the balcony. We relax a while before retiring and we don't want to raise any suspicions even among the sisters, I trust them all completely but the fewer that know the better."

They went and sat but Michael was unable to relax. His mind was racing and he was very concerned especially since Cassondra felt that defeating Baylor would be so difficult if not impossible. How could he be so powerful and yet no one had been able to detect him before this and what of Elaina she would've been killed if Cassondra hadn't intervened. There were so many questions in so few answers.

"I can feel that you're very tense Michael and not very relaxed."

"Yeah there are so many things on my mind. He got two glasses of water and turned them to a light sweet wine and gave one to Cassondra.

"Let's talk for a while Cassondra but not about anything important.

Just talk tell me a little about you, do you have a boyfriend or do you go anywhere to have fun."

"No Michael, we don't have emotional attachments. We just guard and guide and help protect the people and the world."

She took a sip of the wine. "What is this I like it?"

"It's wine have you ever tasted wine before."

"We don't have taste or feel much of anything except contentment when we can help we don't eat or drink and can not sense flavors. Your people are blessed to be able to feel and taste and enjoy."

"That's terrible you spend your existence helping us and yet you can't even feel what we do."

"Everything exists for a reason Michael we don't always understand why."

Then Evie entered the room.

"Hi Mike, Hi Elaina, I heard you two had a wild time today."

Cassondra turned and said, "hello your Evelyn"

"of course, what did you do get hit in the head."

"Oh no! I'm just still a little shaken up after today."

Cassondra looked at Michael with that I almost mess that up look.

"Mike can I have some wine."

"Sure Evie." He waved his hand and handed her the glass. Cassondra leaned over and said "isn't she too young to have wine."

Michael replied "it's only wine flavored there's no alcohol in it."

Cassondra just leaned back and smiled. Evie sat and they just talked and enjoyed the view before breaking up to go get some rest. It took Michael a while to get to sleep that night. He was worried about Elaina even though Cassondra said she would be all right. After tossing and turning for what seemed like hours he finally drifted off to sleep but not a restful sleep as his dreams turned into nightmares one after another. But one thing was common in each nightmare Elaina was in trouble and he did see her off in the distance but no matter how he tried or how fast he ran he couldn't reach her. He abruptly woke and looked around it was morning already.

11

HE GOT UP BUT DIDN'T feel as rested as he normally would, in fact he felt as if the weight of the world was on his shoulders. He went to take a relaxing shower under the gentle waterfall hoping that would help. He was right, after a short while of the soothing waterfall he felt a little better. At least he wished for the days when he and Evie were back in their box and the only worry was where he was going to earn his next few bucks. Michael finished bathing and got dressed when he exited the bathroom Durell was already setting the table for breakfast. Evie was already there and sitting at the table.

"Hi Mike." She said.

"Hello Michael," said Durell.

"hello Durell, how are you today?"

"I'm fine Michael," she paused and then added "I heard how you and Elaina drove off the dark one and his minions yesterday. It must of been amazing to see."

"Yes, Elaina and I make a good team, would you care to join us this morning."

"No thank you Michael I've already eaten and have a lot to do, but thank you anyway."

Michael shook his head in acknowledgement and she bowed and left the room. Evie turned to Michael. "Hey Mike, is everything okay with Elaina she's acting a little strange."

"What you mean strange, how."

"She keeps calling me Evelyn instead of Evie and seems to have forgotten things we talked about already."

"Don't worry about it Evie she's probably still shaken up after our battle yesterday, it was pretty rough. I'm not quite 100% myself."

Minutes later Cassondra entered the room.

"Hello Michael, hello Evelyn, how are you both feeling this morning."

Evelyn just looked at Michael then turned and said, "fine Elaina, how are you feeling?"

"Very well thank you."

They all just sat and ate without much conversation. After breakfast Evie said she'd see them later and left to train and do her chores. Michael said Cassondra "Evie is getting a little suspicious, she's close to Elaina and notices little things that Elaina does, for instance Elaina calls her Evie not Evelyn and she said you were unaware of things she and Elaina had discussed."

"She doesn't know something is wrong does she?"

"No I told her your little shaken up after our confrontation with Baylor."

"Good, I'll try to be more careful may take quite a while before Elaina will be strong enough to survive on her own. Now Michael, what do you normally do we don't want to raise suspicion."

"Well most days Elaina and I would train for an hour or two. Then I would go to the library to study or meet with you."

"Well the training part is out, the minute we started the others would notice I'm not Elaina, we don't fight physically."

"That's okay we can tell the others your shoulders hurt and were not going to training until it's completely healed because we don't want to make it worse. Then I'm going to tell them that you're going to help me with my studies. That way you can avoid the others as much as possible."

"Good thinking Michael, the less time I spend with the others the better, less chance of being discovered."

"Now Michael do you have any suggestions on how to deal with my senses and feelings. Breakfast was amazing the tastes flooded my senses I almost said something but thought Evelyn, I mean Evie would think something was wrong."

"No I don't, I guess you just have to deal with them until you get use to it. For us it's a normal thing but you never have and now suddenly it's all just hit you, just try and relax."

"That's what I keep telling myself relax, relax, relax but even that doesn't help because I don't know how."

"Well there are a lot of ways to relax. Like last night we sat in just looked out at the horizon and talked."

"Yes that was very comforting it made me feel good."

"Yeah Elaina and I and sometimes Evie do that all the time. You could also take a bath or shower that can be very relaxing."

"I know humans need to clean themselves and although I have heard of showers and baths I don't see how that can be relaxing. What exactly are they?"

"Wow, you really do have strange gaps in your knowledge don't you."

"Well I've never had contact with the people before Michael. Like most of my kind we have watched over the human race since the beginning, but very few of us ever have direct contact with them."

Michael asked her to follow him. He led her into the bathroom and showed her his pool and waterfall. The sun was up in the light shimmering off the falling water. Cassondra was stunned."

"Michael this is beautiful, and you bathe here regularly?"

"Almost every day, some days if I'm in a hurry I'll just wash up but most days I drift out into the pool and let the warm water from the falls beat down on me it's very relaxing. As I've told Elaina, you're welcome to use it whenever you like just let me know ahead of time so that I don't accidentally walk in on you."

"I'm looking forward to trying it, maybe later this evening, but what should we do now so we don't get the other suspicious about Elaina."

"Well I think we need to go to the gym like we normally would and do some light exercise. I'll let everyone know that you can't train because your shoulder is injured and we don't want to make it worse. Then after a short while we'll leave and go to the library. I'll do some studying and we can spend the rest of the day there so were not around the others. We'll have a light lunch brought there."

"That's good Michael, but how long can we do this without the others getting suspicious."

"As long as we have to I guess. I hate lying to them but we have no choice. Cassondra, let me ask you a question. What would happen if the others of your kind found out, they wouldn't turn you into one of those devils would they."

"No Michael, my crime is one of compassion not evil. But they would strip me of most of my power and banish me to the human realm with no memory of who I was or where I came from."

"That's terrible, for compassionate beings you're not very forgiving especially when it's for a just cause."

"I'm sure our rules were created for a reason and they've never been flexible."

"You mean you don't know why these rules were made or even who made them, does anyone?"

"I don't know, perhaps the Magra does, he's our leader."

Michael said, "that sucks" and Cassondra laughed.

The rest of the day went as planned they spent most of the day in the library the evening was spent as usual relaxing and talking the next couple of weeks went around the same way. Hiding in the library during the day and relaxing in the evenings occasionally joined by Evie. Cassondra was loosening up thanks to her new found feelings. She was even laughing and filling Michael in on some of the things the guardians normally wouldn't.

"Michael, what are you going to do when you find Baylor and his base of operation. One-on-one you're not a match for him, you have the power I can sense it but he has the knowledge and skill not to mention he may have hordes of evil creatures with him. I know you don't want to risk others, but you can't face them alone. You need to bring as many of the others as possible with you."

"Before we worry about that we have to find them and so far they haven't been very successful which is why tomorrow I'm going to call Dade and Richard and try to work out a new plan."

The following day Michael sent word first thing to Dade and Richard that they should meet at noon so that they could discuss what progress has been made at finding Baylors base and work on a plan to narrow down the possibilities. Dade and Richard arrived precisely at noon and the three of them went right to the conference room cut up some fruits and vegetables along with fresh juice was waiting for them.

"I had them lay out some snacks because we may be here all afternoon." Said Michael. Richard started by filling Michael in on where they were in the research and the areas that they may have eliminated.

"There's one thing Michael. We were originally concentrating on the deserts, but further investigations say we may be looking for wastelands. It's difficult getting accurate descriptions from those creatures since they don't use the same terms we do and interpretation can be very difficult. So we've shifted to wastelands but have not entirely given up on deserts."

"How many teams do we have searching." Asked Michael

"4 teams of eight."

"Why so few."

"None of the mage or orders want to thin themselves out too much in case of an attack."

"Well we need at least three more teams and reduce them to six all the other orders will be on alert and will respond to aid any that come under attack. I'll lead one of the teams myself."

Dade looked at Michael with concern.

"Okay Michael," Richard said, "it's been four hours I'll head back and inform the others of the change in plans".

After Richard left Michael and Dade sat and talked "Michael, I put together a team but I don't think it's a good idea that you go there's plenty for you to do here."

"I know my studies and training are important Dade, but I think it's even more important that I take the lead in the search. Not because I feel I'm better than the others but to set an example and help build their confidence in me. I think that's important if they're going to follow me."

"I don't know how one so young can be so wise."

"I learned a lot from my father, pride, honor, humility and courage are the things he always stressed the most. It's almost as though he knew I'd need to fall back on these skills."

"All right Michael, I'll have the team here first thing in the morning with enough provisions for two weeks if I can't get here before you leave good luck and please keep us posted."

"Thanks Dade.

Dade left and Michael return to his room where Cassondra was waiting.

"Well how did it go Michael."

"We've come up with a plan were expanding our search Dade is getting a team together and I'll be going with them tomorrow morning."

"And of course I'll be coming with you."

"No Cassondra I need you here."

"Why Michael you may need my help."

"It's more important that you stay here Cassondra, I've been concerned ever since the Dragon sword disappeared. I trust the sisters of the Temple but the sword didn't get up and walk out. Someone took it and the enemy couldn't have gotten in at least not without setting off the alarms. I need you to keep an eye on things and alert me if anything happens while I'm gone."

"What of the others they might realize I'm not really Elaina."

"I don't think that's a problem you've learned enough to fool them just stay close to Evie."

"Okay Michael, but I don't like you going without someone covering your back."

"I told you I'll be with a team of wizards"

"I know but I'm still worried about you."

"Now you're sounding like Elaina, I thought guardians didn't worry about things."

"We normally don't worry but these feelings are so overwhelming I sometimes don't know what I'm doing."

"If we find anything we'll inform the others and not take any action until help arrives maybe we'll even return to base to coordinate an attack."

Cassondra walked up to Michael put her arms around him and kissed him. It was a warm passionate kiss, but when she realized what she was doing she pushed away with a look of shock on her face. She put her hand to her mouth and said "Michael I'm so so sorry I." But she couldn't say any more she ran from the room. Michael called to her realizing she was embarrassed by what happened but she just kept going without looking back. A few moments later Evie entered the room.

"Hi Mikey, I just saw Elaina running down the hall did you insult her again."

"No Evie, not this time."

"Oh good, because she really likes you."

"Yes Evie, and I really like her too."

"Evie, I'm leaving tomorrow and may not be back for a couple weeks so stay close to Elaina and help her out if she needs it."

"She's not going with you."

"No I asked her to keep an eye on things here and she may need your help. She still not 100% even though she acts like she is."

"Yeah I've noticed she still a little out of whack. Of course I'll help, me and Elaina get along great." After relaxing for a little while they broke up and went to bed. Michael tossed and turned for quite a while he was confused about the kiss Cassondra had given him. He didn't know why she would do it unless maybe it was Elaina's thoughts and emotions that caused it. She was after all very shocked and surprised with what she had done. Michael felt it best not to bring up the subject again and just forget it happened. The next morning Michael got up early he went straight for his bath he wanted to get one more shower under the warm soothing waterfall before leaving since he didn't know when he would be able to enjoy it again. After a shower he got dressed. He was feeling exceptionally well on this fine beautiful morning. Upon exiting the bathroom he found Durell setting the table for six.

"Hello Durell are we expecting company."

"Yes Michael, Dade sent word he would arrive shortly with your team." Michael walked up to her waved his hand and produced a lovely violent rose that he handed to her.

"Thank you Turel."

"For what Michael"

"well you do so much for me and I never seem to have time to say thank you, so thank you."

"Why thank you Michael."

Turel smiled bowed turned and walked out admiring her gift. A short while later Dade arrived he entered Michael's room with four others Michael recognized Thalia but the others were not familiar.

"Hello Michael, how are you?" Said Thalia

"fine and how about you."

"I'm good."

Michael asked, "how is Luke?"

"Oh he's doing fine, he's working hard to improve."

"Well Michael," said Dade "this will be your team we had to draw lots, everyone wanted to come. Thalia didn't have to draw, I thought a familiar face would be best."

"Great ! Let's all sit and have a bite to eat and get to know each other."

As they ate Michael started the conversation.

"Well everyone I'm Michael, now I know Thalia and of course Dade but I have not worked with the rest of you before let's start with your names since I'd rather not point and say hey you."

They all laughed.

"I'm Paul said the first one sitting to Thalia's left."

"I'm Tony" said the second.

"I'm Angus" said the third with a deep Scottish accent. "But everyone just calls me Scotty."

"Well Scotty I take it you're not from around here"

"no I crossed the seas and came here to join the gray order."

"But there is a mage and wizarding order over there why didn't you join them."

"I wanted to be with the best."

"Cool, well welcome aboard Scotty." Then Dade turned to Michael

"Michael are you sure you want to do this yourself, you are one of the main targets if they get you to turn, or take you out they will have won. The others wouldn't have the heart for prolonged fight if they see you can be defeated."

"Dade I have to do this, you know I do. If I'm going to lead the mage Council I need to lead by example." Dade paused

"okay Michael, but in case you run into trouble send a signal I have a dozen wizards standing by at all times."

Michael and Dade walked off while the others were eating breakfast.

Michael asked, "this team, can I depend on them if we run into trouble."

"Yes Michael, I know the kind of young I did that on purpose I felt that you would feel more comfortable with wizards closer to your age. But even with the limited experience their very good and they're all looking to prove themselves. Thalia is probably the best of them."

"Yes I know I can depend on her. They seem like a nice group."

"By the way Michael I don't know how long you'll be gone when you get back I'd like for you to meet with the entire gray order. They've been looking to meet with you, you've met some of them and the others are looking forward to getting together. I would have set it up sooner but something was always getting in the way. We'll make it a real banquet."

"Sounds great Dade, give us a couple weeks and whether we find anything or not will be back for a break. We can set it up then. We'll probably be ready for some rest and relaxation by then."

Looking around Michael saw Evie coming down the hall.

"Hey Mikey" she said "getting ready to leave."

"Yeah ! Where is," he almost slipped inside Cassondra, "where's Elaina."

"She's not coming, I thought at first she was just sad that you going without her but after we talked I felt she was embarrassed about something, what happened last night?"

"None of your business peanut."

They returned to the others and Michael laid out his plan. Michael's strategy was simple he showed them the maps he had enchanted with a spell that showed any magical activity they would then teleport to that location and check out the area paying special attention to the areas that could be shielded to prevent detection.

"Now to prevent confusion this map only works on a limited range about 1000 miles so we'll have to move each day."

Thalia asked, "Michael what area will we were working in."

"The next couple of weeks we'll be working the northern continent. We'll start in the far north and work our way south."

"Should we really bring anything special with us."

"No bring as little as possible, we need to travel fast, anything we need we can summon magically at night. We'll find secluded areas and set up tents or small shelters but when we get a signal we need to move fast. I think part of the reason we found nothing so far is that at the time word of an incident comes in and they react whatever was going on is over and no clues are left. With this map we can react the same time something happens."

Thalia nodded, "okay Michael when do we leave."

"We'll all relax here until we get the first signal. Just stay at the ready once we go will be gone at least a couple weeks."

Michael waved his hand in his team's clothes change to more casual wear jeans, boots, shirts and light jackets.

"Once were out we don't want to draw attention these clothes will help us blend in."

"aye, I like these" said Scotty.

Michael laid the map on the table and walked to the balcony. He stood there looking out deep in thought when Thalia walked over.""Thalia, you're looking good in those clothes."

"Thank you Michael, nice of you to notice. You look worried is everything okay?"

"I don't know, trying to keep the plan as simple as possible but I wonder if I'm overlooking something."

"Yes the plan is simple and that's good it makes it easier to change it quickly if necessary."

"Tell me Thalia, what you think about the rest of the team."

"They're all very good, I've worked with Tony and Scotty before and Paul has an excellent record."

"That's good we'll need everybody working together if we run into trouble."

Dade walked over to them and said. "If you're set Michael I'll be leaving I'm meeting with Richard, I'm going to help to coordinate the other teams."

"Okay Dade, don't forget to let them know that if they don't find anything within the two weeks it's time for a break. We don't want anyone out too long without rest, week off and then fresh teams."

"Okay Michael I'm off."

Thalia asked, "tell me Michael why did you choose the northern continent for our area, having most of the actual attacks taken place across the sea."

"Yes exactly, except for that large attack on the nuclear power plant all the other attacks took place overseas but that may be the point. Keep us looking there while their base or bases are over here over the last month I've detected many magical incidents here but no attacks I think they're trying to keep us away until they're ready for a major strike, of course that's just supposition."

"This is nice Michael, out here on the balcony such a beautiful view."

"Yeah this is become my favorite place to come and relax and think."

12

A SHORT WHILE LATER THE FIRST signal came in it was in the Eastern part of the most northern continent. The team assembled and were off in a flash they landed in a rural Valley with fairly dense forest everywhere. They looked around but saw nothing.

"Are we in the right place," asked Paul

"yes" said Michael "I can still feel the energy"

Thalia looked at Michael a little confused, "but Michael there's nothing here to attack nothing worth anything."

"You're assuming it was an attack of some kind we know only that a magical incident happened."

Michael Dug small hole and poured a little water into it from his canteen. He then held his hand over the water and concentrated in the water he could see an image of an oval doorway opening. Just then a sound behind them of leaves rustling, they turned and out from the trees came a huge hairy creature walking upright Michael immediately cast the spell which stopped the creature dead in its tracks. He walked toward the creature carefully examining it the creature stood about 8 feet tall with hair covering its entire body.

"What is it Michael," asked Tony. Michael smiled at his team.

"I think it's Bigfoot."

"Thalia said, "Bigfoot I always thought they were myths, what did you do to it."

"Nothing it's only temporarily paralyzed if we don't release it this spell should wear off in about an hour or so the question is did this thing open the doorway itself or did someone else open it and send him through and if so why. I wish Elaina were here so she could read his mind. All right everyone stand back while I release it."

"Why Michael, you said the spell would wear off."

"Yeah but what happens if a bear or a wolf or something comes along and it's still paralyzed it could get hurt or killed we're not here to harm a legend were looking for the enemy base, let's not lose sight of our mission."

Michael waved his hand spoke the ancient language and the creature came to life it looked at Michael and the others and turned and ran off.

"This is a mystery for another time." Said Michael by this time the sun was going down so Michael asked the others to clear an area where they could set up camp. They magically cleared the shrubs and brush and remove the couple of trees Michael summoned the tents and some food and started a fire, a few lounge chairs and they were set to relax for the evening. After dinner Angus and Paul went to their tents while Tony and Thalia sat with Michael sitting back watching the stars. It wasn't as nice as sitting on the balcony but Michael still found it relaxing. After a time Michael got a strange feeling Tony had fallen asleep in his lounger so Michael whispered to Thalia "Bigfoot is watching us"

"how do you know" asked Thalia

"I can feel him watching behind us"

Thalia turned quickly and you could hear the bushes.

"He's gone, he ran off I think you startled him."

"I startled him, my heart is in my throat,"

"I sense he means us no harm he's just curious. Let's get some sleep tomorrow is another day."

The following day they were up early ready to go. Then a quick breakfast. They didn't have to wait long when another signal came in it was in a small town much further south called Robbinsville. Michael teleported them there being careful not to appear in front of anyone. The map indicated that the incident was on the next block over.

"Okay follow me and be ready for anything."

When they got to the next block they saw nothing except a young boy playing with a ball.

Thalia asked, "could he be a demon in disguise?"

Michael replied, "no he's just a boy, I'd say about nine years old"

"then what created the magic."

"I wonder" said Michael. He raised his hands creating a triangle with his thumb and forefinger's recited the spell looked through the triangle and smiled. "He's a young wizard in the making. He doesn't even know he's projecting magic. It's a spell I read in my books for seeing those with magic and it works."

"But he's too young to have magic Michael"

"not really Thalia, I read in my books that those with magic are born with it they just don't know it and can't use it till a short time after puberty. Then they can be taught to use it. I think these maps will be a great tool for the wizarding orders to find and track wizards early on. Well let's move on this isn't what were looking for right now."

The next signal came a few hours later from the backwoods about 600 miles west the current position. When they arrived they saw nothing so Michael checked magically.

"hmm, another magical doorway was created here." They searched the area but couldn't find anything.

"We'll set up camp here" said Michael. The others prepared dinner and set up camp Michael sat by the fire looking a little sad. The others gathered around the fire and Thalia decided to ask "what's wrong Michael"

"oh nothing really I just hoped we would've found something. I didn't expect to find their base right away but I did hope for something we could use."

"Michael we've only been at it a couple of days, the others have been searching for months."

"You mean you guys aren't even a little disappointed."

"Not at all" said Scotty with his deep accent.

"Look at the things we discovered already" said Paul, They all shook their heads in agreement.

"Yeah I guess you're right, it must be a spell to reverse these magical doorways so we can find where they're coming from. When I get back to the library that will be something to look for."

Thalia said "when you find it that will be an adventure I definitely want in on."

"I think that something we should all be in on."

"Absolutely" said the others. Early the following morning another signal was detected Michael said to the others "we have another signal." But he just looked at the others from moment.

"Well are we going Michael?"

Michael looked at them, "this signal is in the middle of a large lake I guess we can teleport to the side and see if we can see anything."

The others looks surprised. When they arrived they could not see anything that could have created a disturbance. Michael told the others to look around while he checked out the area of the magical activity. He stretched out his hand lifted off the ground and floated out over the lake when he reached the spot he created a shockwave straight downward into the lake parting the water all the way to the bottom but could see nothing he then floated back to the shore and waited for the others. But they were also unable to find the cause of the magical activity so it went for the next several days they received signal after signal when they arrived they would either find the cause or not, but were getting no closer to finding the enemy base. On the ninth day they received the message from Dade telling them to return to Ghostra immediately.

"We should go Michael"

"yes of course, Dade wouldn't have sent the message if it wasn't important. Leave everything" said Michael, "we need to go now. They may be under attack." They gathered together and teleported back to the temple.

13

W HEN THEY ARRIVED DADE AND Evie were waiting for them. Evie ran
to Michael. "Mike Elaina is hurt."

"What you mean hurt" asked Michael.

Dade said "she collapsed Michael, we don't know why."

Michael turned to the others "you guys can wait in my quarters I've got to
go see her. On the way he Filled Dade in on what happened, what they found."

Michael and Evie ran off to the medical facility. Michael stopped at the
doorway Elaina was lying in bed unconscious several of the sisters were by
her bedside he walked to the foot of the bed Muriel the head of the facility
and a certified doctor was tending to her. Michael asked "how is she."

"She's alive, other than that she's very weak Dade tried reviving her with
magic but was unable to."

"What happened"

"we don't know, she was in the training room but just sitting on the
sidelines when suddenly she collapsed she's been in a coma ever since."

"There is a spell I read about for transferring energy to a person."

"Transfer from who" asked Muriel

"not from who but from where" said Michael. "If I can do it I'll draw
energy from the air itself ultraviolet energy, electromagnetic energy it's all
around us I'm going to try and channel it through me and into Elaina. I don't
know if it'll help but it might."

Michael went to Elaina's side raised one hand over his head and put the
other on Elaina's head. He closed his eyes and began reciting the spell in the
ancient language. The hand above his head began to glow and down the arm
and across the body began to glow all the way to the hand on Elaina's head
he held a connection for a moment and then released his touch everyone
watched in awe. Michael dropped to his knees by her side and called her

name. Elaina slowly opened her eyes she saw Michael next to her she smiled and said his name. Muriel said, "well done Michael, well done." Michael looked up and said

"can we have a moment alone please."

"Of course Michael" said Muriel. "Alright ladies give them some time together you can see her later." The others left, then Evie said "I'll see you in a little while in your room Mikey."

"Okay Evie," he turned to Elaina "how do you feel."

"Weak Michael, I feel like I don't have the strength to lift myself up."

"Don't try, just rest for now your strength will return you just have to heal. Where did Cassondra go she was supposed to take care of you until you are well."

"I don't know Michael, one moment she was there and then suddenly she was gone like she was pulled from my body and I had this feeling of fear that I think I got from her. You need to go see if she's all right."

"There will be time for that later right now I'm not leaving until I know you're all right. Right now you need your rest get some sleep Dade and the others are in my room I'm going to tell them we're calling off the search for a while I'll explain what was going on later."

"I know what was going on Michael, even though Cassondra was in control I was still in here and know what was happening."

"Get some rest"

"yes Doctor" said Elaina with a smile.

Michael returned to his room where the others were waiting. "Well team were going to have to postpone our search for a while I need to stay here. I need to make sure Elaina is okay and I need to see my guardian because there may be a problem."

"Anything we can help with," asked Scotty

"No thanks guys this is something I need to take care of myself."

Thalia said, "Michael why don't you let me take the others and continue to search while you do what you have to do here."

"I don't know Thalia, it could be dangerous."

"I can handle it Michael trust me."

Michael wasn't sure so he called Dade aside. "What you think Dade could she handle something like this."

"I think she's ready Michael I have wizards with a lot more experience but she's powerful and ready to lead. I think you will be a good experience for her."

Michael turned to the team. "Okay Thalia, you take the lead, here is the map. Dade get another member for the team we need a four-man team. Sorry Thalia I mean four person team." Thalia just smiled.

"Go back to where we left the gear start from there and I expect you back here in a week."

With that they gathered together and teleported away.

"Michael do you have another enchanted map." Asked Dade

"yeah I do why?"

"I'm planning on leading a second team starting in the lower part of the continent. The more we get out the better and faster our chances of finding their base. Besides I'm curious to see some of the things you found."

Michael went to the cabinet and got the second map, he handed it to Dade and said only " good luck". Dade nodded and left Michael returned to the medical facility Elaina was still asleep and Evie was sitting next to her bed.

"Has she awakened at all Evie."

"No Michael but she needs her rest."

"Stay with her I'm going to go see my guardian spirit."

"Okay Mike, ask why she left Elaina."

Michael was surprised. "You knew Evie?"

"Of course I knew I'm not dumb you know."

"I didn't mean it like that I'm just surprised anyone knew. Does anyone else suspect."

"I don't think so Mikey, at least no one has said anything."

"Good I need to find out what happened. She wouldn't just leave Elaina like that knowing her condition. I'll be in the sanctuary come and get me if she needs me."

"Sure Mikey, go do what you gotta do I'll watch her".

Michael left and rushed to the library he ran to the doors of the sanctuary and hesitated, what would he say to her, he was both angry and concerned. He decided to suppress his anger until he found out why she left Elaina the way she did.

He entered the sanctuary and walked to the altar a strange feeling came over him he felt something was wrong. Michael called Cassondra but nothing happened. He called again and a figure appeared but it wasn't Cassondra it was another spirit. She hung there in the air with a glow surrounding her she too was very beautiful.

"Who are you and where is Cassondra." "My name is Kurana I will be your new Guardian and guide."

"Like hell you will, what happened to Cassondra."

"She violated our laws and has been taken before the Magra."

"What is that."

"That is the leader of our kind he and the Council will judge and sentence her."

"Sentence her for what. She didn't do anything except help Elaina and I, isn't that what she supposed to do."

"We cannot interact with your world Michael it is forbidden."

"I need to speak to your Magra and This counsel."

"They will not come here Michael, they will do what they must."

"So will I, if they won't come to me I will go to them."

"That's impossible Michael, no human has ever been able to cross the vail to our realm."

Michael steamed out of the sanctuary and went to his office he removed two books from the shelf he remembered reading about a spell to open dimensional portal's, doorways to other realms. He sat down and began scanning the books, he knew it was in one of these books. After a short while he found what he was looking for he entered his private sanctuary and magically sealed it behind him, he then drew the symbols from the book on the floor and ignited it. He held out his arms and began reciting the spell he concentrated on where he wanted to go. Since he had never been there before he had no path to follow it was much more difficult to create the doorway so he concentrated on Cassondra suddenly the doorway opened Michael took a deep breath and entered. Upon exiting the portal at the other side Michael felt as if he were walking on air a light misty cloud floated all around him he waved his arm in the clouds parted. The sun shined bright. All around were strange but beautiful vegetation, flowers and vines and what looked like coral from under the sea, all were bright and colorful. A handsome man appeared before him.

"Hello Michael, I'm very impressed, no human has ever pierced the vail between our worlds before. Everything I've heard about your power seems to be true."

"Who are you" asked Michael.

"I am the Magra."

"I want to see Cassondra where is she."

"She is confined until her sentence is carried out."

"What sentence, are you planning on sending her to the dark realm."

"No Michael, what she did was not evil but it did violate our laws. She will be stripped of her powers and memories and placed on earth."

"You can't do that, all she did was what she was supposed to do protect me and save someone I care about who you almost killed when you took Cassondra away."

"We cannot intervene Michael we can only guide and advise, she knew this and violated our laws."

"Guide and advise how convenient to just let us do all the fighting and dying while you sit back and guide and advise. Well Cassondra showed me that she actually cares about us and right now she is the only one of you that I trust. I want Cassondra back as my guardian I won't except anyone else."

"That is not possible Michael our decision has already been made and we don't accept your ultimatum."

"Oh that wasn't an ultimatum that was my request. This is my ultimatum, Cassondra will be returned to me as guardian or your days of guidance in advising are over. If she's not returned I will destroy your sanctuary and will have the other mage do the same. If we can't trust you than we don't need you. Show me you have our best interest at heart. Show me you have compassion for one of your own who just stepped in to help or your days of advising and guiding are done and you will be reduced to just watching and hoping we do the right thing."

"You can't do that Michael."

"Just watch me, the choice is yours, how is that for an ultimatum."

Michael turned away the anger swelling within them. He recited the spell to open the portal and with the force he hadn't even realized he possessed blast open the doorway home. He walked into the portal which disappeared behind him. Another Guardian appeared next to the Magra. "he is even more powerful than we first thought" said the guardian. "He meant what he said, what we you going to do."

"I'm tempted to let him try it on his own. If he stumbles and falls a couple of times maybe he will realize we truly trying to help. But with this powerful darkness they're facing they will need our guidance and advice."

"Sir right now he doesn't trust us, he wants Cassondra, he cares for her and he trusts her."

"But our laws have been with us since the beginning of time how can we just make exceptions when it's convenient."

"Maybe we should, we blindly follow our laws without ever asking if they were originally intended to be adhered to so strictly. Maybe we should be using wisdom to interpret our laws."

"What do you mean."

"Cassondra broke the law but why. Michael was in the middle of the terrible battle barely holding his own when Elaina was struck he turned his attention away from the battle if Cassondra hadn't done what she did Michael may have been killed. Where would they're world be then."

"You make a good point Kurana, I think we need to assemble the Council."

"What of Michael Sir do you think we should tell him everything."

"No tell him what he needs to know he's young and inexperienced we don't want to overwhelm them. Besides some things humans just can't handle it all."

14

MICHAEL EXITED THE PORTAL BUT wasn't in his sanctuary. He appeared to be in a garden the flowers and foliage were beautiful, for a moment he thought he had been pulled back by the guardians but this was not the same place. On the path in front of him he saw a figure begin to materialize as it appeared Michael was prepared to fight but when the figure fully appeared Michael saw that it was an elderly man wearing purple robes who walked a little closer and said, "hello Michael, I've waited a long time to meet you."

"Who are you", asked Michael.

"My name is Zaxor and I'm your grandfather."

What! If this is some kind of trick I'm ready for anything."

"This is not a trick Michael I am actually your grandfather."

Michael was at a loss for words he had no idea how to respond but he was skeptical to say the least. Just then another figure began to appear on the path coming toward them, it was a very attractive woman in a blue silk gown and white robe she was wearing a delicate crown on her head. She Looked at Michael as though she had been waiting for him for a long time.

"Michael", she said as tears began to form in her eyes. "I'm Noreen your mother."

Michael's face turned suddenly grim. "That's impossible my mother is dead, she died when I was born."

"No Michael, I was brought back here when you were only three months old."

"You mean you abandoned me and dad and while were at it where is here."

Zaxor spoke, "we'll explain everything Michael once we reached the Palace, but first we'll bring the one who is been watching you to make sure you're safe. Maybe that will help you believe we are who we say we are."

"Someone watching me and you think I'll believe someone who has been hiding in the shadows spying on me."

Without another word Zaxor waved his arm and opened a portal when someone came through Michael was shocked it was Evelyn. "Evie?"

Noreen said, "Michael this is Evell your sister."

"My sister," now tears began to well up in Michael's eyes. "All this time Evie."

"Hey big brother, you don't know how I wanted to tell you."

"Well why didn't you".

"I swore to grandfather not to tell until the time was right. Plus he put a spell preventing me from saying the words just in case I slipped."

Michael turned to the others "then you really are my mother." She choked up when she tried to answer she just nodded. They were both crying at this point, she just ran over and threw her arms around her son. Evie smiled and ran over and hugged them both. She looked up then said "come on grandfather group hug."

He smiled and walked over putting his arms around them all. When they were done hugging and crying Michael looked around at the place you just found out was his home.

"All happening too fast for me to grasp. A few minutes ago I was an orphan with your young girl I was taking care of who was like a little sister to me. Now I find out my mother is alive, I have a family and this young girl really is my sister and she's been watching over me."

"I know it's a lot to take in all at once Michael I wish there was an easier way" said his mother. But you need to get the whole story of what is actually going on and what you're up against."

"You mean you know what's happening in our world."

"Yes, and considering what has happened and what is happening you need to know the whole story. But not here, let's go back to the palace and I'll explain it there."

"The palace, you live in a palace."

"Yes Michael, your mother is the Queen of the land of Rayne and I am first counselor, you and your sister are the Prince and Princess." Said his grandfather

"this is getting crazier and crazier."

"Don't worry Michael, you'll understand when were done explaining." They started walking and disappeared and reappeared in front of a large castle. It wasn't like the quick motion of teleporting which can leave you a little disoriented until you get accustomed to it. It was just an easy comfortable fading and reappearing. The castle was amazing it looked like stone but it shimmered and it's pattern seems to change as if it were alive. There didn't appear to be a way in unless you counted the windows which are rather high up. However as they got closer a doorway seemed to form in front of them as they entered the doorway closed behind them.

Grandfather said, "thank you Gelva."

Michael asked, "who are you talking to."

"The palace of course, I don't think we thank her often enough."

"Her? You talk like it's a living thing."

"It is Mikey" said Evie. Michael just shook his head. When they got inside they entered a large dining room. Zaxor asked Michael to sit and he poured him a cup of juice. It was a purple liquid Michael had some and said, "this is delicious what is it."

"It's called Gurro it's a fruit that grows here."

Evie was already gulping hers down.

"Michael, the first thing you need to know is that there are two lands in our realm separated by great bodies of water similar to the oceans on earth. Each land is named after the monarchy ours is the land of Rayne. The other is the land of Diecis. Baldor is one of the Diecis. In our land the people live in peace and prosperity. In the other they are ruled by the Diecis monarchy. They are brutal and rule by force the people are treated badly. They would even try to conquer our land if they didn't know we were much more powerful. Story began over 2000 years ago when the king of the Diesis family Graygle with his lust for power tried to attack our land. Your great-grandfather Creighton Rayne and his force turned back the attack. Devastating their forces and much of their power. They fled back to their land to avoid total destruction but Graygle still had his lust for power and his need to rule. So he used the portal to go to the other world and attempted to get the greatest wizards of the time with promises of wealth and power once he conquered realm. Many joined when they realize he had power they had never seen before. Others saw his power as well and his evil and band together to oppose him and those who joined him. That's when the great wizarding wars began when Creighton realized what was happening he opened a portal and went to that realm with two pet dragons. he created the Temple of Ghostra and became the first Dragon mage. With his power and his dragons he ended the wars. With his defeat Graygle fled back here. Many innocent people had been killed. None of the wizard dared to challenge the Dragon mage. No one knew him by any other name and he wouldn't let them know of our realm. He found 12 with good hearts. Some were wizards some were ordinary people without magical ability, he gave them powers beyond what any wizard on earth possessed. With them he formed the mage Council he then took the best of them and had him take his place as Dragon mage. the original priestesses of the Temple were a religious order trained to fight to protect themselves and others from the devastation of the wars. Creighton made the Temple their home. They've been loyal guardians of the Temple and aids to the Dragon mage ever since. But Michael, there was one flaw in the plan that Creighton hadn't foreseen. Over the centuries the power of all the mage have become weakened. Perhaps through marrying those with no powers or of lesser power or maybe just the spirit that is passed on became slightly less with each generation."

Michael's mother went over to her son and took his hand.

"Michael, you have to restore the power to the mage but no not all of them in the Council, some have become corrupted you need to do as Creighton did look into their hearts restore power to those with good hearts and take away the power from those who have been corrupted and replace them."

"How? I don't know how to tell the good from the bad and I don't know how to give or take away magic and where is this magic that I'm supposed to give them supposed to come from."

"Magic is all around us Michael the warmth of the sun, the flow of the wind, the universe itself is power you simply have to draw that power and as far as how, when you get back somewhere in your private sanctuary there is a magically hidden safe and in it you'll find four books of very powerful magic that Creighton himself put there 2000 years ago. It ancient magic very powerful and much of it long forgotten the safe can only be opened by one of our family and the books can only be read and absorbed by us. each book has a magical symbol on it they can only be learned in the proper order as each builds upon the previous book. The symbols show the order." She handed Michael a piece of parchment.

"Don't try to learn to much at once or the power can overwhelm you. It will probably take years to read and understand and master all four books. Don't push it Michael that's very important spells. The power you need to give and remove power is in the beginning of the first book or if you will the beginning of your journey." Noreen took Michael's hands in hers and as she closed her eyes both their hands began to glow and Michael felt a surge of power and he was actually able to feel her love for him, she opened her eyes and looked at him with tears in her eyes.

"Now Michael, you'll be able to touch someone and see what is in their heart."

"I need to get back and see how Elaina is mother. She was hurt badly and magic doesn't seem to help none of the normal healing spells seem to work."

"Okay Mikey I'm ready" said Evie.

"I don't know Evie things are getting a little hairy right now you might be better off staying here" said Michael. "He might be right" said Zaxor.

"No way, Mikey may need me plus I have friends there."

"What do you think mother? Asked Michael

"I think she's determined to go and even though I want you both to stay safe here, she's right she may be of help or at least moral support now that you know who she is."

Grandfather said, "before you go Michael you may need this." He went to the cabinet and took out the sword.

"That's the Dragon sword how did he get here."

"I took it from your room, I knew it would draw you here, but it belongs to you and you will need it." Michael removed the replica and his grandfather handed him Dragon's breath which glowed the instant Michael touched it.

"The sword recognizes its master" said grandfather as he put the sword into it's sheath Michael heard a voice in his head it was Elaina.

"Michael hurry, were under attack.

"What is it Michael" asked Noreen

"it's Elaina! The Temple was under attack I need to go now".

"I'm coming with you" said his mother

Zaxor said "majesty if there under attack it will be dangerous"

"I won't abandon my son again I'll be fine and I'll return when it's over."

"As you wish"

"come Michael, we can open a portal within the castle."

They ran outside where Noreen waved her hand and open the portal they ran into it and reappeared in Michael's private sanctuary.

"Evie wait here you'll be safe here"

"oh come on Michael"

"I mean it Evie."

"All right I'll stay here"

15

Michael and Noreen ran to the hallway and could hear the battle raging as they rounded the corner they could see Dade in several wizards along with the sisters of the Temple battling fiercely but hordes of demons along with dark magical creatures were about to overwhelm them through sheer number. Immediately Noreen began launching lightning **bolts** into the advancing creatures in rapid succession Michael joined in with balls of fire which exploded on contact Dade and the others shocked by the sudden onslaught coming from behind them stood aside as Michael and Noreen advanced driving the dark creatures back Michael moved in front of the others most of the creatures were in full retreat when Michael saw a black cloud moving down the hallway toward him.

Dade yells "death Beatles one bite and we'll be dead within minutes." There were hundreds maybe thousands of them Noreen yelled, "Michael you're sword" Michael drew his sword uttered the words and flames lept from the sword filling the corridor in front of them Noreen cast the spell that sent the wall of fire traveling quickly toward the enemy. The flame sped down the hallway leaving nothing but ash in it's wake. When the last of the creatures had either fled or been incinerated the flames died down with a single word from Michael the sword shut down and he returned it to it's sheath.

"Dade turned to Michael "you got your sword back where was it."

"That's not important right now Dade, what happened"

"Thalia and her team were attacked. Thalia returned here hours ago. The others didn't make it back. The attack started about 20 minutes ago I don't know how they could have broken through our defenses. They never should've been able to get through. We didn't know where you were no one is heard from you for three days."

"Three days, I've only been gone a few hours."

Noreen said, "you went to the realm of the spirits Michael, time doesn't work the same there."

Dade looked shocked, "Michael you went to the world of the guardians, how." But Michael wasn't listening he had noticed the high priestess kneeling by several of the sisters who had fallen in the battle, he ran to her.

"Are they all right," he asked

"Sister. Mary is dead, the others are hurt but I think they'll be okay, thank God you came when you did.

"I heard Elaina call she said the Temple was under attack. Where is she?"

Tears had filled her eyes but there was a look of confusion on her face Michael you couldn't have heard Elaina she still unconscious and medical."

"But I know I heard her."

Noreen said, "your bond to her is very strong Michael."

Then she walked over to the body of sister Mary. She moved her hand over the body her eyes closed.

"As I suspected her spirit is still here. Their bond to the temple is also very strong." She put her arms over the body and began a magical incantation. Suddenly sister Mary began to breathe then slowly opened her eyes. Everyone was shocked. But the look of disbelief gave way to joy. The high priestess turned to Noreen took her hand and kissed it "I don't know how you did it but thank you."

Michael picked up sister Mary and carried her to medical while the other sisters followed on stretchers. Michael put sister Mary in her bed and quickly went to see Elaina.

"Mother this is Elaina, I can understand why she's not getting any better. She was healing when Cassondra was inside her."

"She's not getting better Michael, because she was cursed by powerful evil magic. Give me your hand Michael and I'll show you how to cure this magic. She stood behind him and held his hands over Elaina's body and spoke the spell in the ancient tongue. Slowly Elaina opened her eyes looked at Michael and smiled then closed her eyes again. Michael turned to the mother and asked what happened

"nothing happened, she'll sleep for a while and when she awakens she'll feel much better tomorrow she should be good as new." Michael looked around to make sure no one was close by and then said "thank you mother."

She smiled and held her son.

"I need to go back Michael, if you need us you know now how to reach us. Take care of your sister and come home whenever you can."

Just then Evie entered the room, ". Well I guess you guys forgot all about me. You would think when the shooting was over somebody would come to get me." Michael was embarrassed, "sorry Evie but we have been busy, you're here right on time mothers leaving."

"Already Mom, can you stay a while."

"I would really like to Evell but I don't want to give your grandfather a nervous condition. When you come visit bring Elaina she's a lovely girl and I want to get to know the young woman who has stolen my son's heart." She hugged them both and left. Michael turned to Evie.

"Evie I need to go to the library and see if Cassondra is back then I need to go to my sanctuary and see if I could find those books. If anything happens or if Elaina wakes up and wants me come get me otherwise I'll be back as soon as possible."

"Okay Mikey I'll take care of it." Before leaving he went over to the Matris to see how the injured were doing.

"How are they doing Matris."

"They'll be fine Michael, thanks to you and the woman you were with. She is more powerful than anyone I've ever seen. Who is she?" Michael paused thinking what to say looking for the right words "she's someone very special. I'll be back shortly to check on everyone if I'm needed Evie knows where I'll be."

When he got to the library he went to the door to the guardian sanctuary and he hesitated. What if Cassondra is there, what would he do. He gave his ultimatum and he Would have to stick to it. He would break all ties to the guardians but what would be the consequences of not having their help. Was he going to far demanding a change their rules for him, after all they have been around forever and he's only been a mage for a year and a half and he's telling them their wrong. Many thoughts flashed in his mind. No, in this he felt he was right. They say they want to help but don't want to get involved, they'll punish their own for actually helping when it's needed. He entered the sanctuary and walked to the altar he looked around for a moment and then called her name. There was no response he called again. This time a figure appeared it was Cassondra, Michael smiled and felt relieved.

"Cassondra, I was beginning to wonder if I'd ever see you again."

"Michael, good to see you too from what I've seen you created quite a stir. The Council is meeting and from what we've heard our whole structure of rules are being reviewed."

"Good They should be."

"In the beginning Michael the rules given to us was simple help the people but don't let them know you exist. All the other laws or rules sprang up around that.

Every time one of us made an error or problem arose new rules were added and as happens with laws eventually it gets out of control and they began to add punishments for violations of the rules. It's not the way it was supposed to be, but now thanks to you things will change."

"I don't know anything about that, I only know that I trust you and I couldn't let them punish you for doing something that had to be done."

"Well I have to go for now Michael, I've been asked to appear before the Council. I think they're very concerned that you don't trust them. I'll keep watch call if you need me."

"Okay Cassondra till later."

After Cassondra left Michael rushed to his office and entered his personal sanctuary. He began searching for the books of the ancient magic. He looked around the altar but found nothing. There were no cabinets or doors that he could see exept for the one they saw earlier, then he noticed on the far end of the room an area of the wall that seemed out of place, seemed to move like the ripple of water on a calm lake it was barely noticeable. He walked to the spot and reached out and touched the area which immediately opened to reveal another small room when he entered he saw many magical items weapons cloaks clothing and other items that he couldn't classify. But there on the table were the four books that he sought. Odd red glow surrounded them. As he approached the book on top of the others rose into the air Michael took the book and noticed a symbol on the cover indicated that this was the first book he had to study. He opened it and began to read. The words and symbols seem to float off the page and enter his mind he was able to understand every word every spell without studying or translating as he read he could feel the energy and power of each spell each incantation as if the book were imparting not only the knowledge but also its power the more he read the more he wanted.

Michael had never felt anything like it the energy was coursing through his body it was intoxicating he completed the first couple of pages and continued on until suddenly he became lightheaded stumbled and fell to one knee the room was spinning he grabbed the desk to stabilize himself then he remembered what his grandfather had said about going slowly or he would get overwhelmed by the power. He realize that he had overdone it from his first session he put the book down and went and sat while his head cleared. After a short while except for a slight headache he felt much better. He can still feel the rush of energy. Michael went back to the infirmary when he arrived Dade was standing in the doorway.

Michael asked, "Dade how is Thalia"

"she'll be all right Michael she's resting now.

"Have you heard anything about the others."

"No Michael, we sent a team but they found nothing. I feel responsible I thought they could handle it without you I should've gone with them."

"It's not your fault Dade, don't start second-guessing you decisions. Everyone has to take responsibility sometimes. You could never have known it would be an ambush."

"It's as if they knew they would be there."

"What are you saying Dade, do you think someone betrayed us."

"I don't know, I can't see anyone who knew where they were turning trader I trust them all still how did they get into the temple without someone with access helping them get past the defenses. I just don't know."

"How many wizards are in the gray order."

"19 counting Thalia and the three that are missing. I'm still holding out hope that they are still alive."

"I need to meet with them all as soon as possible we need to know who we can trust."

"I'll show you take my hand." Michael held out his hand and Dade a little apprehensive placed his hand in Michael's. Michael read his mind and heart Dade had a good heart he believed in what they did. Michael sensed someone who enjoyed helping others like teaching others to be the best they can be. When Michael told this to him, Dade said, "well anyone who knows me could figure that."

"Would they also know that Luke is your son."

Look of shock came over the Dade's face. "No one knows that."

"I know, "said Michael

"Michael, you have abilities I've never seen before even in a mage."

"I read a lot"

"you're being evasive Michael and let's talk about the woman who came with you. She has powers I never knew existed. I've always believed almost anything is possible but I would never have believed someone could be brought back once they were dead, and then as quickly as she came she disappeared. I don't suppose you're willing to explain that."

"I wish I could Dade, I trust you is much as anyone. But there are some things I can't even tell you. their answers I just found out myself and I'm sworn not to tell. Maybe someday but not now."

"Well Michael, I look forward to that day, in the meantime I'll make arrangements to bring the others here to meet with you." When Dade left Michael went to the infirmary and went straight to Elaina's room Evie was sitting next to her bed, "HI Mike" she said

"hey Evie, how is she doing"

"okay I guess, she's been in and out since you've been gone, she needs her rest but she's been fighting it, she's stubborn like you."

"Thanks Evie, you're all heart."

"I know, you don't have to tell me. I'm going to go rest for a while I'll be back later."

"Okay thanks Evie"

Michael sat beside the bed and took Elaina's hand, it felt good to hold her hand. Elaina opened her eyes and looked at him.

"Hi Michael," she said faintly, "they told me you were away. I was worried about you."

Michael asked, "you were worried about me, you're the one in bed barely able to move."

"I know, but they said you were gone for days alone and then everyone was running around and said we were under attack I heard terrible noises and I tried to call out to you but couldn't."

"I know Elaina I heard you calling."

"How I couldn't even get the words out."

"I know, but I did hear you, I heard you in my mind and I came right away just in time thanks to you."

"But where were you Michael."

"I'll explain everything, but for now just rest I'll be here."

Elaina relaxed and soon fell back asleep, Michael stayed by her side thinking about what a long day it had been. After a while he fell asleep in a chair next to her bed still holding her hand. Next morning when he woke Elaina was already awake sitting up and looking good as new.

"Hello sleepyhead," she said

"Elaina you look much better today."

"I feel fine Michael, ready for action."

"Let's not push Elaina."

"Michael, they told me that when you return you were with a woman who helped you defeat the enemy, and help cure me and brought sister Mary back when she was dead. Is that true?"

"Yes Elaina, it's all true."

"How is that possible, who is she where she from? No one knows anything about her and she vanished as quickly she came. Michael if she's that powerful how is it no one has ever heard about her."

"Calm down Elaina, this evening we'll have dinner together Evie you and I, and I'll explain everything that you need to know if you promise that you won't repeat what I tell you to anyone."

Elaina couldn't understand why he didn't want the others to know, but Michael felt it was important that was enough.

"Okay Michael, I promise."

"Now Elaina try and get some rest I have some studying to do in the library."

"Rest! Michael I've had nothing but rest I need to move around, get some exercise workout."

"Okay but don't overdo it, take it slow."

16

MICHAEL HEADED FOR THE LIBRARY, he knew how important it was for him to continue studying the ancient texts, plus he liked the feeling he got learning the spells and energy they gave him it was almost intoxicating. He studied most of the day taking it slow reading no more than a couple pages at a time and resting in between. His grandfather was right the spells to give and take away magical powers were toward the beginning of the first book. Every once in a while he would try a couple of the nondestructive spells or enchantments. He couldn't believe the power the book contained. He created a small whirlwind, made a ball of energy that gave off light and warmth, he could summon animals and they would follow his commands. Spell after spell of powerful magic. Finally he had enough for one day as he returned to his room he wondered just how he was going to tell Elaina everything and how he was going to explain the mysterious woman everyone was so curious about. But he was determined that he would not lie to her. But he also wondered how it would affect the relationship, would she feel the same knowing he was actually from another realm, another world. When he got to his room he found no one else had arrived yet so he sat at the table dinner was already there but he was going to wait for Elaina and Evie before eating. He sat thinking. Suddenly the door to the bathroom opened and out stepped Elaina. She was still wet with a towel wrapped tightly around her. Michael looked up and for a moment she took his breath away.

"Oh! Hello Michael I didn't know you were here yet, I hope you don't mind but I took advantage of your offer to use your bath I was sweaty from working out and figured I'd indulge myself, it was amazing I could've stayed in all day it felt so good." Michael fumbled for words.

"No that's fine, I'm glad you enjoyed it." He looked away not wanting to stare at her.

"Evie went to get some clothes in my room, I forgot to bring clean clothes and she offered to go while I bathe." Michael decided to change the subject.

"So Elaina, how are you feeling after your ordeal."

"Much better now after getting out of bed and moving around and that bath just topped off the day." Just then Evie arrived with Elaina's clothes.

"Oh! And what have you two been up to." Michael and Elaina both blushed and looked at each other "Michael quickly responded, "nothing at all I just got here and didn't know Elaina was here."

"Okay, okay did you tell her about mom yet."

Michael quickly looked at Elaina hoping she didn't hear that. He wanted to explain everything to her gently without shocking her. He still wasn't sure how she would react.

"Your Mom, I thought your mother died when you were born."

He gave Evie an angry look and she looked away like nothing happened.

"Get dressed Elaina, we have a lot to talk about I can't concentrate with you wrapped in a towel."

"Really, well that's interesting." She took her clothes and went into the bathroom.

"Sorry Mikey, I thought you told her."

"I'm going to but I want to do it slowly so that she doesn't freak out, and I don't want her to think less of me because I'm not from this world. Also I wanted you to be here."

"Is that what you're worried about, she cares about you and not just because you're the Dragon mage. She wouldn't care if you are from the moon."

"I hope you're right Evie, because I'm going to tell her everything."

"Good Mike, it's always best to come clean."

"Yeah just like you did right."

"Sorry Mike, but I swore to grandpa I wouldn't say anything to you until they felt the time was right."

Moments later Elaina emerged from the bathroom and came and sat at the table by Michael and Evie.

"Okay Michael, you said you wanted to tell me everything. Well I'm ready."

"Are you sure you don't want to first eat food, looks great."

"That's okay Michael, we can eat while we talk."

"All right then, what I'm going to tell you maybe a little difficult to believe and I don't want you to freak out. Michael hesitated for a moment. Elaina I would like you to meet my sister." Michael pointed to Evie.

"What do you mean, I thought Evie was someone you took in and helped."

"Yes that's what I thought, but I found out that she is actually my sister."

"I don't understand did your father have a child with another woman."

No she's my full sister same father same mother."

"But I thought your mother died when you were born."

"So did I, but the woman who came back with me and helped the drive back the attack and save sister Mary and you was my mother. Let me start from the beginning." Michael began to relate everything that happened and what he discovered from the time he was told that she collapsed until now making sure he covered everything except what he learned about the ancient books, which he felt he shouldn't share with anyone at this time. When he finished he looked at Elaina. She was staring in his direction as if in total disbelief.

"Elaina" he said "Elaina are you all right."

"Michael that's the craziest thing I've ever heard."

"It's all true Elaina, Evie can verify everything."

"Oh no Michael, I do believe you but it's just amazing. You are the descendent of the original Dragon mage." Michael just nodded.

"Michael, who the original Dragon mage was, where he was from, and where he disappeared to is the biggest mystery in the entire magical world. Our order wouldn't even exist anymore if it weren't for him."

"And you don't hate me."

"Michael why would you think I would hate you."

Evie said, "he thought you wouldn't like him when you found out we're from another realm."

"I could never change how I feel about you Michael."

See I told you Mikey, oh! By the way Elaina when you guys have the time mom wants to meet you." Elaina looked at Michael.

"Really Michael, she really wants to meet me."

"Yes she does, she said I should bring you the first chance we get."

"I'd be honored Michael, why would she want to meet me I'm nobody special."

Michael was thinking of an answer when Evie blurted out.

"She said she wants to meet the girl who stole my brothers heart."
Michael blushed while Elaina just smiled.

"Thanks Evie, don't you have somewhere to be." Evie laughed out loud.

"What's the matter Mike did I embarrass you."

"Michael answered quickly, "no! Well maybe a little."

"Don't worry Mikey, it's not really a big secret everybody knows."

"Everybody," asked Michael. Evie just shook her head.

"Well I've had my fun I'll be going now."

"I was kidding Evie you don't have to go."

"I know Mike, but I have stuff I need to get done, I'll see you tomorrow."
After Evelyn left Michael and Elaina went to sit at the balcony.

"Elaina, we need to talk."

"I agree Michael, we need to talk about what happened when I was injured."

"Yes that's exactly what I wanted to talk about. I know you feel that
you need to be with me whenever I go somewhere, but I think you see how
dangerous it can be with what's happening right now, you were almost killed
when I saw you fall I didn't know what to do."

"Yes Michael, and that's what I want to talk to you about your loss
of control and almost got yourself killed. Michael I don't have to see how
dangerous it is I know how dangerous it is. You don't seem to grasp our role
here Michael. As much as you feel that you need to protect us. We are here
to serve you in the temple and fight with you and help you to do what must
be done. I'm your personal aide sworn to stay by your side for as long as I live
you can't change that because you're concerned for my safety, and what you
did when I fell was dangerous and foolish. You took your mind off the battle
you could've been killed and as much as I care about you we need to keep
our relationship purely professional. I will not be the cause of your death."

"And I will not be the cause of yours. Tomorrow I'm going to where
Thalia and the others were attacked to see if I can find out what happened
to Paul Tony and Angus. You can come along but if we run into trouble
I'm teleporting you back here so you can find Dade and send him to help."

"But Michael"

"no butts, that's my condition for letting you come with me, he's too
strong I can't protect us both and fight him at the same time if any other
dark creature we'll fight together. Deal"?" She looked in his eyes and could
sense that he meant it. "Okay Michael I'll play along for now it's a deal."

"Good now let's get some rest we'll leave first thing in the morning."

The next morning Michael woke early. He went to the bathroom but didn't even take time for a nice bath. He just washed and dressed. When he was done he found Elaina already waiting for him she was dressed in her warrior uniform of his colors Michael thought she really looked good but didn't say anything. He was still concerned about taking her with him and hoped he was doing the right thing. Breakfast is already there so they ate quickly. After they ate Michael turned to Elaina.

"I'm not expecting any trouble but just in case remember our agreement."

"I remember Michael and you need to stop worrying about me."

"I'm not worried, I'm concerned, I know you can take care of yourself but without magic you are extremely vulnerable. They may target you more than me hoping I'll drop my guard to protect you."

"Michael no matter what you do you can't lower your guard for me."

"I won't have to if you fight smart and seek shelter if necessary." Elaina nodded. Michael took her hand in a flash they were gone the reappeared in a canyon, it was dry and nothing but rocks and cliffs on both sides.

"This was the last place they transported to. The attack must of happened somewhere around here."

"Michael I'm sensing something up ahead where the canyon narrows."

"That makes sense it looks like a good place for an ambush, come on let's head that way and see if we can find any clues. As they approached the narrow section of the canyon Elaina picked up a thought.

"Stop Michael" she said

"what is it" he asked

"there is a mage in two wizards up ahead somewhere."

"Good it may be one of our team."

"No Michael, it's Raymond the desert mage and two of his wizards I read their thoughts for a moment before they close their minds. Michael look."

Three creatures were heading their way from a little further up the canyon about 200 yards ahead. They were ugly creatures dressed in rags. They stood about 8 feet tall and moved toward them very slowly.

"What of those ogre looking things."

"I've heard about them Michael, they are Bogen's there slow but very strong and Michael will have to fight or run, magic doesn't work on them, it has no effect."

"We can't take the time to fight them for Raymond and his wizards will attack while were occupied. So we'll have to take care of them quickly with magic."

"But Michael I told you magic doesn't work against them."

Michael just smiled and waved his hand while muttering incantation. The right side wall of the canyon trembled and fell right on top of the Bogen's.

"Magic may not work on them but works on everything around them."

"That's crazy Michael, but I don't think anyone thought of that before."

"Raymond and the others are hiding in that small cave up ahead on the left." Said Michael.

"Are you sure Michael? How do you know?"

"I saw one of the fools look out quickly when I dropped the wall on those creatures."

"Michael another Bogen coming from behind us."

"At least it's only one, do you think you can keep him occupied while I take care of Raymond and his friends."

"Michael are you sure you'll be all right there's three of them and one is a mage."

"Yeah I've been practicing, when they attack I'm going to go down like I'm hurt that will draw them closer I want to get them all so they can't report back. Don't freak out when I go down just pretending as you said keep your mind on what you're doing. If You can't bring that thing down don't worry just keep it occupied."

"Okay Michael, I'll take care of it, you be careful I hope you're right about being able to handle them if you go down for real were going down together."

With that said she drew her sword and headed back to deal with the oncoming creature. Michael kept going forward to what he knew was a trap. The whole time thoughts were running through his head. What defensive spells would he used to make it look like they defeated him what counter spells would he use once they approached but the thought that kept flashing in his mind was whether he was strong enough to overpower all three of them even with the powers he's gained in his studies but he couldn't let Elaina know he had doubts. He kept moving forward. He picked what he felt was the most likely place for the attack and prepared himself. He looked back Elaina had just engaged the Bogen. He hopes she can handle it but knew she was right he had a trust her more. Still he thought she was in a coma just a few days earlier. Focus he kept telling himself focus. Then it happened they sprung from the cave and together fired a blast of energy at him without hesitation he created a tight shield around himself the energy that struck the shield was absorbed. He quickly fell to the ground maintaining the shield in case of another attack. He waited as they approached he wanted to get them close so when he trapped them so none of them will be able to escape. Then he heard footsteps someone running toward them.

"Oh look", said one of the wizards "Little priestess is running toward us with her sword"

thats when Michael jumped up and cast a binding spell around the three of them. They were caught completely by surprise.

"Are you all right Michael?" Asked Elaina

"I'm fine how about you?"

"I'm good, our ugly friend is down for the count. I didn't kill them but he will think twice about attacking again."

"Good job Elaina, but why were you running they were about to attack you. I had to attack sooner than I would've liked to."

Sorry Michael, I knew the plan but when I saw you go down I felt."

Michael interrupted "like I did when you went down."

Elaina knew what he meant she had criticized him for doing the same thing she had just done, she ran to protect him just as he had run to protect her.

Yes Michael, I guess so but it's my duty to protect you." She tried to rationalize a response.

"Yes Elaina just as is my duty to protect you and not just because of the way I feel about you personally, we're a team and we work well together. I wouldn't feel comfortable working with anyone else. Now let's get this bunch back home."

With that they transported them all back to Ghostra. When they arrived he sent word to Dade. Dade arrived within minutes with three of his wizards.

"The Trader and two of his wizards. This is amazing news. We can extract some major information from them. We'll notified the mage Council they're coming to take Raymond they have facilities to hold and interrogate mage. We'll take the wizards and get what we can from them unless you have other plans Michael."

That's fine I have no special plans for them. But I don't want them hurt."

""That'll make it harder to get information."

"Maybe but I don't want us to stoop to their level get what you can but no physical abuse."

"As you say Michael, but I doubt we'll get much information."

"Oh you'll be surprised that the information we'll get, but I want to give them a chance to give it to us freely before we use other methods."

"Okay Michael, will take care of it and I'll make sure everyone understands your orders." With that Dade took the prisoners and left and Michael and Elaina went to his room.

"It's been a very good day" said Elaina

"yes it has, tomorrow is also going to be a good day. I want you to come with Evie and me to meet my mother."

For a moment Elaina was speechless. Then she gathered her composure and said, "you mean to actually travel to another world, another realm."

"Yes, unless you're not ready for something like that. I don't want to rush you into anything."

"No Michael, I'd be honored to meet your mother and thank her personally and to travel to another world is something I've never dreamed possible."

"Good and first thing tomorrow after we make sure there is no trouble anywhere we'll go. and now have some dinner and relax. During dinner Evie showed up.

"Hey guys, what's happening I heard you caught a couple of traders today."

"HI Evie, would you like some supper."

"No thanks I already ate. I just came to sit with you two. So what happened was it exciting."

"I wouldn't quite put it that way, but we got the job done."

"Don't listen to him Evie, it was very exciting" said Elaina.

"Cool, I can't wait till I'm able to go out on missions."

"Evie, I'm going to take Elaina to meet Mom tomorrow if everything's okay here."

"It's really great Mike can I come along."

"Sure Evie I want you there too."

"That's wonderful, Mom really wants to meet her."

They went out to the balcony and sat for a bit. After a while Elaina said, "If I'm going to meet you mother tomorrow I should try and get some rest."

"Okay" said Michael. "I'll see you in the morning"

after she left Michael asked Evie "you think I'm doing the right thing. I mean I don't want to rush things maybe mom's not ready yet or maybe I'm rushing Elaina."

"Mike you always overthink everything. Mom wants to meet Elaina and Elaina wants to meet mom. It's a great idea anytime is the right time to just go with it."

"You're right Evie, thanks."

They sat for a long while Michael fell asleep in the chair just after Evie left. Next morning Michael woke early still in the chair first thing he did was make sure there were no messages to indicate there was any trouble. Durell brought breakfast while he got cleaned up. Elaina and Evie arrived shortly after and he sat and had a quick bite.

"Are we going Michael" asked Elaina.

"Yes everything seems to be quiet. They didn't send any messages so yes were going."

He took them to his study in the library. Waved his hand in the door to his sanctuary opened.

"Michael, no one ever knew there was a hidden room here."

"This is my private sanctuary. My place to study and practice away from everyone even the guardian's can see and hear."

Michael walked to the altar closed his eyes raised both hands and muttered his incantation. Immediately the portal open to his own realm.

"I'm nervous Michael" said Elaina

"don't be just take my hand."

She and Evie took Michael's hand stepped into the portal. The pass-through arrived at the garden where Michael landed before. The trees were green multicolored flowers were stunning. The sky was deep blue and the sun was shining.

"Oh Michael this is beautiful" said Elaina. "This is like a scene from a beautiful dream"

Michael and Evie both smiled. Just then Michael's mother appeared. She was wearing a light pink and blue dress with a delicate crown upon her head.

"Michael, Evell, I'm happy to see you both and you bought Elaina. Hello my dear welcome to our world."

"It's an honor to meet you." She hesitated not quite knowing how to address her.

"Just call me Noreen, we don't stand on formalities here."

As they walked toward the palace Elaina noticed something flying overhead. She turned to the others not knowing if they saw it.

"Michael did you see that was that the Dragon."

Noreen answered, "yes they live here at the top of that mountain in the distance. They are our friends."

"How many are there."

"Oh about one half a dozen I guess. Dargus is their leader. Perhaps later I'll introduce you." Elaina was speechless, she looked at Michael even he was a little surprised. After a few minutes to compose herself Elaina said,

"everything is so beautiful here."

"Thank you" said Noreen, "the people here take a great deal of pride in keeping everything especially the gardens perfect Zaxor and I also like spending time working the gardens."

"You mean physically not with magic."

"We don't use magic for everything. There is no sense of accomplishment if you don't get your hands dirty once in a while. would it surprise you to know that I often cook for Zaxor, myself and the staff who help us in the castle."

"Yes, back home rulers don't work they have others do it for them."

"Well we're not rulers, we are leaders and it's always best to lead by example. We often go to the local villages and help with whatever new projects they may have going on."

Evie said "there is another land Elaina and they are led as ours is. Some of the leaders of the other land are really bad. It's the land of Deices where Baylor is from they treat their people very badly."

As they approached and the castle recognize them the doorway formed in the wall they entered. "was that door there before".

"Not exactly, the door formed out of the wall when the castle recognized us."

"This place is truly amazing."

Noreen said, "follow me and I'll give you a glimpse of our lands."

"Cool, are we going to the tower mom." Asked Evie.

Noreen looked at her and nodded. They walked to the end of a long corridor and passed through a large wooden door and suddenly began to ascend straight up toward the top of the tall tower. Elaina slightly caught off guard for a moment clutch Michael's hand. They passed several levels with doors leading to different floors in the castle and then continued all the way to the top where they stepped onto the stone platform which went all the way around the top of the tower. They looked out and saw forests and fields everywhere Dragon Mountain off in the distance surrounded by clouds and they could see several villages scattered about.

"This is my favorite place to relax and reflect on any thoughts or problems." Said Noreen

"mine to" said Evie "I would come here all the time. I find it very relaxing."

"Oh this is beautiful, and so peaceful I could spend my whole life right here." Said Elaina. Noreen smiled and Michael stood there amazed.

"Come it's nearly lunchtime and I'm sure your grandfather would like to meet Elaina." When they arrived at the dining room the table was already set and a young lady was just bringing out a bowl of fruit.

"If there's nothing else my lady I'll be leaving, my boyfriend and I are going to have a picnic."

"No nothing else, thank you to Kiva and give my regards to your mom. Tell her I'll visit soon."

Elaina said, "that's a strange conversation to have with a servant."

"Kiva isn't a servant, the local villagers stop by and help out occasionally. Just as we go and help out at times. Like when the crops are due for harvesting we all help each other."

Michael said "but you have magic to do those things."

"We don't use magic for everything Michael. It would take all the fun and friendship out of life." Elaina said, "I think that's nice."

"Noreen smiled and said, "shall we eat."

Moments later grandfather entered. He came to the table and greeted everyone.

"Hello Michael, hello Evie and this must be Elaina."

"Yes sir" she said.

"Sir, I like her already but there are no sir's here, I'm just Zaxor."

They sat in a and talked about everything and nothing they just got to know each other. Fruits and vegetables most of which Michael and Elaina had never seen before but they tasted amazing. When they had finished Evie said "Elaina would you like to see my room, can I show her around mom."

"Of course Evell, if she would like to. When you're done you'll find Michael and I in the garden."

"Come on Elaina I'll give you the tour."

"Okay Evie let's go." She looked at Michael and shrugged her shoulders who laughed as she followed Evie. Grandfather turned to Noreen and said, "you two go ahead I'll clean up and join you when I'm done."

Noreen and Michael went and sat in the garden. "It's good to have you and your sister here with us and Elaina seems like a wonderful girl."

"It's good to be here, it's nice having a family again."

"I sense something is bothering you Michael what is it."

"Oh nothing really, I was going to ask your advice about Elaina. Every time we go out I fear for her safety she so vulnerable but I don't want to insult her by not letting her come along she feels as do the rest of the sisters that it's their responsibility. Apparently it's the way it's been done since the beginning. You're a woman mom tell me how can I keep her safe without hurting her. She's determined to throw her life away if necessary to protect me."

"I'm glad you asked Michael, I've been meaning to talk to you about this very thing when the time is right. I guess the time is right now. Michael she's proud and courageous and you're right when you say vulnerable. Also she's human which means she will only live a normal human lifetime while you will live many human lifetimes and I can see in your eyes that you love her. There was only one solution, if you're sure she's the one you want to spend your life with you have to give her the power."

"What power, you mean the power of a mage."

"More than that Michael, you need to go all the way and make her like one of us."

"But I didn't think I was allowed to do that and is that even possible. I thought the rules forbid giving anyone power unless they were on the mage counsel."

"Michael the rules were made 2000 years ago by Creighton your great-grandfather and they lasted all this time, but times have changed and the rules need to change to match the times. You don't seem to grasp the fact that you are now the Dragon mage and you need to adjust the rules. Besides your great-grandmother was originally human. She fell in love with Creighton and he with her and when they returned here they were married.

You see he faced the same dilemma you do now. If you love her and she loves you and I can tell you both do then you need to give her the power."

He hugged her and felt as if the weight of the world had been lifted from his shoulders. They sat and talked for a while until Evie and Elaina arrived. Noreen said, "follow me I've something to show you."

They followed her to the top of the hill where she performed a series of gestures which ended with a bow. Michael Elaina had no idea what she was doing but then in the distance they saw a dragon flying toward them bigger and bigger it Got as it approached them. It was a magnificent creature which landed right in front of them.

"You called to me your Majesty" said the Dragon but not in words Michael and Elaina heard him with their minds.

"Yes Dargo, I'd like for you to meet my son Michael and his aide."

Darga looked at Michael and Elaina. " Ahh, the young Prince has come home." The Dragon bowed to Michael and Michael returned the honor.

Noreen said "he is only here for the day. He is the new Dragon mage and has much to do."

"Wonderful" said Dargo, "young Prince when your mission is complete and you return home I would be grateful if you could bring my children home with you. They've been away for too long."

"I'd love to, where can I find them."

Noreen said, "Michael, the two dragons on top of the temple are Dargo's children."

"You mean the two stone statues."

Dargo laughed, "they are not stone statues young Prince they are only hibernating, waiting to be awakened when needed by a true descendent of Creighton."

"I had no idea" said Michael. "When my mission is done and evil is put back where it belongs I will bring your children home."

"Thank you young Prince, and if you need their help you can awaken them and they will help all of my clan have sworn their loyalty to your house."

With that he bowed again and flew off to tell the rest of his clan that a Rahyn is once again the Dragon mage of Ghostra

"it was amazing" said Elaina, "I can't believe those are real dragons on top of the temple."

"I never would've guessed it either" said Michael

Evie looked troubled.

"What's wrong Evie" asked Michael

"I still couldn't hear him communicate."

"That's because you don't have your magic yet sweetheart" said Noreen.

"But Elaina heard him and she doesn't have any magic either."

"But Elaina is sensitive to people's thoughts Evell, you haven't develop that skill yet."

"Michael we better get going or the others will be wondering where we are and I know we need to keep all of this a secret."

Elaina walked over to Noreen and said, "thank you so much this is been an amazing experience."

Noreen hugged her "you're most welcome and you must come again soon. Do you hear that Michael soon."

"Yes mother I hear, we'll come back as soon as I possibly can, I promise."

She hugged her son and Evie with tears in her eyes. Michael, Elaina and Evie turned and left. They shortly arrived back in Ghostra and headed back to Michael's room.

"Michael I can't even begin to tell you how happy I am that you shared this day with me. I never would've believed a place as wonderful as that existed and your mother is amazing."

"It was a great day and I'm glad we had it together."

They were holding hands as they walked. Evie looked at Michael then Elaina, "all right guys chin up, don't get mushy on me now." And she started to laugh. They looked at each other and began to laugh along with her. When they reached Michael's room it was already getting dark and dinner was on the table. they sat and ate and talked for the rest of the evening. When Elaina and Evie left Michael stayed up a while longer. He was very excited about tomorrow when you take Elaina to the sanctuary and give her magical abilities beyond even those of a mage.

17

THE NEXT MORNING MICHAEL GOT up extra early even though he knew the spell as it was imprinted in his mind. He didn't really want to leave anything to chance. He went to the sanctuary and open the book and reread the spell three times until he felt felt he was ready. He went to the training center to get Elaina. He saw Evie at the far end training with her instructor but he didn't see Elaina. He asked Evie if she had seen her but she said that she hadn't. Michael thought that she may have overslept since they were up kind of late last night so we went to her room everything was neatly in place her bed was made up but there was no sign of her. Well he thought maybe she had gone to his room when he was late getting to the training center. He ran to his room he was beginning to get a little concerned. This was not like her when he got there he didn't see Elaina but Dade was there.

"Dade I wasn't expecting you, is something wrong."

"No I just came for Thalia she's being released today and I'm here to take her home. Michael is everything all right you look upset?"

"not exactly, I can't find Elaina"

"Well she has to be here somewhere she can't very well have left the temple."

"Did you check the great Hall, she may be at prayers, or maybe medical, she may be visiting Thalia, especially if she knows that Thalia is leaving today."

"Yes you may be right let's go."

When they got to the infirmary Michael looked around but did not see Elaina. Thalia was already dressed and sitting down waiting.

"Hi Thalia have you seen Elaina I've been looking for."

"No Michael I'm sorry but I haven't."

"That's okay, how are you feeling?"

"Much better, I'm ready to get back to work."

"Well don't push yourself too hard."

Michael offered her his hand to help her up, when she took his hand he was hit with a wave of images and thoughts. He let her go and said. "Thalia! It was you, you're the one who betrayed us. Even as he said it he couldn't believe it. He never would've suspected her. They looked at Michael in disbelief. Thalia's face turned red. Dade turned to Thalia.

"Is this true" she didn't answer. "How could you, you help them get through the defenses. Everyone here could have been killed."

Thalia began to cry, "I'm sorry Dade I didn't want anyone to get hurt."

Dade she's the reason we can't find Elaina. She brought her to the enemy last night, I saw it in her thoughts."

No Michael you must be wrong, she wouldn't do that."

"Yes, I did. All along I should have been Michael's aid. Not some girl with no powers. I earned the honor, she can't protect you I can."

"I'll take her Michael, we'll deal with her

"what are you going to do with her?"

"Traders have to be dealt with in your traditional way their put to death."

"That's barbaric."

"That's how it's always been done Michael I don't like it anymore than you do."

"That may have worked a thousand years ago but we should be more civilized now, if not were as bad as Baylor and his evil army."

"Michael she turned Elaina over to them, she may be dead already and Thalia knows a lot about our plans and defenses."

"I know Elaina still okay, I'd know If she were hurt, as far as what she knows that won't be a problem."

Michael raised both arms and began to mutter an incantation in the ancient language suddenly and Ora formed around Thalia. What appeared to be a shadow image of Thalia raised into the air and quickly vanished. Thalia stumbled as though temporarily disoriented. Michael turned and walked toward Dade. Thalia reached for her wand and pointed it at Michael. She said with a tear in her eye, "I'm sorry Michael" and she cast a spell, but nothing happened. She tried again still nothing. Dade who had been reaching for his own wand when he saw her reach for hers looked confused.

Thalia said, "what did you do to me."

"I've taken away your powers you are no longer a wizard."

She fell to her knees "no! That's not possible, you can't do this to me."

Dade asked, "how is that possible Michael her magic was part of her."

"Yes and I remove that part." He turned to Thalia who was still on her knees crying, "you turned on your team. Then you put everyone here in great danger and turned Elaina over to the enemy. We can no longer trust you, you're no longer one of us."

"You should've let them kill me I can't live like this."

"Michael walked over to her and put his hand on her head. He recited another incantation and Thalia collapsed.

"Is she dead" asked Dade.

"No, I've taken away her memories she'll have no knowledge she was ever a wizard. When she wakes take her to the police in the town she came from, tell them she was found wandering and doesn't seem to have any memory of who she is. She may have family who will claim her or at least get her the help she needs."

"All right Michael, I'll take care of it."

"Thanks Dade, in the meantime I'll try and find out where Elaina is and get her back."

Michael went straight to the Guardian sanctuary and called Cassondra.

"Elaina has been taken is there any way you can track her."

"I'm sorry Michael, but wherever they have her it must be shielded with powerful magic."

"That's what I thought, if they hurt her to get to me."

"Focus Michael, they may suspect you care for her but I doubt they realize how much. They must've taken her for a reason we need to find out what that is."

"You're right, I can't let on that my feelings are anything but professional."

He then went to his study and began scanning through his books hoping to find something that would help them find a way to track where Elaina was. Suddenly he heard a voice in his head. It was Baylor.

"Hello Michael, I thought I'd contact you and let you know that I have something that belongs to you."

Michael knew that is much as you wanted to rip his heart out you couldn't show it.

"So you're the one who took Elaina. I'm impressed how did you get into the temple."

He didn't want Baylor to know he discovered Thalia.

"That's not important Michael, just know that I have your little girlfriend."

"Girlfriend, Elaine is simply my aide."

"No Michael, I heard that you have feelings for her."

"Of course I do but no more than for any of the other priestesses, we're a little closer because we work together. But looking out for her is the same responsibility I have toward her and the others."

"Well maybe I was misinformed about your feelings for her, but I'm sure you don't want her killed."

Michael felt the panic rising within him but he couldn't let on so he responded as calmly as possible.

"Let's get to the point Baylor, what do you want."

"A trade, I'll exchange your priestess for Raymond."

"Well that's interesting, why is he so important to you. I know you don't care about him."

"It's not your concern Michael, do we have a deal."

"Well I don't know, if he's that valuable to you maybe I should keep him."

"Do that and you lose your little priestess, what do you say."

"Well any one of the sisters are worth 10 of that Traitor, so all right you can have him. Just bring her here and I'll give you the traitor."

"Michael you know I'm not that stupid. Meet me the same place as last time and come alone only you and Raymond."

"After what happened last time why in the world would I trust you."

"Because you have no choice."

"That's where you're wrong you're the one who has no choice. If you want him I'll meet with someone other than you. Send one of your underlings send them along with Elaina and we'll make the trade no tricks or Raymond dies and I'm gone."

"How do I know I can trust you."

"Because unlike you I keep my word."

"All right Michael, all I want is Raymond our time will come, but this time all I want is to make the trade."

"Okay we'll meet in two hours."

Michael immediately sent word to Dade to bring Raymond to the temple. When they arrived Michael filled Dade in on what was going on.

"Michael, if he has vital information that Baylor wants we can't give him up until we find out what it is."

"I don't care what it is Dade. They have Elaina and they will kill her if we don't give him to them."

"Michael I know you have feelings for Elaina but."

Michael interrupted, "Dade my feelings for her have nothing to do with it. I would do the same for any of the sisters here or any of our wizards or any civilian. I won't sacrifice anyone for fear of what he may learn."

Michael pulled Dade aside and whispered, "besides whatever he knows now won't do Baylor any good when he gets him. I promise to deliver him I didn't promise he would have his powers or his memory."

Dade smiled, okay Michael what you want me to do."

"Prepare the gray order if he doesn't keep his word I may need your help to take Elaina by force."

"All right Michael we will be standing by."

Michael took Raymond into his room to wait for the appointed time. As they sat Raymond continued to smile. A smug kind of smile.

"Well Raymond you seem to be in a good mood considering your predicament."

"You lost again Michael, why don't you just give up you can't win. If the mage counsel didn't bind me I'd show you now what real power is."

"Wow, I'd like to see what real power is so here let me unbind you." With a wave of his hand a few magical words Raymond was released much to his surprise. He responded quickly with an attack spell which Michael deflected sending some of it back at Raymond knocking him onto the floor. Raymond stared in disbelief.

"I wouldn't try that again if I were you. Next time I'll send it all back at you. What's the matter Raymond you're not smiling anymore."

"It seems you've picked up a few tricks Michael, but it won't help you."

Michael raised both of his hands and began to recite the spell of disenchantment Raymond's body began to quiver and glow a deep red in a shadowy figure left his body as if the spirit rising and disappearing. When it was over Raymond said "you can torture me if you like but I'm not giving you the information Baylor wants." "I don't want it, I don't care what information you have. By the way I wasn't going to torture you I was removing your magical powers."

A look of fear came across Raymond's face, and the smile returned.

"You can't do that, no such power exists. I'm a mage I was born a mage, always be a mage."

Is that so why don't you try something simple like levitate that glass."

Raymond looked at Michael a bit confused. Why would Michael ask him to do a simple thing like that. he raise his hand and without warning launched an attack spell at Michael, but nothing happened.

"No, no it can't be," he screamed.

"Why do you all try and attack me when I've taken your powers." He said calmly as if he knew Raymond would attack. Raymond was still ranting in disbelief.

"It's not possible you can't do this, it's not possible." As reality set in. "What will I do without my power."

"Well without magic to extend your life you will live a normal life span. But I don't want to make you suffer too much so I'm also going to remove your memory which will serve two purposes. First you won't realize what you lost or should I say what you've given up, and secondly you won't be able to give Baylor the information he wants so badly."

"Why would you do this to me."

"I'm surprised you would even ask that question. You betrayed everyone and everything the Mage stand for. You've lost sight of who we are and why we exist and joined one who would destroy the world as we know it and enslave everyone."

As he spoke his anger grew then with a wave of his hand he unleashed the spell that would remove all of Raymond's memories. He turned and walked away upset with himself for letting his anger overcome them. Raymond slumped into the chair unconscious a few moments later Dade arrived.

"All is ready Michael if you call we'll be there in an instant."

"Thanks Dade."

"What's wrong Michael" asked Dade.

"I don't know, I felt bad when I took his powers and then lost my temper when I wiped his memories I felt the same way with Thalia but I thought it was because we were close, but he was Raymond after all he's done it still felt wrong somehow."

"You're a good man Michael and you don't like hurting people. But what you did was necessary taking Thalia's powers and memories hurt me to, but it had to be done. Having responsibility means doing things you don't like just As much as things you like."

"I know, but it doesn't make it any easier."

"They never will, if it ever gets easy that's when you need to worry."

"Yeah I guess you're right. Well it's just about time let's wake up sleeping beauty here."

Michael shook Raymond who woke right up. He looked at Michael and said hello where am I and who are you? Raymond looked at Michael with a confused look.

"I don't know who I am or how I got here, wherever here is."

"Well I'm going to take you to a friend of yours. His name is Henry and he can tell you more than I can okay."

"A friend of mine? I don't recognize the name are you sure he can help."

"He should, he knows you better than I do, I only know your name it's Raymond."

Raymond seem to be grasping for any memory or Anything familiar but there was nothing.

"Come on Raymond let's go."

"Raymond, are you sure that's my name."

"Yes I know that for sure."

"Okay let's go I want to meet Henry maybe he can help me."

If you can't remember Raymond then you don't remember the new teleporting technology. See that doorway it's really a gateway that will take us where we need to go."

Michael didn't want Raymond to freak out when they arrived since Henry would know something was wrong as they headed toward the door Michael whispered to Dade. "Standby just in case."

As they passed through the doorway Michael transported them to the meeting place. When they arrive Michael looked around. About 30 yards ahead was Henry and one of his wizards and although he couldn't see him anywhere he felt Baylor's presence not too far away.

"You were supposed to come alone Henry."

"What's the matter Michael, are you afraid."

"Oh yes I'm terrified can't you tell. Send Elaina to me and I'll send Raymond to you."

Henry gave Elaina a shove and she started walking toward Michael her hands were tied behind her. Michael told Raymond to walk slowly to Henry. About midway Michael cast a protective spell and an invisible shield formed around Elaina. He didn't trust them with Baylor close by. Not that he trusted Henry any better. The moment Raymond reached Henry Michael heard Baylor in the distance. He yelled now and Henry fired a lightning bolt at Elaina which deflected off her invisible shield. Michael immediately sent a fireball hurling toward Henry and his wizards sending them's diving to the ground. Michael ran and grabbed Elaina in a flash they were gone. When they arrived back home he untied her.

Elaina threw her arms around Michael and said, "I'm sorry Michael I didn't know. Thalia turned me over to them. She said she needed my help."

"Slow down Elaina we know all about it and Thalia has been taken care of."

"Oh Michael, you didn't kill her."

"No" said Dade as he approached them. "I see you made it back okay."

"Yeah that was little touchy but we made it."

"Michael if you didn't kill her, tell me what you did to her." Asked Elaina

Dade spoke first "he took away her magic and her memory. He did the same thing to Raymond the mage."

Elaina looked at Michael with a shocked look. "You can do that."

Dade said, "He sure can, it surprised me to."

Michael just looked at them for a moment then turned and walked away.

"What's wrong" asked Elaina

"it bothers Michael to do that to a wizard or mage he's got a good heart and I just hope it doesn't get him in trouble."

"What do you mean"

"he hesitates when he has to do anything that he feels may hurt someone physically or emotionally. That could cost him in battle."

Elaina looked at Dade and said, "I trust Michael to do the right thing at the right time without hesitation."

"I hope you're right Elaina we can't afford to lose him. Anyway I'm glad you're okay."

"Thank you Dade."

Dade turned and left and Elaina hurried after Michael. When she got to his room he was sitting at the table is back to the door. She walked toward him and without turning his head he said to her, "I miss my cardboard box, my simple life where my only problem was where could I find work and how can I keep Evie safe."

She walked up behind him and put her arms around his neck to comfort him.

"You bear a heavy burden Michael, but I can't think of anyone better. With the Dragon mage I know we can win this."

"Elaina I need to ask you a question and I need you to answer me honestly."

"What is it Michael is something troubling you."

"Sort of, I need to know how you feel about me."

Elaina was taken back, this was not a question she expected. Michael looked away waiting for her response. She hesitated before answering.

"Well Michael, you're the Dragon mage and I respect and honor you and I'm proud to be your aid."

"Elaina you know that's not what I mean."

"Michael this is not a conversation we should be having."

"This is exactly the conversation we need to have, it's important. Alright let me put it point-blank stop beating around the bush, do you love me."

Elaina knew all along what he meant, but she couldn't say it, shouldn't say it. She was afraid to tell him how much she loved him. Her heart was pounding, her nerves were Peaked she felt her hands shaking.

"I can't love you Michael, it's not right I'm a normal I will age and you won't sooner or later you will have to choose another aid and then another and another and I'll have to watch and." The Stress became too much she began to cry and ran out of the room. Michael paused to think, then he followed after her, he passed Evie in the hall.

"Mike, Elaina just ran by and she was crying did you say something to hurt her again."

"No Evie, I just asked her if she love me."

"Whoa way to go big brother. She was heading toward her room."

"Thanks Evie" he said as he hurried down the hall toward her room. he arrived at her door and knocked.

"Please go away, she said.

Michael didn't believe she really wanted him to leave so he took a chance and entered her room. She was lying on the bed still crying he walked over and sat next to her. "This is important"

"I guess that means you do love me."

She sat up and threw her arms around him. "Yes I love you Michael, but I meant what I said I've been told how it works. I'm young now so I may be able to be your aid for 20 years maybe a little longer. But eventually I'll become more of a hindrance than a help and you'll be forced to choose someone else, and I'll have to watch as someone else take my place at your side.

"You don't want to love me. You say you shouldn't love me, but you still do that's all that matters because I love you too."

"But Michael"

"no but's, no regrets it just is. Elaina I need to go see my mother. I won't be gone long but if anything happens call me and I'll come right away."

Before she could say anything he was off. When he reached the sanctuary he quickly opened the portal and headed home as he raced toward the castle his mother sensed his arrival and was on her way to meet and intercepted him midway.

"What is it Michael, what happened?"

"She loves me mother."

"Is that all, I could've told you that."

"But like you said I want to make her one of us."

"Then she is the one you want to spend your life with."

"Yes she is."

"I'm glad Michael, I like her."

"But the problem is the spell I have is to make a mage. How do I make her like us."

"You need to perform the spell here."

"Here"

"to be more specific up there and she pointed to the top of the nearby mountain. At the top of that mountain is an ancient stone altar. The spell must be performed there and with all your heart. The top of that mountain is a special place. There it seems all the elements and all the forces come together in perfect harmony. When you can bring her here I'll take you to the path that passes around and through the mountain to the top."

"Why can't we just teleport up."

"You can't teleport up there you'll have to walk."

"But that will take forever."

"A day, maybe a bit more and once you get there don't try to rush it, remember how important this is, do it right."

"I don't like leaving the temple for that long, what if something happens."

"Don't worry Michael your sister can watch and send the message of anything happens and I'll take care of it for you, and send you a message."

"But I thought you said we couldn't teleport up there how can you get a message up."

"The reason is not that you can't teleport. On the mountain especially at the top your magic will be amplified many times normal, that's why the mage spell will take her far beyond the mage. But if you try to teleport there is no telling where you could wind up. You'll see what I mean when you get there."

Alright mom, I'll go back and make arrangements. We'll come back as soon as we can."

"Good, and I'm going to rush to tell your grandfather."

When Michael got back to the temple he headed straight to Elaina's room he knocked and when she said come in he entered. She was still sitting on the bed and was no longer crying.

"Elaina I need to take you home."

"Your home world Michael?"

"Yes"

"okay I'd like to see your mother and grandfather again, and just being there. The calm and serenity fill you up, but don't we have things to do here?"

"It's nothing so important you can't wait a couple of days."

"Days, Michael we've never been away that long is something wrong?"

"No everything is fine, we have things to do there that will take a couple of days. So pack for three days just in case I'll tell Dade we'll be gone so he can beef up security, and if anything happens Evie will let us know."

Elaina was confused about why Michael being so secretive and nervous, because since coming to the temple years ago she has never been away from it until Michael came and even then only for a few hours never overnight. But if Michael said they have to go then it must be important and she would follow him anywhere. So she told Michael okay and went to get her things together. Michael left to make arrangements with Dade and Evie. Dade was a little upset that Michael wouldn't tell them where they were going or why but trusted in Michael enough not to question it. When Michael explained to Evie that they would be gone a couple of days that if anything happened she should contact their mother. She had an idea that this was a personal trip and not business. Even though he had Dade and Evie standing by he was little worried, seemed whenever he was gone something would happen. Just my luck he thought to himself. But everything was in place and he felt that this had to be done as soon as possible. When he arrived back in her room Elaina was ready as he requested. She wanted to question him more about why this trip was so important but decided not to. She figured she would find out soon enough. Besides spending a couple of days away with Michael and his family sounded nice. They walked to the library talking about general things. Both of them avoided talking about anything important or about their feelings. Which helped to put Elaina at ease. When they reached sanctuary Michael immediately open the portal. He smiled at her and held out his hand she took it and they entered the portal together when they step through the other side Noreen was already waiting.

"Mom, I didn't expect you to be waiting for us."

"Well from your enthusiasm I knew you wouldn't be gone very long."

She walked up to Elaina and hugged her. "How are you Elaina."

"I'm fine just a little confused. When Michael said to pack a few things that we would be gone a couple of days. I love being here I haven't been away from the temple for so long since I arrived there many years ago."

"Elaina are you telling me you don't know why you're here?"

"To visit I thought."

Noreen looked at Michael, "Michael you didn't tell her why you brought her here."

"Well I just thought, not exactly."

"Oh Michael, did it ever occur to you that she may not want this."

Michael started to turn pale, he was in such a hurry to get this done he didn't even think that she may not want this.

"No I'm sorry, that thought never occurred to me."

Noreen just shook her head. She put an arm over Elaina shoulder and said. "Elaina walk with me, we have to talk and when we;re through you have a decision to make. Michael you wait here."

They walked a short distance to a secluded area full of colorful flowers and with an amazing view out into the countryside. There was a bench there and Noreen asked Elaina to sit so they could talk.

"Noreen what is this all about and if it's not for a visit why am I here."

"Elaina Michael loves you very much and wants to spend his life with you. There are however things that would make the union between you impossible. The biggest problem I'm sure you know is your lifespan. There is magic, powerful magic that could fix that. Michael brought you here to make you one of us."

"You mean he could extend my life so I could be with him forever."

"Yes but the way to do that is to give you the same magical powers we have."

"You mean like a wizard or mage."

"Much more powerful than either a wizard or mage. You would be as powerful as we are you would in fact be one of us. You;ve seen Michael's power, well he's just beginning to come into his own, he doesn't even realize his true potential yet."

"To be honest with you Noreen, magic scares me. I don't know if I'm all that thrilled to have magic powers, but if it means Michael and I could share our lives together I'll do anything, plus if Michael didn't have to worry about me as much, he'll be less likely to get hurt looking after me. I love Michael so much but I never dreamed we could actually be together."

Noreen added, "sometime after this war is over you and Michael can be married and return home to live."

Tears were now welling up in both their eyes. They stood and hugged again. They walked back to where Michael was waiting. He looked into their faces and saw tears in their eyes was this a good sign or bad he wondered.

"Well" he said.

Noreen decided to toy with him a little. "She doesn't want magic Michael, it scares her."

Michael's expression sank, his heart seemed to stop. Then Noreen continued, "but if it means you can be together she'll do whatever it takes. Michael smiled and his eyes began to tear.

"Michael are you crying" asked Noreen.

"Michael quickly responded, "no, it's probably just allergies."

The women just smiled. "Come on I'll walk you guys to the foot of the mountain where the pass begins."

When they got to the base of the mountain Noreen gave them some last-minute instructions.

"Just follow the path, it winds around and in some areas through the mountain. Once you start up don't try to use any aggressive or transportation spells when you reach the top wait until nightfall before performing the spell. That's when the mountain's power will be greatest. About midway up you will see a shelter carved into the mountain you can spend the night there and push onto the top in the morning. I'll see you when you return I love you both – good luck."

18

Michael and Elaina looked at each other and started on your
journey up the mountain. Darkness was closing in on them when
they reached the shelter Noreen had suggested. It wasn't much more than
an area cut into the mountain with a carving on either side one of a Wolf
like creature standing upright the other looked a little like a large cat with
human features.

"That's curious Michael what would you suppose they represent."

"I don't know" he replied "probably just decorations."

Michael took a large sleeping bag out of his bag and placed it on the
ground. "There we go, big enough for both of us. I don't think we need to
get inside it's such a beautiful night we can just lay on top and look out at
the stars."

"Yes I noticed them, they are so much brighter here than I've ever
seen before."

Michael took out some water and food. They ate and talked and joked
and laughed, each avoiding talking about anything serious that might ruin
the evening. Finally they decided to get some sleep. They went and laid
down on the sleeping bag Elaina snuggled up to Michael and put her head
on his shoulder. They stayed looking at the stars for a long time without
saying anything then Elaina said "Michael, tell me about magic."

"Are you still nervous Elaina."

"Magic scares me Michael I'm not sure I'll be able to control it. What if
I hurt someone, what if I hurt you. I've always admired those with magical
powers especially those who use it to help people, which is why I was so
proud to be chosen to be your aide even before we got close. But the thought
of me using magic scares me."

"Elaina first of all you don't control magic you become part of magic and

Frank DeCario

magic becomes part of you. You learn to control yourself and with all your training in meditation I'd say you're at least halfway there already. The rest I'll teach you as Cassondra taught me. Second just the fact you're worried say is you have all the love and compassion to use your magic without fear of hurting anyone."

"Thank you Michael, I guess I can't go wrong as long as I put my faith in you."

Michael kissed her on the forehead. "Let's get some sleep we've got a big day tomorrow." They woke early next morning feeling very refreshed. "Michael I had the weirdest dream last night. I dreamt I was flying and you are flying right next to me."

"That is weird I had the same dream except I had trouble taking off and you helped get me off the ground."

"Michael that's the same way my dream started out but you helped me. What do you think it means?"

"I don't know but this is definitely a strange place. Come on we better get going." When they reached the top they surveyed the area. They saw the stone altar off to one side with a large stone fire pit full of wood. Directly in front of the altar was a shiny stone circle on the ground with magic writing on it.

"Michael if people don't normally come up here where did all the wood come from."

"I'm not sure maybe the mountain knew we were coming."

"You don't really think that do you."

"Elaina at this point I would believe anything. It's been quite a hike up here let's rest a while, it will be dark soon and I want to be fresh for the ritual tonight."

They sat and rested. No one said it but they could feel the power of this place. Night fell and Michael started the pit on fire using two sticks since he didn't want to use a fire spell as his mom had warned. It was a little difficult but he finally got it going he had Elaina stand on the stone circle and he went to the altar. He was very nervous since he had never done this spell before. Elaina could see that he was as nervous as she was. Not knowing what to expect she shut her eyes tight and Michael began. He used all his concentration. He didn't want any mistakes. The Stone Circle Elaina was standing on began to glow and little specks of light began to appear around

146

her as he continued the stone got brighter and brighter and the sparks of light began to appear all around her almost like little fireflies, until they were completely surrounding her she wouldn't open her eyes but called to Michael as she began to hear a crackling sound.

"please Michael hurry, it feels like electricity is dancing all around me."

Michael wondered if this was supposed to happen. He wanted to finish quickly but was afraid to rush the spell or break his concentration. The light from the stone she was standing on rose up and enveloped her the hundreds of specks of light that had surrounded her seemed to enter her body. There was a sudden flash of bright light, so bright Michael had to turn away. When he looked back she was lying on the stone circle. He ran over to her and checked, she was still breathing. He put an ear to her chest, her heart was beating steadily. He wondered if he should do anything, when suddenly he became very dizzy. He thought he saw a figure moving toward him just as he lost consciousness. When he woke Elaina was curled up next to him her head on his shoulder when he looked around he realized that they were at the foot of the mountain Michael shook Elaina and she woke right up.

"How do you feel he asked."

She looked around for a moment and then said, "I feel fine, but how did you get us all the way down the mountain so fast."

"I didn't after the ceremony you were out, and I passed out and just woke up here."

In the distance they saw Noreen approaching. "Are you two all right" she asked.

We seem to be fine, but we don't know how we got down the mountain."

"The mountain holds many secrets Michael, best not to question it."

Elaina asked, "did it work Michael."

Noreen said, "I can feel her power, but there is only one way to find out for sure. I don't want you to use any magic on your own till we show you how to control it, so here's what I want you to do." She walked over to Elaina and whispered in her ear. Elaina looked at her, you could see the doubt in her eyes.

"Take my hand Elaina, I'll help you control it." Elaina took Noreen's hand, she pointed her hand at a large boulder of 10 yards away and mumbled the spell Noreen had told her. A bolt of lightning flew from her hand striking the boulder splitting in half. Michael smiled.

Noreen said, "well that answers that question."

Elaina just looked down at her hand and said, "WOW"

Noreen turned to her son "Michael I think Elaina should stay here a couple days so that I can start teaching her some control over her power. There is no telling what might happen if she went back without some control of her new powers."

"A couple of days, it took me weeks to gain control enough where I felt comfortable."

"Yes but we have ways to help her with her abilities."

"Okay mom. If you think it's best, is that okay with you Elaina?"

"Yes Michael, I would definitely feel better knowing I won't hurt someone accidentally."

"When she gets back Michael you'll have to continue her training and start her reading and learning spells, in the beginning it's probably better to start with defensive spells."

"I will mom, and defensive spells are definitely first thing on the agenda."

"I'll see you in a couple of days Michael."

Michael watched as they turned and headed for the castle. He wished he were going with them but knew he had to get back. When he got back to the temple he went to see Cassondra. Since Evie hadn't contacted them he assumed there were no problems. When Cassandra arrived. She asked where he had been.

"I lost track of you nearly 3 days ago Michael where were you hiding that I could feel your presence."

"Yeah sorry, I was busy working on something very important."

"Well are you keeping secrets from me now Michael."

"Maybe a couple, you have your secrets and I have mine. Believe me if I thought it was something you needed to know I would tell you."

"Okay for now Michael, what can I do for you?"

Obviously she didn't want to push the issue since there were many things she would like to tell him but knew she couldn't.

"I was wondering if any of you have been able to determine where this evil has been hiding, where their base is?"

"No we haven't and that is of great concern, it has to be shielded by some very powerful magic that we have not encountered before. Normally we would have a general idea of where our mage are due to the bond between us. But since Raymond and Henry stop meeting with their guardian and join the evil that bond has become fractured. Henry's guardian can still feel his magic but is unable to locate him. Raymond however can no longer be felt we don't know why."

Michael was tempted to tell her that Raymond no longer had his magic, but wasn't sure if he should let her know he had that power. He thanked her for the information and headed back to his room. When he got there he found Evie standing by the balcony. When she saw him she ran and hugged him.

"Mikey, I was beginning to worry. I didn't know if you would be back today. You were gone almost 3 days."

"Sorry Evie I came back as soon as I could"

Evie looked around for Elaina, "where is Elaina Michael is she alright."

"She's fine Evie, she's going to stay behind so mom can help her learn to control her magic."

"So you were really able to do it, you gave her magic. That's awesome."

"Yeah it's amazing, now I don't have to worry so much when were in a battle."

They sat and Michael filled her in on everything that happened over the past couple of days.

"Well Mike, I can't wait until I get my magic. I've been doing all the mental exercises so that I'll be able to control the magic when I get it. What is my magic never comes to me."

"Don't worry Evie, it will come to you when it's time.

"Yeah I hope you're right, but it will probably be a couple years yet before I get my powers. What will I do in the meantime."

"Well Evie you can keep practicing, you can start reading some of the books and scrolls in the library. But mostly just enjoy yourself have fun. When the magic comes to you, you're going to find that with it comes great responsibility sometimes you'll wish it never came. everyone thinks that because I'm the Dragon mage I have some great wisdom to guide me. When actually most of the time I have no idea what I'm doing. I just make what seems like logical choices and hope I don't mess things up too badly."

"Well Mike, everyone seems to think you've done a good job so far, and the sisters all respect and admire you. They would follow you to the ends of the earth."

"Yeah that's what I'm afraid of, I worry that's exactly where were headed."

"There you go again, stressing over things too much Mike. Stop overthinking it just go with your feelings. They've done fine so far."

"Thanks Evie, when did you get so smart."

"I've always been smart, you just never noticed before."

He smiled and vigorously rubbed her head. The matriss of the order entered the room. She approached Michael and bowed.

"It's good to have you back Michael, but where is Elaina."

Michael looked at her for a moment wondering how much you should tell her.

"Do you remember the woman who helped us when we were attacked."

"You mean the one who saved sister Mary's life, how could I ever forget her."

"Yes, her name is Noreen, and Elaina is with her and she'll be there for a couple of days."

"What is she doing."

"She's training."

She looked confused and had many questions but simply said, "thank you Michael" and left.

The next few days Michael spent most of his time studying the ancient texts and practicing its powerful spells. He was almost half of the way through the first book and found that very few of the spells were combat spells. The few that were seems very powerful and a little frightening. He was learning to control the elements themselves. There were spells he didn't even feel he should practice for fear of doing irreparable damage. He studied and practiced hard since he felt they were getting close to finding Baylor's Lair. It also helped to keep him from dwelling on how Elaina was doing. It's been almost a week and still she hasn't returned. When she finally returned to his room Evie was there waiting.

"Hey Mikey, it's getting late and your food is getting cold. Should I have someone warm it up."

"No thanks Evie, I'm not really that hungry."

"You gotta eat Mike, you have to keep up your strength and I know you haven't eaten since this morning. I guess you haven't heard from mom or Elaina yet."

"No not a word I'm beginning to get a little concerned. I mean I know she's with mom and I shouldn't worry, but I keep thinking what if something happened and they don't want to tell me."

"No way Mikey, if anything happen you be the first to know."

Just then the head of the order entered the room.

"Hello Michael, I'm sorry to bother you but have you heard anything from Elaina, many of us are beginning to get worried."

"No I haven't and I'm beginning to get a little concerned myself. If I don't hear from her by tomorrow I'll go find out exactly what happened and I'll let you know as soon as I return."

"Okay thank you Michael, I'll say good night."

Michael turned to Evie, "you don't think mom will be upset if I just popping while their training do you."

"Heck no, mom would love to see you anytime. She would rather we be there all the time but she knows how important your mission is."

Michael ate a little bit and he and Evie went to sit at the balcony. He missed not having Elaina there with him. He went to bed late and had a hard time getting to sleep. His mind was bouncing from one thought to another. When he finally got to sleep it was not the usual calm restful sleep but restless with dream after dream some actually bordering on nightmares. The next morning Michael woke late and sitting next to his bed was Elaina and Evie.

"Elaina your back. How are you is everything all right."

"Yes Michael I'm fine, I had a great time and learned a lot. Everyone here said you've been very edgy lately."

"Well I wouldn't go that far but I was getting concerned. I expected you days ago."

"I know but Noreen said the reason it took longer because I wasn't born with magic. She said wizards and mage are born with magic in them and even though it's dorment it's there so your whole life your body becomes accustomed to the power until finally it emerges that is just a matter of learning to use it and to control yourself. With me my body wasn't use of the power so it took more time to get used two it then actually learn to control it."

"Then your going to control it well."

"Well I can use it now without hurting anyone, but the control still needs a little work. In the beginning it was a different story."

"Why what do you mean."

"Well at one point I was all over the place. But your grandfather is okay and assured me that his hair will grow back."

Michael said "what". But Evie just began to crack up laughing. Elaina turned bright red. Michael just looked at her for a moment before he too began to laugh.

"Elaina said, "it wasn't funny" and she began laughing too. "Well it wasn't funny at the time."

She looked at Michael and said you might get up sleepyhead we have some training to do. Oh yeah and your mom said if things don't go right with the training and you need help go there for advice or help I think she just likes when we visit."

"Okay just let me get Washed and changed and we'll head to the sanctuary."

"Michael I think we should go to the gym first. We should keep our normal routine so that no one gets suspicious. Noreen said the fewer people that know I have magic the better at least until the time is right."

Michael went to get ready. Evie went to the bathroom door. "Hey Mikey can I come with you and Elaina while you practice. I know I don't have my powers yet but I should prepare for when I do."

"Sure Evie, no problem."

So they went to the combat training area the way they normally did for a quick workout. Everyone was glad to see Elaina and rushed over to greet her. They went through their training so as not to raise suspicions and then heading to the library. They went to the study and Michael handed Elaina one of the books he has set aside and asked her and Evie start studying it,

"you shouldn't have any trouble with this book is not written in the ancient language. By the way did my mom teach you any of the old language."

"No, she showed me what it look like there wasn't time for that."

"Okay we'll have to start on that later."

He went To the sanctuary of the guardians and walked to the altar and called Cassondra. She appeared almost immediately.

"Hello Michael, how are you today."

"I'm fine Cassondra, have you found anything further on possible locations of their base."

"We feel there is more than one base. We think there are three."

"Three, and we can't seem to find any of them."

"Well Michael we believe one is in the northern continent, one is in the southernmost continent in the third is in the frigid zone. We haven't been able to narrow it beyond that so far."

"But that's a big help Cassondra. We can begin to narrow our search areas to these places."

"Michael a lot of people have been hurt recently. There have been fires and major accidents that we think are being caused by evil magic. No open attacks since you stopped the one on the nuclear plant, but it's only a matter of time before they try again."

"Thank you Cassondra, this information may help us find them before they can try again."

"One more thing Michael, we have just sensed a new power, very powerful at and it seems to be coming from here, from someone in the temple. You wouldn't know anything about that would you?"

Michael realize he had not thought to shield Elaina from detection. Now came the dilemma. Should he tell Cassondra the truth and ask her to help with the training, or keep the secret. The trusted Cassondra but she was still a guardian and if he told her about Elaina he would have to explain everything. Including the secret kept from them about the first Dragon mage. He felt there must've been a reason that Creighton didn't tell them so he decided to play dumb even if she didn't believe him.

"I have no idea, are you sure you're not reading some of the wizards that have been coming and going."

"No Michael, this is much more powerful than a wizard."

"I don't know then, but I;ll have a sister search the temple in case someone got in and is hiding."

"All right Michael, of course you will keep me informed on what you find."

Michael could sense the disbelief in her voice. "Of course" he said.

After she left he went back to Elaina.

"Elaina I need to put a concealment spell on you because the guardians have sensed your magic."

"Oh really, what happened."

"Nothing, I denied knowing anything about it, but I don't think she totally believe me."

"Can we actually shield it from them?"

"Yes, it's a powerful spell the same one my parents used on me. But it means for now anyway you can't use your magic anywhere in the temple except my sanctuary. They can't penetrate there and they can't enter either."

"But what if were attacked again?"

"Well that's a different story if that happens we'll do what we have to, besides I'm not going to keep it from them forever only until you got enough training I don't want them getting involved or knowing until then."

"Okay Michael. I've got some questions about what I've been reading."

Things went on like this for the next couple weeks with Michael concentrating mostly on defensive spells and teaching her the ancient language. While she was training Michael continued his studies of the great books. His training was going slowly the more powerful the spells became the less he was able to digest in one sitting. he thought no wonder his mother said he could take years to master it all. Some days Evie would go with them and study the books. She would try using the spells she was learning but couldn't since her powers had not come to her yet. Michael could tell that she would sometimes become a little frustrated. But she didn't give up she kept on trying. They work during the day but make sure they relaxed in the evening they would sit on the balcony and talk about anything but Magic and just take in the beauty.

19

ONE MORNING IN EARLY SUMMER Dade arrived. He and Michael sat while Elaine and Evie went to start their morning workout. Michael could tell that Dade had something important to talk about.

"What is it Dade?"

"We've found an enemy base, it doesn't appear to be the main base. Two small doesn't fit the description we've gotten the prisoners we've interrogated. But there are at least a couple hundred creatures there with our order and maybe the blue order we could probably wipe them out easily."

Michael thought for a moment.

"Maybe, but this could be our opportunity to find the rest and maybe even Baylor himself. Station a few wizards close by. Have them shield their powers and observe. They have strong shielding around their base, so any teleportation will have to be done from outside. If we follow any time any of them leave they may lead us to the main base. If a large group leaves follow and send word, they may be on an evil mission and we can intercept them."

"Okay Michael, that sounds like a plan." "Oh and Dade I need you to come back later, I want to take a look at the base."

"Okay Michael, I was going to go see it later myself."

After Dade left Michael went to joined the others in the training room. But when they were done with their morning training, Michael didn't go with them to the library. Instead he went back to his room to get cleaned up and wait for Dade. After about an hour Dade returned.

"Okay Michael everything is set are you ready to go."

"Yes I'm ready, let's go"

"Dade waved his wand and he teleported to the site overlooking the enemy base. Three members of the gray order where there. Dade introduce them.

"Michael this is Walt, Miguel and Ron. They will be watching the area during the day. Three others will switch off and watch at night for any movement that we can track."

"That's good where is the base."

"Over here Michael." He went to the edge of the hill.

"You see that cave opening down there, that's apparently the only way in or out. This is about as close as we dare get. We don't want to alert them to our presence."

"Good, you have a Birdseye view from up here."

"We have the area cloaked so that they can't detect this magically."

"Are you sure they're in there."

"We saw two of them come out earlier, but nothing since. We're pretty sure there are quite a few in there."

"You guys wait here," said Michael, "I'm going to get a closer look"

"Michael that may not be wise."

"That's okay Dade, I'll be fine."

Michael started walking toward the cave. About 20 yards away from the others he cast the spell and disappeared. Walt turned to Dade. "Where did you go, he just disappeared."

"Invisibility, it does exist."

Ron said, "invisibility, I thought that was just a myth. I mean I know we can cloak ourselves from magic detection but true invisibility."

Dade said, "I heard rumors that the first Dragon mage had the power of invisibility but wasn't sure it was real. I don't think any of the other Dragon mage had that ability but Michael must've found the spell."

Michael carefully walked down to the cave. He wasn't sure they wouldn't be able to see or feel his presence. He moved slowly and carefully so as not to make any noise. He entered and started walking through a tunnel. It looked like an old mineshaft about 100 yards in the shaft opened up into a large cave. There appeared to be about 200 creatures. Some Michael recognized others he hadn't seen before. Many of them appeared to be arguing with each other. This is good Michael thought, they're not used to working together. He looked all around still hoping none of them could see or sense him. Off to the side he can see one of the devils wearing a cloak and sitting watching the commotion. Toward the back on the right hand side he saw a demon going into the side tunnel carrying a wand that was very odd because this type of demon's doesn't have any magic and wouldn't need a wand. He headed toward the back of the room being very careful to avoid getting bumped into since they didn't know he was there. He entered the short passage and at the end was a room. When he got there he saw Scotty and the other missing wizards who are magically bound. They looked as if they had been beaten but none look seriously injured. The demon was toying with them hitting them with a wand and laughing. He kept saying in a horrible little voice "you will talk you will tell us."

Michael knew if he took them with him the other creatures would know he was here or at least that the wizards had escaped. Either way they would abandon the site. He thought for a moment but knew he couldn't leave his friends behind. He waited for the demon to leave and made himself visible. "Michael," they said almost at the same time.

Michael said, "come on I'm going to get you out of here. he removed their bonds and waved his hand and made them all invisible.

"Follow me and be careful not to bump into any of them. Remember they can't see you so if you're not careful they can walk right into you."

Quietly they walked out and passed all the creatures in the main cave and up to where Dade and the others were waiting. Michael made everyone visible they were shocked to see their friends alive. They ran over and hugged and shook their hands. They began talking while Michael and Dade stepped aside.

"This is wonderful Michael, where did you find them."

"They were in a side room inside the cave. Apparently they were being held all this time and beaten for information."

"But these wizards don't know anything that they don't already know."

"I know Dade, but maybe they don't know that, or maybe they beat them just because they like beating them."

"You know Michael, when they realize they're gone they'll know the site is been compromised and abandon it."

"Yes I know, which is why we'll leave two wizards behind. I'll make them invisible and they can follow this bunch wherever they go and then report back. In the meantime you can take the team to the infirmary at the temple."

"What about you are you coming."

"Something is not right."

He asked Scotty, "Scotty how did they capture you. I think a couple of you should have been able to get away."

We couldn't Michael, we were suddenly unable to move. One of them must have used some kind of spell or enchantment that stopped us dead in our tracks."

"Did you see Baylor was it his spell."

"No we saw nothing that looked human, only those hell spawns."

Michael turned to Dade, "something's not right. None of these creatures has the power to paralyze a group of wizards I doubt they would even know how, and then they prevented wizards from using their powers to escape. None of the creatures I saw could have that kind of power. You go ahead Dade I'm going to stay here a while with Walt and Ron."

"Okay Michael, I hope you know what you're doing."

Dade gathered the group. He raised his wand and then in a flash they were gone. Michael turned to Walt and Ron and cast in invisibility spell "we need to get closer weight behind those bushes by the entrance to the cave." They went and they waited. About an hour later a being appeared, floating in midair at the mouth of the cave. He called in "come out were moving to another base. Hurry before the wizards arrive."

Then he opened the portal and the creatures began exiting the cave and entering the portal. Michael said to Walt and Ron, "go through the portal and see where their going then let Dade know."

"Michael is that what I think it is."

"Yes, that's a guardian and he's helping them."

"What are you going to do?"

"I'm going to find out why he's helping them, go quickly before he closes the portal."

"Be careful Michael, you can confront him their to powerful."

Then they quickly entered the rift. When the last of the creatures transported away and the portal was closed Michael became visible.

"Why would a Guardian be helping Baylor and help him release this terrible evil on the world."

The Guardian turned and saw him, "Michael, the great one everyone is talking about. Why you ask, maybe you haven't noticed the world is tearing itself apart and no one can do anything about it. Were not allowed to interfere all we can do is watch and guide them through their thoughts. But none of them listen to us anymore. Their greed and selfishness seems to rule their actions, so I've decided to take action."

"By helping Baylor and his hell spawn."

"Better they should live under evil sadistic ruler then continue on and wipe themselves out completely."

If you just give us a chance were going to get more involved in helping them see the light. The mage can help prevent the destruction and help put them on the right path."

"That's what many of my kind are hoping. That you will lead the mage to prevent the inevitable destruction and help to put them on the right path." Well we don't believe it and your time is come to an end."

With that he began to attack Michael with powerful spells. But Michael was ready for the assault you blocked the incoming spells and countered with spells of his own. The battle raged on for what seemed like forever. Several of Michael spells made it past guardians defense but had little effect.

"Even with your power, your spells can't hurt me Michael."

That's when Michael realized that the Guardian was floating and not actually in this dimension which is why his attacks had no effect. then Michael remembered the spell he had learned called dimensional lock. He let loose with the spell which created a pocket around the Guardian locking him between dimensions in effect paralyzing him. He was floating unable to move a look of shock on his face. Michael laughed when he learned this spell he couldn't see what good it could be. Michael called to Cassondra, "Cassondra if you can hear me I need you here."

A moment passed and Cassondra arrived. But before she could ask him what he needed she saw the figure floating a short distance away. "Meingan" she said, "what happened here Michael."

"Well apparently your friend here has been helping Baylor and his evil horde with their plans of conquest as well as helping them evade our detection."

"What did you do to him, or should I say how did you do this to him and what exactly did you do to him."

"I'll explain later, right now Cassondra I'd like to know what you're going to do with him."

"He will be brought back and judged by our leaders."

Cassondra muttered some words and three guardians appeared, one Michael remembered as their leader. They look at Michael and then at Meingan. They approached Cassondra "you called us what is happened here."

She explained to them what had happened. They approached Meingan and looked at Michael curiously.

"Your even more powerful than we first thought Michael. A normal mage could not have done this."

"Then you should be glad I'm not a normal mage."

"You can release him now Michael, we'll take him from here and do What must be done."

Michael released Meingan and they immediately overpowered him with their magic. Michael looked to Cassondra and then teleported back to the temple. When he arrived Evie and Elaina were waiting

"Michael are you all right, we were very worried when the others arrived without you. They said you stayed behind because you felt something was wrong. You should've waited for me Michael as powerful as you are you still need someone to watch your back."

"I'm sorry Elaina, but I thought we were just going to observe the base. Things just snowballed from there. Next time I go anywhere you'll be with me."

"Okay, were you right was anything wrong."

"Yes, but let's go sit in my room it's a long story."

We got back to his room he explained what happened. Evie and Elaina listened very carefully neither could believe what they were hearing.

"Michael why would a Guardian do something like that. We always heard how good they were, how they were here to help us. How can you possibly believe that being enslaved by evil was best for the people."

"I don't know Elaina, but in some warped twisted way he reasoned in his mind that it was for the best. But the worst part is that from the way he was talking he may not be alone. There may be other guardians who agree with him."

"What are you going to do Michael."

"First I need to speak to Cassondra, and I want you to come with me."

"Me too Mikey" asked Evie

"no Evie not this time. I want to keep some things secret and you're one of them."

He saw her disappointment so he added, "you are my ace in the hole Evie, in case I need you as backup."

"Okay Mike I think I like that."

Michael raised his hand and cast the spell that removed the shielding from Elaina.

"There I removed the spell that shielding your power from detection."

"But Michael. The guardians will be able to sense my magic now."

"Yes exactly, let's go."

Elaina just shook her head and followed Michael as he headed toward the library. They reached the door to the sanctuary and Michael turned to Elaina. "Wait here until I call you."

"All right Michael, but are you sure you want to do this."

"This is the surest I've been about anything in a long time, I trust Cassondra but I need to know if the trust is misplaced before I tell her everything."

Michael entered the sanctuary and walked directly to the altar and called Cassondra. She appeared quickly floating before the altar.

"Michael you may have been infiltrated, we sense a powerful magic within the temple."

"No Cassondra we have not been infiltrated. The present you sense isn't the enemy."

"What you mean Michael I know none of the other mage are here."

"I'll explain but first I need you to come completely through the rift into this realm."

Cassondra was confused but did as Michael asked she stepped out onto the floor Michael immediately cast the spell.

"I've just sealed the room so none of the other guardians can see or hear us."

"Michael what makes you think anyone would be listening or watching us."

"I think they have been from the beginning. Listening in on our training in our conversations and everything that's going on between us in here."

"That's crazy Michael why would any of my people do that."

"Cassondra, when I was speaking to Meingan I got the impression that he is not working alone. That other guardians are behind him maybe even some of your leaders."

That's insane Michael, none of our leaders would support such foolishness. Meingan is being dealt with."

"I hope you're right but if you are wrong you will have a choice to make. Whether you will come here with us or stay in your realm forever."

"What you mean Michael." Her look suddenly turned very serious.

"Cassondra if it turns out I'm right and there is a much bigger conspiracy, I'm prepared to seal off your realm completely. Preventing any of the guardians from ever crossing over again."

"That's impossible Michael, no such spell exists and even if it did no mage has that kind of power."

"Trust me Cassondra, the spell does exist and I'm quite capable of using it."

"You can't do that Michael, it's our whole reason for existing. We've been guides and guardians so long we don't know anything else."

"Do you call what Meingan was doing guiding or guarding the people?"

She put her head down, "no Michael, but let us deal with it. Don't assume all of my kind are as foolish as he."

"I'm not doing anything that drastic without proof. I may be wrong, I hope I'm wrong. But if it turns out I'm right I can't allow them to destroy this world. Now Cassondra I want to show you the power you been sensing."

Michael closed his eyes and projected his message to Elaina's mind. "Elaina come in."

A moment later Elaina entered through the barrier. Cassondra looked at her, stunned she turned to Michael.

"It's Elaina, Michael how is this possible she had no magic."

"Well she does now, I gave it to her."

Cassondra said nothing for some time. She turned back to Michael and Elaina.

"Michael you're even more powerful than we imagined."

"Cassondra I'm telling you all of this because I trust you. I don't want any of this to go beyond this room."

"But Michael this information would give the others the confidence they need to trust that you can do what you say. That you and the mage can prevent any more destruction of your world."

"No Cassondra, please I need you to promise me that you won't say anything."

"Okay Michael, I promise I won't say anything as long as you don't want me to. I'm happy for you Elaina."

She walked over and hugged her.

"Thank you Cassondra, we appreciate everything you've done for all of us."

"If you unblock the room I'll returned to my world. I have a lot to think about. By the way Michael I can sense another magic within the temple. Not nearly as strong but it's there."

"The room stays blocked but you can pass back and forth but only you. I don't want any of the others to have access to the temple."

Cassondra shook her head in agreement and passed on to her world.

"Well Elaina what do you think." I think it's wonderful that you feel you can trust her. I trust her to but are you sure you should've told her everything."

"I didn't tell her everything just enough I need to know where her loyalties are. I trust her but I'm not sure she won't tell the others what I told her. I need to know, besides I didn't tell her about our world or any of our plans."

Elaina looked at Michael and smiled.

"Why are you smiling Elaina."

"You said our world Michael."

"Well it is our world. Your part of our world now and always will be."

She hugged Michael and just said "thank you Michael. But Michael Cassondra said that she sensed other magic in the temple. Can someone be hiding here."

"Come on Elaina I have an idea about that."

On the way out of the library Michael picked up a book as they headed for his room. When they arrived and Evie was sitting at the table waiting for them.

"Hi guys" she said.

"Hello Evie" they both said.

Michael walked over to the table and said, "Evie hold this book for me will you."

"Sure Mike," she took the book and almost immediately a flame appeared in Evie's hand just as it had for Michael when he first picked it up in the library so long ago. Evie was caught off guard and quickly dropped the book.

"What was that Mikey, what did you do?"

Michael smiled, "I didn't do anything Evie that was all you. It seems your powers are just beginning to develop."

"Really Mike, I did that."

"You sure did, you're not quite there yet but it's beginning to show."

"That's why Cassondra said she felt another magical presence, it was Evie." Said Elaina

"yes I thought she was sensing Evie when she said it, but I didn't want to let on. I don't want any of them to know Evie is my sister, or that she's developing power. Not until I'm completely sure we can trust Cassondra not to say anything to the others. Evie I'm going to shield your magic from detection."

"But Mike that won't keep my powers from developing will it."

"No Evie it will only keep the guardians from sensing them."

"Mikey I'm so excited. Can I go and tell mom and grandfather."

Of course Evie, tomorrow we'll go to my sanctuary and Elaina can open a portal to our world."

"Michael I have never done that I don't know if I can."

"Sure you can I'll show you how and you can do it. Come on it's been a strange day let's go relax on the balcony."

They went and talked a while. Evie grew tired and left for her room. Michael and Elaina stayed a little longer. Michael was mesmerized by the beautiful night but when he looked over Elaina had fallen asleep. He couldn't bear to wake her so she gently picked her up and carried her to the bed and just as gently put her down. He looked down at her sleeping and smiled. Then he went back to the loungers. He drank in the splendor and the beauty of the night a little longer before drifting off to sleep. The next thing he realized it was morning and Elaina was sitting next to him.

20

"**G**OOD MORNING, YOU SLEPT ON the lounger all night how do you feel?"

"I feel fine, you looked so content last night I didn't want to wake you."

"Well thank you Michael, Evie has been here twice already. She's excited to get going."

"Yes I would imagine she is. I'll get cleaned up and changed and we can get going." Michael got his cloths and went to the bathroom. The pool and waterfall look very tempting, but he knew Evie was in a hurry. So we just washed and changed. On the way to the library they were stopped by the matriss of the order.

Michael said "I'm sending Elaina in Evie on a mission but it's nothing dangerous they'll just be gone short while."

"Certainly Michael, when they're away I'd like to have a word if you're not too busy."

"Not at all I'll come see you shortly."

"She nodded and walked off. The three continued to the sanctuary once there Michael brought Elaina to the altar you whisper the spell to Elaina and told her when she uses a spell think of where she wants to go don't think the spell, feel the spell.

"Remember Elaina think only where you want to go but feel the spell."

"Elaina did it and the portal opened. "I did it" said Elaina.

"Okay you two go ahead through and I'll go see the matriss as promised."

When he arrived she greeted him gracefully. "Hello Michael how are you feeling."

"Fine, what can I do for you matriss, you said there was something she wanted to discuss."

"Yes Michael there is. Michael something is going on that you're not telling any of us, and if Elaina is aware of any of it she's not sharing either. We are here to help and serve you, but I feel we're being left in the dark and don't know what to expect next. It's of great concern to me. There is very little we can do if we don't know what's happening."

"You're right, I'm sorry I haven't been more open with you, but things have been happening fast and I just didn't think to update her closest friends. There will always be some things I can't tell anyone I hope you realize that. But most things I should be sharing with you and the rest of the sisters of the Dragon order."

Sisters of the Dragon order. We've never been called that before. I like it. Yes Michael I understand there may be some things you need to keep to yourself. Just so we know what's happening so that were not caught by surprise."

"When Evie and Elaina return will gather everyone together and bring you up to date on what's happening."

"Thank you Michael, we were beginning to think you didn't trust us after what happened with Thalia."

"Not at all, those here and a select few others are the only ones I can trust completely."

She smiled and he saw tears well up in her eyes. He had no idea they felt so deeply about him not trusting them. He walked over and hugged her.

"You are all my close trusted friends."

He turned and walked off before he too began to tear up. A little while later Elaina returned.

"Hi Elaina where is Evie."

"She decided to stay a little longer. She wants Noreen to start training her. She explained to Evie that her power needed to mature before she could actually do anything. But you know Evie she was excited to get started."

"Good For Evie she's really looking forward to it."

"I know how she feels Michael. When I realized I really had magic and I cast that first spell I can't describe the feeling it was just amazing and a little frightening."

"Well while you were gone the matriss expressed concern that we haven't been keeping them up on where we are and what's happening. I told her we would let them in on everything that happened."

"Everything Michael."

"Well certainly not about our world or your magic. But everything else that's happened they have a right to know."

"Are you sure you don't want to tell them about my magic. They'll find out sooner or later."

"I don't want anyone to know until the time is right. If we can catch the enemy by surprise all the better. I trust the sisters completely but they may talk about it to each other and be overheard. Wizards of the gray order are here sometimes and although I think I can trust them I haven't tested any of them except Dade. I saw his heart it was good and loyal. But I keep thinking about Thalia. I would've put my life in her hands and yet she turned traitor. There is an old saying, loose lips sink ships."

"I didn't know you were in the Navy Michael."

"Oh I wasn't I saw that in a movie once."

Elaina started to laugh and then Michael joined her.

"Anyway I'll call Dade we can update everyone as to where we stand in searching for the enemy base, and I'll fill them in on everything else. You tell the matriss we will meet in the great Hall in two hours."

Dade arrived shortly before the meeting at the designated time. Everyone gathered in the great Hall. Michael got up and apologized for not keeping them informed about their situation. He then called Dade up to tell them where they currently were.

"Sisters of the temple." Michael interrupted, "sorry Dade but their now called the sisters of the Dragon order."

"Sorry, I didn't know,"

he went on to explain how Michael had made two of his wizards invisible and they followed the evil horde to a new location and found another base. He said they don't believe it's the main base. Baylor wasn't there and like the first base it wasn't very big. They posted wizards there to observe. He also let them know that they still have search groups out using Michael's maps to try and locate the main base. When Dade was done, Michael got up and fill them in on everything else being careful not to mention Elaina's new abilities or anything of his home world. He explained how Elaina was hurt during a battle and how his guardian took over her body to help her heal. He told of the mage counsel and those who had turned against them. He told of his capture of the Guardian who was helping Baylor and his suspicion that it goes much further than one guardian. When he had finished the matriss stood and spoke.

"Thank you Michael for sharing these things with us. We had no idea everything had become so unstable. As always we are prepared to follow you and fight with you against any evil."

Michael simply said, "thank you"

he and Elaina returned to his room they sat at the table. Elaina noticed that Michael looks stressed.

"What's wrong Michael"

"the way she said that."

"Said what"

"that they would follow and fight with us." Elaina looked confused.

"Don't you see Elaina, it sounds like she means to leave the temple with us and fight hordes of demons and devils and all the other creatures that we'll be facing."

"Yes of course Michael, that's exactly what she meant."

"But they'll be killed. This is what I was afraid of with you, they can't fight magic."

"Wow Michael, all this time and you still haven't learned that we are your armies your personal guard. Whatever you want to call it this is what we're here for. To help you fight evil. You need to get used to it because it's the way it is. Oh and Michael don't underestimate their value magical beings need to think of the spell before they can use it and we can read their minds and know when and what is coming. So our skills and agility can see we're somewhere else when it gets there."

"I hope you're right Elaina, I hate to be responsible for any of them being killed."

"Michael it's possible some may be killed. But you're not responsible. We know the risks, but it's who we are and it's why we're here."

"We need to go" said Michael "I need to speak to my mother."

Elaina didn't know why he was in such a hurry to see his mother, but she followed without question."

They went to the sanctuary, opened the portal and crossed over. When they got there they hurried to the palace. Upon entering Evie ran up to them.

"Hi Mike, you come to visit. Mom's been showing me some tricks to help me develop my magic."

"That's great Evie, you can show Elaina what you've learned. I need to talk to mom for a couple minutes."

Noreen and Michael walked out to the garden.

What is it Michael, you look troubled."

"The sisters of the temple are determined to fight alongside of me and Elaina and I'm concerned they'll be hurt."

"Michael stories tell us that when Creighton rescued them and brought them to the temple they swore their loyalties to the Dragon mage and all of his successors. During the wizard wars they fought at Creighton's side and fought well even though the wizards had their magic. I think you underestimate their abilities. But if you concerned in the ancient texts that you're studying is a spell for you to create runes that will give them a measure of protection against magic. They won't protect against everything but the runes cluster skills will make them a formidable warrior in battle."

"Thanks mom I knew you'd come up with something to ease my mind. Maybe I am underestimating them, but this will make me feel a lot better."

"We can collect the crystals to make the runes in the cave at the base of the magic mountain. I don't know if there are crystals in the human realm that will work, so you better get them here and take them back with you."

"Mom there is one other thing that's been bothering me. Eventually I need to upgrade and create new mage, but I can't bring them all here in order to give them power."

"You're very powerful Michael, and getting more so every day but you still may not have the power to draw the energy from around you and channel it into others. Soon you won't need help to do it, but for now, well come with me."

"They went to Noreen's room. She opened the drawer and handed him an amulet.

"The energy in this amulet should help you do what you need to do."

Michael could feel the energy emulating from the amulet. He put the chain around his neck and tuck the amulet inside his shirt.

"I can feel the energy mom."

"Yes Michael it 1qis very powerful."

"One more thing is been bothering me mom. All of the Mage are men there are no women on the Council. I've seen some of the female wizards there magic seems as powerful as the men, but no female mage, why is that."

"I don't know Michael, maybe because the original mage counsel consisted of all men and their power only passed to other men. Remember when the Council was formed women with magic were suppressed not allowed to develop their power and if they tried they were probably killed. You're talking 2000 years ago Michael. Those were barbaric times in their realm and women had no rights and Creighton had to go with the times or would've been much more difficult to bring peace."

"Well I think the first Magi replace will be a female mage."

"Well good for you Michael, but you may meet with some resistance."

"Like you said I'm the Dragon mage and head of the Council, and there will be no denying her power. I'll bring her into the Council before I bring the others up to full power. That way she will be more powerful than any of them that should help them accept her."

"Good idea do you have anyone in mind."

"No not yet, but I'll find someone."

"I'm very proud of you Michael."

"Thanks mom"

"here are the crystals you need to create the protective runes. We keep them around the castle as decorations and because of their power. You'll find the necessary spell in the first of the ancient books since you know the spell you're looking for just hold the book concentrate on the spell you need and the book will open to the proper page."

"Wow, I didn't know the book could do that."

"Well you need to know spell you're looking for in order for it to work." They walked back to where Elaina Evie and grandfather were waiting. Grandfather asked to speak to Michael alone. They went into the other room.

"What is it grandfather, what's wrong."

"Nothing's wrong Michael, but I need to tell you a story. Now I know your mother told you about a long time ago when the Deices try to conquer our land and were defeated. But she didn't know the details of the war. When they attacked they had a horde of creatures with them. Horrible creatures they stood upright and were pale in color. They had curled horns on their head and sharp fangs and stood about 7 feet tall. They also had a strange power some sort of mind control. Many because of their magic we think were immune to their power others were not. Those who were not just stood there as if in some sort of trance and were torn apart. These creatures were destroyed. The reason I tell you this is that we've never seen those creatures before or since. We don't know where they came from but we know they weren't from our world. I don't know if Baylor knows of this or if he can get more of them. But you need to know and be prepared just in case."

"Thank you grandfather that's good to know if he does have these creatures we need to be ready."

They walked back to the others.

"Well Elaine are you ready to go."

"Yes Michael I'm ready."

"How about you Evie, are you coming with us or do you want to stay a while longer."

"No Mikey I'm ready."

"They gave their hugs and said their goodbyes and off they went.

21

W HEN THEY ARRIVED BACK AT the temple Michael told Elaine and Evie to go and find out who among the sisters was the best fighter. The best in combat. They didn't understand why he wanted this information but they didn't question his request. Meanwhile Michael took out the ancient books. He took book 1 and concentrated on the spell he needed to create the protective runes, and the book instantly turned to the spell. He read the spell and absorbed its power. He then laid out the crystals one for each sister in the order and carefully cast the spell. The crystal glowed and ancient symbols were suddenly etched into the surface and golden chains formed out of them so that they could be worn around the neck. Michael took the runes and went back to his room to wait for the others. When Elaine and Evie arrived he asked them what they had found out.

"Well Michael everyone seems to agree that aside from our instructors, the best fighter is Durell."

"Durell? You mean our Durell who brings us our food and keeps our rooms clean."

"yes Michael, Why?"

"Because she will be the next mage to replace either Raymond or Henry."

"What! Michael there has never been a female mage. The others won't accept her."

"She will have the power of a mage and they'll have no choice. This is not the Middle Ages, they need to get over themselves, but first I need to ask the matriss and Durell. Because if she accepts. She would be leaving here after she's trained to take over their area of the world and I know how much you all care for each other and for the temple. So the final choice will be hers."

Just then Dave arrived with news.

"Michael we just got word the enemy we were following just arrived at what appears to be another base."

"About time, I was expecting the report days ago, what took so long."

"They moved several times. I guess they wanted to see if they were followed before going to their base. But they didn't know our wizards were invisible. Oh by the way there still invisible, they don't know how to break the spell."

"Oh right, we'll have to fix that. But first come with me this concerns the wizards as well as the mage."

Along the way Michael filled Dade in on what he wanted to do.

"That's a bold move Michael, but none of the sisters have any power."

"I can take care of that. What I want to know is what you think and how the other mage will react."

"You mean you can give someone power as well as take it away. I've never heard of a mage with your power. There is something more to you than just a mage."

"I don't actually give power Dade, the power comes from all around us. But I can harness those forces into a person or remove them with magic. Come with me Dade I'm going to talk to Durell."

They talked as they walked.

"Dade what is your assessment of those in the mage counsel, you know them better than I do."

But before Dade could answer sister Reina came walking toward them dragging what appeared to be a little gnome like creature who was kicking and screaming.

"Michael, I found this little guy inside one of the storage rooms."

The little gnome looked at Michael and Dade and dropped to his knees.

"Please don't kill me sir, I mean you no harm."

"Who and what are you and how did you get in here."

"I am a vizzen sir."

Michael looked at Dade who just shrugged. "I've never heard of them"

"is that your name or what you are."

"It's what my people are called sir."

"Well what your name."

"I am eight sir."

"That's a number, what is your name."

"I don't know sir I'm just eight, my master just calls us by our number."

"What do you mean, who is your master."

"The devil Maison was my master since I was born."

"So you're a spy."

"No sir, were not smart enough for something like that we are just slaves we do what we're told and we are beaten a lot. Those who really do bad are killed."

"How did you get here."

"During the last attack our master brought some of us with him I think to use as shields. The others were killed but I ran and hid."

"That attack was weeks ago. You telling me you been hiding here since then."

"Yes sir, I couldn't get out and didn't know where to go even if I could get out."

"Well eight, touch my hand."

Frightened and shaking the little vizzen reached out and touched Michael's hand. Michael quickly sensed fear and confusion, but also a childlike amazement and a good heart.

"All right little guy you can stay here and help with the chores, unless you would rather leave."

"Oh no sir I'd like to stay."

"Sister Reina will show you to your room and introduce you to the matriss and the other sisters."

"Yes sir, thank you master."

"There are no masters here. We all work together. Oh and sister Reina ask the matriss if she could find a name for him. We Can't keep calling him eight."

Reina laughed, "of course Michael I'll take care of it. Come on eight."

Dade asked, "are you sure that's a good idea Michael he could be a spy."

"No he's not, he's just a scared little creature. Besides what else would we do with him, he has a good heart so I'm not going to harm him and if we sent him away and they find him they can force information from him remember he's been here for weeks."

"Well I suppose you're right, but what can he do here."

"I don't know, I'm sure the matriss will find some chores he can handle. Come on let's find Durell see if she'll accept the challenge."

"Michael I think I'll go back in your room. I think this is something you need to discuss with her in private. She may not speak freely with me there."

"All right, I'll meet you back with the others."

Michael proceeded to Durell's room and knocked on the door. When she opened it she seemed surprised to see him standing there.

"Hello Michael," she said.

"Hello Durell may I come in, I'd like to speak to you."

"Of course Michael, please come in."

"Durell I have something to ask of you."

She quickly responded "anything Michael, whatever you need."

"Don't be so quick to accept. It's something that will take you away from the temple permanently. Of course you will visit, you will always be welcome here."

"Then you're looking to send me away Michael, did I do something wrong."

"No, nothing like that, I would like for you to become a mage to replace Raymond. But you would have to take over responsibility for his area and his wizarding order. You don't have to accept. We don't really want to lose you but I have to replace him on the Council and would like to replace him with a woman, and I would like it to be you."

Durell just sat there staring at him in disbelief.

Finally she spoke, "Michael I don't have any magical power unless you consider the ability to read others thoughts magic. But I'm certainly not a mage."

"I can take care of that Durell, what I need to know is whether or not you're willing."

Her head was spinning. She was caught totally by surprise.

"Michael what do you think I should do?"

"I'm sorry Durell, but this is not a decision I can help with. But I know the thought is a bit overwhelming. You don't have to decide right now. I wouldn't expect you to make a decision like this right away. Think it over, talk to your friends, talk to the matriss. Take your time."

"Michael can you really fix it so that someone with no magic can have the powers of a mage?"

"Yes" Michael took her hand, "think carefully"

with that Michael turned and left her to think it over.

When he entered the room Elaina, Evie and Dade were waiting. Elaina approached him "well Michael is she going to do it."

"I told her to think it over it's a big decision to make, and I don't want her to make it in haste."

"Then Evie asked, "Mike is a true they found a little creature hiding here."

"Yes Evie, he said he's a vizzen. There slaves to some of the demons. Nothing to worry about he's harmless."

"Are you sure" asked Elaina.

"Yes I'm sure, but you have the opportunity to read his mind. He will be staying here for now." "Speaking of reading thoughts. Can I speak to you privately."

"Sure Elaina", Michael turned to Dade Evie and said, "excuse us we need a private meeting."

They left the room. "Michael I didn't want to talk in front of Dade he doesn't know I have magic now. Michael I think that my ability to read thoughts has been enhanced because my magic."

"Well that's good Elaina isn't it."

"I guess but I'm having trouble controlling it, sometimes I'm getting others thoughts even when I'm not trying to. It's a little unnerving. It actually seems like I can read thoughts even from those who are trained to block their thoughts. Here at the temple we spent long hours not only learning to read thoughts but also how to block our thoughts. But I can read the thoughts of others, sometimes they just pop into my head even when I'm not trying."

"It could be a problem if you get distracted in a battle. It could help but it could also hurt. I think it's important that you learn to control that. There's a book I came across in the library that may help. If not will go home and see if mom can help. Right now I need to go with Dade to check out the new base you feel up to coming along?"

"Of course Michael if you're going I'm going with you."

"Maybe we should bring Durell with us, what you think."

"That's a good idea, before she decides she should see what were up against." "Okay you go get her and I'll tell Dade were ready."

Short while later they all met in Michael's room. Durrel and Elaina were dressed in their combat uniforms sword in a sheath across their back and carrying a staff weapon.

Michael said, "Durell we don't expect any trouble but if there is any hang back we'll handle it."

"Thanks for your concern Michael, but if there is trouble I'll fight as you should know by now."

Elaine and Dade laughed and Michael just shrugged and shook his head. In a flash they disappeared and reappeared at the site above the enemy base a voice spoke from the bushes to the right

"we're here Michael but were still invisible."

Michael waved his hand and muttered the spell to cancel the enchantment. The Wizards appeared in front of them.

"We've been watching since yesterday. There has been a lot of activity but nothing to indicate their planning anything."

"Good, you both must be tired Dade will send a relief you can get some rest."

"We been sleeping one at a time so that someone is always watching."

"You've done a great job."

"Dade spoke, "you two head home. Two others are waiting, send them to this location we'll stay until they get here."

"Yes sir" with that they teleported away.

"Still no Baylor. That concerns me, you think he would at least show up with instructions once in a while. How is he communicating. Dade you and Durell wait here while Elaina and I check out the base."

Durell responded, "Michael you brought me along. I should go with you."

"You did say you wanted her to see what we were up against." Said Elaina.

"All right but while were invisible remember if you're not careful one of them could walk right into you and blow our cover so be careful to avoid them. Also we won't be able to see each other so stay behind me by touch and when we enter stay to the right side unless someone is coming toward us."

They moved to the opening of the cave and proceeded to slowly enter. Once again there was a long tunnel which led to the cave where the creatures were all congregated. There seem to be no kind of discipline some were sitting eating what look like raw meat. Some were fighting over scraps. Small fires were burning all around. the devil set on a large rock in the corner. He looked down and slapped at something. That's when Michael realized it was another vizzen. The poor little guy looked terrified. Then down one of the side tunnels they heard a scream.

"That sounds human," said Elaina.

Michael said "come on stay close".

They walked down the corridor to another room and saw to creatures whipping two men and a woman. Anger boiled up and Michael and he sent to fireballs which instantly incinerated to creatures. Then he Elaina and Durell became visible. The three prisoners were frightened out of their wits. One of the men was aimlessly staring the other said, "who are you what were those things. Ranting wildly, the young woman dropped to her knees and kept saying "they took my brother."

Michael whispered "quiet" and they all looked at him terror still in their eyes.

He asked the woman, "where did they take your brother."

She looked at him with tears in her eyes. "They killed him right there and dragged him out."

Michael said, " I'm sorry but we need to get out of here."

He turned to Elaina and Durell "I'll distract them and you two get these three out."

Elaina looked at Michael "why not just make us all invisible."

"Because this needs to stop, we need to stop hiding and I've had enough. Besides these people are all in shock and that would give us away"

"How you plan on distracting them. If it involves using yourself as bait, no way."

"Elaine it's important that we get them out of here a few fireworks and I'll be right behind you."

"All right Michael but don't take any chances."

Michael made himself invisible and went back out to the main cave Elaina and the others went as far down the tunnels they could without being seen and waited. Suddenly Michael appeared about 50 feet from the entrance and started his assault on the demons. In the confusion Elaine and Durell started toward the entrance with the prisoners, but just then about two dozen devils and other magical creatures ran out of a side cave and began counterattacking Michael. Several of the creatures spotted the prisoners escaping and charged Elaine and the others.

"They're trying to surround Michael" said Durell as she drew her sword. Elaina shouted for her to get the others out.

"But Elaina you can't fight them alone."

Elaina quickly turn to the oncoming enemy and began firing lightning bolts to clear the way for Michael. Durell stared for just a moment shocked at what she was seeing. Then she grabbed the prisoners and headed them out the tunnel. Michael blasted his way to Elaina smiled and said, "let's get outta here."

Upon exiting the cave Michael turned raised his arms and cast a spell that shook the ground and collapse the entrance to the cave.

"Well that was kind of scary" said Michael, "it should take them a while to get out of there." Durell walked over to Elaina. "That was amazing Elaina, I didn't know you had any magic."

"No one knows and Michael wants to keep it that way for now."

Michael said, "she was great wasn't she."

"I thought you were going to be angry with me," said Elaina.

"Well you are here to fight along with me right."

She smiled and said, "right"

"come on let's get these people out of here, their minds must be splintered from what they've seen."

Dade and the others came running down the hill. "What happened Michael and who are these people."

Michael didn't want to talk in front of them. The woman was crying and the men looked as if they were in shock. So he pulled Dade away from the others.

"Dade these people were captives. They were being beaten and I think those creatures were using humans for food. When we first entered some of them were fighting over meat and when we were leaving I went a little further in to distract them and saw human skeletons. The girls brother was killed and he may have been the meat they were fighting over."

"Damn animals, you should've killed them all."

"I might have if I had Dragon's breath with me."

Dade asked, "what are we going to do with them."

"I think we should bring them back to the temple with us, help them rest and heal before we release them. Then we'll wipe any memory of what happened."

"Well Michael, why don't we just wipe any memory of what happened and see they get home alright."

"Because Dade, they suffered and are traumatized and confused. When Evie and I were living in a box in an abandoned warehouse we met a lot of homeless people. Sometimes someone would have bad things happen to them but their minds would forget it like it didn't want them to remember it. But it would eat away at them and sometimes they would hurt themselves or someone else. These people need to come to terms with what has happened to them especially the girl who's brother was killed right in front of her."

"I never thought of it that way Michael. You get so used to magic we sometimes forget that it can't solve everything."

"Let's get out of here," and with that Michael transported them all to the temple. Once they arrived the sisters took the people to the medical area and Michael and the others went to his room.

"Sorry Dade that I messed up our stakeout. Seems wherever we go there's trouble. Now we have to start all over again and find their main base."

"It's not that you find trouble Michael. It's that you save lives. First our wizards then these people if it weren't for you they would all wind up dead, and as far as finding their base we found them before and we can do it again."

"I guess you're right but this time I had help."

He looked over to Elaina and Durell and they smiled.

"Dade I'd like to meet with Richard and his master wizard in three days could you arrange it."

"Sure Michael and I'll put our scouts back out with your maps so we can continue our search."

Dade turned and left just as Evie arrived.

"Hi guys, how did it go, was it exciting."

Durell looked at Michael not sure if she should say anything to Evie.

"It's okay Durell Evie knows everything."

"Durell walked over to Evie, "yes Evie it was very exciting."

Evie said, "oh man, I missed it again."

Durell turned to the others, "Michael I would be honored to be a member of the Council."

"Are you sure Durell, some may not like a woman mage."

"Yes Michael I'm sure, I will deal with their prejudice and eventually earn their respect."

"Good, we'll start first thing tomorrow, for now let's just rest we've had a busy day.

Moments later the matriss entered with their dinner along with their new little friend.

"Matriss you didn't have to bring our food we would've gotten it."

"It's no problem Michael I like helping."

"Well have you found the name for a little helper."

"Yes we've decided to call him Herbert."

"Well Herbert how do you like your new name."

"It's amazing, I've never had a name before master, oh I'm sorry I mean Michael Sir."

Durell walked over to the matriss, "matriss, I decided to accept Michael's offer."

"I rather thought you would, you've never been one to back away from a challenge, and I know you'll make a great mage. Remember you'll always have a place here my dear."

"Thank you maîtriss," she said with a slight bow.

The matriss turned and left with Herbert bouncing along behind.

The rest of the evening they just sat and talked about what happened during the day. The following morning after breakfast they went straight to the library and to Michael sanctuary.

"Elaina hold her hand that's the only way she'll be able to get through the barrier."

As they entered Durell said, "no one ever knew there was another room here"

"I know Durell, this room was created by the first Dragon mage."

"How do you know that."

"I was told by a reliable source."

"Durell stand in the circle with the magical symbols around it right over there."

Michael went to the altar, "Elaina stand behind me."

He grasped the amulet around his neck with one hand and raised the other hand toward Durell. As he began to recite the spell to bestow power, the amulet began to glow and the specs of light began to surround her. The whole room began to glow the specs of light entered her body she glowed for a moment and then collapsed. Michael and Elaina went to make sure she was all right, "just sleeping," said Michael.

"Well that definitely wasn't as intense an experience as we had on the mountain."

Elaina laughed, "I hope it worked okay."

"We won't know till she wakes up."

Just then she woke up and looked around. "How long was I out" she asked.

"Just a minute or two, how you feel?"

"Okay, but it felt like I was sleeping for days. Was that supposed to happen?"

"Yes it seems you pass out, it's probably the sudden surge of power."

"But did it work, I don't feel any different."

Elaina walked over to her and whispered into her ear as Noreen had done to her. Durell raised her hand recited the spell and the bolt of lightning shot across the room.

Michael smiled, "well I guess it did."

"Oh my goodness was that me."

Elaina said, how you feel. When I first did it I felt both excited and a little frightened."

"Yes, that's exactly how I feel." Said Durell

Michael said to Elaina, "we need to take her to Cassondra. She'll have to train her so that she is ready to introduce to the Council."

"Michael, she whispered, what about your mother."

"No, she's a mage she will have to be trained as a mage. Besides I'm not sure I want anyone else to know about our world."

Michael went to Durell, you will need some training before you use your magic so that you don't hurt anyone."

"Oh of course Michael whatever you say, I wouldn't want to hurt anyone."

22

THEY WENT TO THE GUARDIANS room where Michael walked to the altar and called Cassondra. Moment later she appeared stepped out into the room. "Hello Michael."

"Hello Cassondra, this is Durell she will be a mage and she will replace Raymond. I need you to train her."

"She had no power, yet now I sense great power within her, did you give her this power."

"Yes, I gave her the power of a mage."

"Who are you Michael? A mage can't create a mage. The power to do such a thing is far beyond that of a mage even if such a spell exists. I know we've had to keep things from each other, but I've tried to tell you everything I could. I know you've kept things from me Michael, but I need to know where you came by such power. I think I've proven to you that I can be trusted, that I only want to help."

Michael looked at Elaina who nodded to him.

"All right Cassondra, you remember telling me what you knew of the first Dragon mage."

"Yes but we know very little about him. We don't know where he came from, but he fulfilled all his promises. He ended the wizard wars and created the mage counsel and then was gone, and turned the mage counsel over to the new Dragon mage."

"Well his name was Creighton and he was my great-grandfather."

Cassondra stared at Michael for a moment as if not knowing what to say. "Well I didn't expect that. But it makes some sense now. He had tremendous power. But Michael if she is in fact a mage she will need her own guardian."

"No Cassondra, I want you to train her I told you I don't trust the others, if you can't or won't train her I'll do it myself, but as busy as I've been it will take longer."

"All right Michael I'll train her."

"Thank you Cassondra."

"Also Michael, about the rest of my people, you may be right. I don't think our leaders are involved but I do suspect a couple high up in the Council and several others are part of this dark conspiracy."

"Just as I thought. Cassondra were getting close to finding their stronghold and when we do you'll have to decide whether to stay here or go back to your realm forever, because I will seal it so that no one from your world can Pass over. I can't risk them joining Baylor."

"When it's over you'll unseal it won't you."

"I don't know if I can, I haven't come across a spell that would allow me to do that. So you'll have to decide whether you will stay or go back. I don't need your answer now, but you need to think about it. In the meantime Elaina and I will leave you with Durell so you can get started."

Michael and Elaina headed back to his room.

"Michael you look troubled what's wrong."

"I wonder if I'm doing the right thing. Starting to question every decision I make.

So many people could be hurt if I'm wrong, and so many lives. The mage the wizards not to mention the sisters all depending on me to do the right thing. What if I'm wrong."

"Michael everyone counts on you and depends on you because everything you've done has been the right thing. You were cast into this role without even knowing who you were or even that you had any power. And yet you've done everything that was asked of you. We here couldn't be more proud to serve with you and even Dade and entire gray order would follow you anywhere and not just because you're the Dragon mage but because they trust you. They're loyal because you've proven yourself to them and those are Dade's own words."

"Really, that makes me feel a little better I respect Dade's judgment. Still every decision I make could cost someone their life." "Believe in yourself Michael, because not making a decision can be even more costly."

"I guess you're right Elaina I got to stop second guessing myself,"

when they arrived at Michael's room Evie was there with another girl not much older than she was. Dinner is already on the table.

"Hi guys, this is Katie she's my friend and she's going to take over some of Durell's duties."

"Hi Katie" said Michael and Elaina almost the same time.

"Hey Mike, can she eat with us tonight."

"Sure Evie."

They sat and ate Michael just picked at his food and ate very little. When they had finished Evie and Katie left and Michael and Elaina went to their favorite spot on the balcony. They sat and sipped some juice but said very little.

Finally Elaina said, "what's wrong Michael you seem troubled."

"I'm missing something Elaina and I can't figure out what."

"What you mean Michael."

"We're getting close to finding Baylor's main base I can feel it, but were not as prepared as we should be. We need more help I need to check the mage on the Council. We need to know which are loyal and which are wavering in which if any can't be trusted."

"Well if you call a meeting and I could get close and read their thoughts, they won't know it's harder for them to block me."

"Yes I was thinking the same thing, and if I shake each one's hand I'll be able to tell their true feelings. Dade should be here in the morning I'll have him set it up for after our meeting with Richard. I'd like to introduce Durell to the others at the same time but I don't think she'll be ready. I don't want to delay the meeting until she is better able to control her powers it's too important."

"Maybe if we send her to your mother to train she'd be ready sooner."

"I thought about that, but like I said I don't want people knowing about our world."

Finally Durell entered Michael's room. "Hello everyone, that was the most exciting few hours of my life."

"Hi Durell, are you hungry."

"No thanks, I'm kind of exhausted. I'm going straight to bed I just wanted to let you know I was back. Good night Elaina, good night Michael."

"Good night Durell."

The next morning Durell and Elaina both came to Michael's room early. Michael had just gotten up. Katie came and dropped off the breakfast and left.

Durell said, well I'm going to go do some more training."

"Don't be in such a hurry, sit down and have something to eat."

"That's okay, I'm not really that hungry."

"Durell you didn't eat last night, now you need to eat something you got a long day ahead of you."

"Maybe you're right," so they sat and had some breakfast.

Short while later Dade arrived. "Good morning Michael, I set the meeting with Richard and his master wizard will be there as you requested."

"Thank you Dade would you like something to eat."

"No thanks, I've already eaten."

"If you're not busy Dade I like you with me at the meeting."

"Course Michael, I'll see you then, but I gotta go now we have a new recruit starting today and I should be there on the first day of training."

Next day Michael, Elaina, Durell and Evie sat together for breakfast. When they were done Durell hurried off the train with Cassondra. Elaina and Evie headed for the gym.

"Are you coming Michael" asked Elaina.

"I'll catch up, you guys go ahead I have a couple things to do first."

Elaina thought that was strange but went along with Evie anyway. After they were gone Michael went to the top of the temple and stood before the two dragons that he originally thought were stone statues he recited the spell he had found in the ancient books and suddenly the dragons began to move. Their color change from stone gray to black and they looked down at Michael.

"ahh! A new young prince of Rayhn" and they bowed. Michael heard them in his mind. Michael returned their bow.

"How do you know who I am."

"Well you're too young to be king, and no one but a descendent of the Lord Creighton could have awakened us."

"My name is Michael and you're right Creighton was my great-grandfather. When I was home I spoke with your father and he said I could count on your help. He also asked if I would bring you both back with me when the war is over."

"A war you say, well of course we'll help we always serve the house of Rayhn. I am Malum and this is my sister Elon. We have been asleep since Lord Creighton asked us to stay and wait. In case we were needed again. We aided in the last wizard wars."

"This war is a little different" said Michael. "The evil from another realm have been let loose by Baylor of the Deices."

"Ahh, the Deices, their thirst for power never seems to end. They should have been destroyed long ago."

"Excellent Malum when we find their stronghold I may need to call on you."

"We will be ready young prince."

Michael returned to his room excited that he was able to make contact with Malum and Elon. When he got there Evie and Elaina were already there.

"Michael where were you, we will looking all over for you."

"Sorry Elaina, but I didn't leave the temple I was on the roof."

"On the roof! What were you doing" she hesitated a moment, "oh my goodness, you were with the dragons. Were you able to wake them?"

"Yes, and they're willing to help. Their names are Malum and Elon. Their brother and sister and their amazing."

"Wow Mike, said Evie. Can I go meet them?"

"Sure Evie, but not right now we have to get ready for the meeting."

The day of the meeting Dade arrived. Durell had already gone to meet with Cassondra. She had been training day and night since she started. Elaina and Michael were in his room waiting when Dade Arrived.

"Did you want some breakfast Dade."

"No thanks Michael, Richard is waiting for us."

"Good let's get going."

Dade raised his wand and in a flash they were gone. On arrival they were greeted by Richard's master wizard.

"Hello Michael, it's been a while."

"Yes too long, I think we need to start having monthly Council meetings to help keep everyone informed." They went in and were greeted by Richard.

"Hello Michael, glad to see you. I hear you've been having an interesting time lately breaking up enemy bases."

"Yes but did you hear about the Guardian I captured."

"No I didn't, you mean you actually captured a guardian."

"Yes he was at the first base and he was helping them."

"What! Why would one of the guardians helped this evil horde, they're supposed to be helping us."

"Apparently he felt that the world would be better off under the control of evil instead of destroying itself which he feels is inevitable and I don't think he's alone in his feellings."

"Wow! This is bad, this is very bad. How can we stop the guardians."

"I'll take care of that, but we need a Council meeting with all the mage and their master wizards. We need to see if any of the others are looking to join Baylor."

"How will you know that."

"Elaina and I will take care of that at the meeting. We have to know who we can depend on. Elaina and one of the other sisters will be with me they'll be able to read their minds."

"Michael we know their ability and can just block our thoughts."

", Elaina's abilities have been enhanced she can get through their blocks."

"Really, how is that possible."

"I've been able to magically do it, but I don't want the others to know that."

"Don't worry Michael will keep the secret."

"I know Richard, If I thought otherwise I wouldn't have told you."

"So when you want the meeting."

"The end of next week, and at that time I'll be introducing Raymond's replacement."

"Wow, that is big. Who is he."

"She is the new mage."

"Did you say she?"

"Yes I did."

"There's never been a female mage before, are you sure she has mage powers and not just a strong wizard."

"Quite sure, you have a problem with that."

"No not as long she can do the job."

"What about the others you know them better than me."

"Well I think most will be okay with it. One or two may not like it too much, but I don't think they'll make trouble over it."

"Which ones do you think won't like it."

"I think maybe Julian and maybe Ryan. They're just so full of themselves they won't think a woman could be a mage, but if she's as good as you say I think they'll come around."

"Julian and Ryan that's the fire and stone mage right."

"Yes exactly."

"Thanks Richard, if you will set the meeting I'll make sure she's ready."

They said their goodbyes and left. When they got back to the temple Michael turned to Dade.

"Well Dade what do you think?"

"I think Richard knows the others better than anyone. If he says that only two may have a problem with it I'd go with his judgment."

"Once she's in she'll be taking over those wizards that didn't defect with Raymond. How do you think they'll take it."

"We've been working closely with them since Raymond left. I think they'll be okay with it as long as she can prove to them she is a mage."

"I want to thank you Dade for bringing me here and helping me when I needed it.

I have depended on you and you've never let me down. I couldn't come this far without you."

"It's my pleasure Michael, you've exceeded all our expectations. I have to admit that before you came I was beginning to doubt we would ever get it together. We have the power and ability to make a real difference in the world. That is our purpose that is what we should be focused on. But the counsel lost sight of that, they had forgotten our purpose. Now it feels as if were back on track and we owe that to you."

"Thanks Dade, that means a lot coming from you. Well the meeting is in just over a week. We'll see how it goes and will find out who was 100% behind us and who may be wavering."

After Dade left Michael went to his room he had a lot on his mind. He laid on his bed and was thinking of all that had to be done, wondering if he missed anything.

Next thing you knew someone was gently calling his name. He opened his eyes and saw Elaina, Evie and Durell standing next to the bed. He looked toward the balcony and saw it was dark outside.

"Oh sorry, I must've fallen asleep what time is it."

"About 730, maybe we shouldn't have awakened you, you seem so peaceful."

"No I'm glad you did, we have things to discuss."

They went and sat at the table and had a bite to eat.

Michael said, "Durell I'm going to introduce you at the meeting next Friday, and you'll take over as the desert mage which was Raymond's order. There are only about seven or eight wizards left that didn't go with Raymond. So will have to replenish their ranks should be about 12 to 18 altogether."

"Okay Michael, if you think I'm ready."

"You been working hard, you are ready as you need to be. Besides Dade, Elaina and I will all be there with you. Elaine as soon as we arrive start scanning the other mage as well as their master wizards, especially as I introduced Durell as Raymond's replacement. If they have a problem with it be sure to speak up but I also want to know what they're thinking."

"All right Michael I'll be ready."

"Now Durell once you take over Raymond spot you will still be here at least until your training is complete your wizards will be bunking with Dade in the gray order."

"That's good Michael, that way I can get to know them better before we actually moved to Raymond's area. Well I may as well get back to my practice."

"Durell come and sit with us on the balcony, you need to take a little time to relax."

"But Michael we don't have much time I need all the practice I can get."

Elaina said "Durell you been practicing day and night studying the scrolls practicing the spells you need to take some time to wind down you'll be no good to anyone if you're burned out when the time comes."

"But you guys are always on the move taking on a lot more than me."

"Yes but we always try to take a little time at night to sit out on the balcony and look at the stars and scenery and talk about anything except work and what's going on. It's like you just let all your cares and worries go and relax. Just Michael and I and sometimes Evie. Come on Durell join us."

Michael poured three glasses of juice and they all just sat relaxed.

The following morning Michael woke early and went to bathe. The soothing water felt great and also help to relax his troubled thoughts. When he was done he got dressed and when he left the bathroom found Elaina and Evie sitting at the table enjoying breakfast.

"Hey guys" he said.

Elaina said " hi Michael, how are you feeling today."

Evie had her mouth full and just waved.

"Well after that wonderful bath I'm feeling much better. Where is Durell isn't she going to join us."

"No she ate early and headed straight to the library. She said that she wants to be as ready as possible when it's time for the meeting."

Just then Dade entered the room and said hello to everyone.

Michael said, "hello Dade would you like something to eat."

"No thanks Michael. I'm just here to give you an update."

The girls finished eating and Elaina said, "we're going to the gym are you coming with us Michael."

"No you to go ahead, I'm going to talk with Dade."

So Elaina and Evie left and headed for their workout.

Dade said, "the meeting is all set and everyone will be there like you requested.

Were also making some progress with our searches we put more teams out."

"That's fine Dade, have a seat let's talk."

"Is something wrong Michael."

"No nothing's wrong it just seems the only time we get to talk is when there's a crisis. We never just sit and talk."

"Oh okay, what you want to talk about."

"Well I'd just like to get to know you and the gray order better, if you don't mind my getting a little personal."

"No not at all Michael, what you want to know."

"Well like how long have you been the head of the gray order."

"Oh, it's been about 30 years or so, that's when my master wizard and mentor asked me to challenge him for leadership of the order. He was over

150 years old and his magic was beginning to fade and he felt I was the best I take over."

"Challenge him? What you mean like challenge him to combat."

Dade laughed, "no Michael it's not combat. Anyone can challenge the master wizard for leadership. Then the mage of the order comes up with a set of tasks which must be performed. The tests include magic, intelligence, and strategies and the winner of the contest becomes the master wizard of the order. He was a great leader but once your power begins to go your age begins to catch up to you rather quickly, after I took over he retired. He lived about another 14 years and enjoyed every remaining minute and passed away quietly and happy."

"Now that's an amazing story, let me ask you has anyone ever challenged you."

Dade smiled, "once, it was quite a while ago we had a new wizard he'd been training about nine months. He was totally full of himself. He thought he was the greatest wizard who ever lived. So the Dragon mage put together a series of brutal tests needless to say he failed but he was a lot more humble after that.

He went on to be a very good wizard."

"Okay now you have to tell me which one of your wizards he is."

"Dade looked solemnly at Michael, "he's dead, when the last Dragon mage was ambushed and killed his aid and two wizards were also killed with them. He was one of them."

"I'm sorry to hear that."

"That Michael is around when the craziness began we don't know if Baylor was leading this evil at that time but we heard rumors of someone or something powerful that was leading them. But they didn't seem very well organized back then."

"Dade how many wizards in the gray order?"

"There are 14 not including myself."

"That means I've only met about half of them. They must think I'm a real jerk, all this time and I've only met half and even then it's always on the run."

"I can assure you Michael that's not the case. They've all expressed great respect for you."

"Still I need to meet with them and I like to do it before the meeting with the Council next week. I know we'll have a party. All of us you me the sisters everyone you can bring the whole order. Recall our search team and we'll have a day of getting to know each other you can also bring Raymond's wizards and will introduce them to Durell. They could use the time to get to know each other.

It will be a day of fun and relaxation. What you think?"

"Well Michael with everything that's been going on, I think it's a great idea."

"Okay then, I'll tell the matrix three days from today."

"All right Michael I'll leave now and let them know you also need to get our team back, till later Michael

"Yeah okay I will, see you Dade."

Michael went off to find the matriss and let her know. Just then it hit him maybe he should have checked with her first before making such a commitment. He went to the gym first hoping she might be there. When he got there everyone was training hard. Michael looked around and sure enough at the far end he saw her talking to one of the instructors. Elaina saw him, but he didn't notice her. He went straight to the matriss.

"Hello matriss, Dade and I were talking and I made a commitment that affects all of us, but now I'm thinking that I should have checked with you first."

"That's okay Michael, what is it."

Michael explained to her what he and Dade had discussed about the party.

"I can cancel it or postpone it if it's not acceptable or too much to get ready in just three days."

"Not at all Michael it's a wonderful idea. Everyone has been working very hard lately in order to get ready to stand by your side in this conflict. I think a party will do wonders for their morale, besides we've never met the gray order except to see them come and go. Don't worry Michael we'll have everything ready when they arrive."

Michael went over to Elaina who had been wondering if there was a problem.

"What is it Michael is something wrong."

"No Elaina on the contrary everything is fine."

He explained to her what they were planning.

"Wow, that's an amazing idea but can we afford to let our guard down for a whole day."

"Yes Elaina we can and were going to. Besides I think everyone needs this time

To unwind."

Over the next couple days everyone was busy getting ready for the party even the work to get ready seem to be raising everyone's spirit. Michael was kept out of the preparation loop and he was happy to stay out of the way. The sisters seemed to be having fun and he didn't want to spoil it. The day of the party arrived and Michael woke early. The sun had just risen it was a couple of hours before Dade and the others would arrive. He went to the table and sat down

. Breakfast was already there warm and fresh he still couldn't figure how they knew when he would awake and have breakfast waiting a few minutes later

Elaina and Evie arrived.

"Hi guys, how are you doing?"

"Fine Mikey, I can't wait for the party to start."

Elaina said, "Michael I brought a change of clothes do you mind if I bathe under the waterfall."

"Not at all what Elaina, I'll go after you. When you're done find Durell.

Tell her no training today get her a change of clothes and have her take a turn under the falls. It will help her relax especially since she'll be meeting her wizards today. She's probably very nervous."

"Okay Michael will do."

"Hey Mikey, can I take a turn in your bath too."

"Sure Evie, you can go after Durell."

"Okay, I'm going to run and get my clothes."

After Elaina was finished with her bath she came and sat by Michael for a moment. "I feel much better now. That is so relaxing."

"I know, when things aren't going quite right and I'm stressed, I so look forward to stepping in the water and just let the waterfall beat down on me. It just makes you feel everything is just right. In fact I'm going to jump in now."

"Okay Michael, I'll go find Durell."

Michael grabbed his things and went for his bath. When he was done Elaina, Durell and Evie were all waiting.

"Durell said, "Michael I could've gotten cleaned up and bathed in my room."

Michael smiled "Elaina please show Durell why it's better here."

Elaina took Durell into the bathroom and a moment later Michael heard "Wow" coming from the room.

Elaina came out and said, "I thought she was going to faint when she saw it."

Michael and Evie laughed. A while later Durell emerged from the bathroom and looked much better.

Elaina said, "well how was it."

"That was the most amazing experience I've ever had. I feel like all this pressure I put on myself had been lifted away."

"Good are you ready to meet your wizards when they arrive."

"Michael, I feel I'm ready for anything."

They all looked at Evie as she ran toward the bathroom with her change of clothes in hand.

Michael, Elaina and Durell Headed to the great Hall to see if everything was ready. When they got there they saw the sisters adding the finishing touches to what was a beautifully decorated room. Michael walked over to the matriss and said, "everything is amazing, you have all done a wonderful job of getting things ready so quickly."

"Thank you Michael, it has been an enjoyable three days and has helped to raise everyone's spirits. We are so looking forward to hosting this party for the gray order. Michael we've been formal long enough please just call me Emily"

"Alright Emily I'll go and wait for Dade and the others to arrive. After the introductions I'll bring them here and we can start the party.

"Ok Michael when you send word we'll start bringing out the food and drinks."

23

I T WAS NEARLY NOON AND Michael knew that Dade and the others would be there be there any time now so He, Elaina and Durell hurried to his room to wait. WHen they got there Evie was sitting at the table." What did you guy's run out on me."

"No Evie we just went to see if everything was ready."

"How did you like it Mike we all worked on it isn't it Fabulous."

"It was great Evie"

"Do you want me to go and help the others finish up Mikey."

"No Evie when Dade and the others arrive I need you to go and tell the Matriss they are here. She knows what to do. Durell you'll be sitting on the balcony, Elaina you'll be at my side. We'll greet everyone and then I'll introduce Durell to her wizards."

At 12 o'clock Dade arrived with the gray order and Raymond's wizards in tow. Michael and Elaina walked over to them while Evie went to tell the matriss that they arrived. The gray order lined up all wanting to shake Michael's hand. Michael greeted each one and introduced Elaina as his aide. The master wizard open Raymond's order came in greeted Michael and introduced each of his wizards. When they had finished Michael announced that the new mage of their order was there. When asked who he was Michael looked at Elaina and they both smiled. Then Michael called to Durell who came walking in from the balcony.

"She's a girl" said one of the wizards. "Can a girl be a Mage."

Michael said, "first off she's not a girl she's a young woman. Second yes females can be a mage and she is a very powerful mage. Her name is Durell."

The master wizard looked at them for a moment. Then he walked over to her and said, "it's a pleasure to meet you Durell." Durell smiled and thanked him then went and greeted the others.

Michael said, "well you will all get to know each other over the next few weeks. But for now let's just go to the party."

When they arrived at the great Hall everyone was commenting on how nice and festive it all looked. The food was already out and they all sat and ate and sampled the various juices. When the dining was over the tables were set to the wall so whoever wanted could munch from time to time. As with most gatherings where no one knew each other things started slowly with friends gathering in their own little groups. The matris instructed the sisters to go and mingle with the different groups and little by little things started to loosen up. Sr. Lorraine was one of the hand-to-hand combat instructors was showing a few wizards some fighting moves and they seem fascinated. Two of the sisters and another group which included Dade had started a game of charades. Other sisters were showing some of the wizards who would never been to the temple before around. Everyone seemed to be having a good time. Durell was getting to know the wizards of her new order. Michael and Elaina walked together talking and mingling with all the different groups. Evie was bouncing from group to group trying to get to know everyone. A while later Dade came over to Michael and Elaina.

"Michael this party is wonderful, everyone is having a great time." Then he added "I think the sisters are reading our minds either that or they are very very good at charades."

They all laughed at that. As evening approached they dimmed the lights and put on some music and some people started to dance while others were talking and laughing. Michael put out his hand, Elaina looked at him and put her hand in his. He led her to the floor and they began to dance it was a slow dance and Elaina put her head on his shoulder.

She said, "Michael this is a perfect day."

"I know" he said "it couldn't have gone better"

the two female wizards in the gray order both came up to Michael and asked if he would dance with them. He really wanted to stay with Elaina but no he couldn't refuse. He danced with each in turn thanked them and went back to sit with Elaina. All the wizards in Durell's new order were anxious to dance with her so she danced with each of them. She really wanted to relax with Elaina and Michael but didn't want to disappoint anyone. It was getting late when Dade gathered the wizards together. He came over to Michael and said "it's getting late will be heading back now it was an amazing day everyone had a great time. They'll be talking about this day for a long time."

"I'm glad it went so well Dade. Everyone including the sisters seem to have fun."

"I'll stop by tomorrow Michael and we can begin to discuss Friday's Council meeting."

"Okay thanks Dade." After Dade and the others left Durell came over to them.

"Durell you look exhausted." Said Elaina

"I am but I'm also feeling good. The evening was a great success and the wizards seem to us accepted me."

"Yes it looks as if you have a bunch of admirers."

Durell blushed "not exactly what I meant." "I know, you did seem to get along fine with them."

"Durell stumbled out of the hall she looked very tired. Evie was sitting at the table fast asleep. Michael woke her and told her to go to bed. He noticed the sisters were already starting to clean up.

He said "ladies please, no more work tonight. Go relax this will still be here in the morning. I want to thank all of you for a wonderful day."

As they broke up Michael took Elaina's hand and left he walked Elaina to her door. He took her in his arms and kissed her.

"Good night Elaina"

"good night Michael" as he turned Elaina said, "Michael do you realize this is the first time we kissed without something being wrong."

Michael just smiled and laughed. Elaina went inside she fell backwards onto her bed her arms outstretched. She felt her world couldn't be more perfect. Michael went to his room he didn't even change, he just lay in bed thinking how lucky he is. He drifted off to sleep feeling good about the day. The next morning he woke and Elaina and Evie were already sitting at the table waiting for him to wake.

"Well you guys are here early"

"we were helping to clean up the hall. Michael it's amazing everyone seems happier their spirits are up and even the work is fun."

Michael said "yeah I still feel pretty good too. I guess we all just needed to let go a little. Well I'm going to go relax in the shower before we get started."

"Okay Michael, will meet you at the training center."

The rest of the day went as expected after training Michael and Elaina went to his study to read and practice while Durell went to the Guardian sanctuary to study with Cassondra. In the afternoon Michael left the others and went back to his room to wait for Dade. About an hour later Dade arrived.

"Hello Michael, how is everything going here."

"Find Dade everyone is in high spirits it's been a good day."

"Same with the gray order everyone's walking on air the party worked out even better than I expected in fact I think one of our wizards has fallen for one of your ladies. He's been walking around humming all day and some of the others said he was dancing with the same lady all day yesterday."

"Really, do you know who"

"no and when you ask him he just smiles."

They spent the rest of the day going over the plans for the meeting of the mage counsel.

That evening Elaina, Evie, and Durell all came to Michael's room. They sat and ate and when they were done they all went out to the balcony to soak up the view. After a few minutes of relaxing Michael said "the Council meeting is in two days, is everyone ready."

Elaina said, "Michael were as ready as we can be."

Durell said, "yes Michael were ready."

Evie said, "well since I can't go I don't need to be ready."

They all laughed and went back to enjoying the view.

Michael woke early the next morning. He skipped his usual bath and just washed and dressed. Elaina arrived a short while later and Michael was still having a little breakfast.

Michael said, "hi Elaina are you ready for tomorrow."

"Are you okay Michael you asked us that last night."

"Oh yeah, sorry I guess I'm a little nervous."

"I thought so," said Elaina "maybe a good workout will help you loosen up."

"Maybe you're right, let's get going I want to speak to the matris anyway."

They hurried to the gym. "You start your warm-ups Elaina while I go speak to the matris."

He went over to the matris who was sitting at the opposite side of the gym and asked her if he could see everyone in the great Hall in two hours.

"Of course Michael, is there anything I should know before the meeting."

"No Emily I just have a gift I'd like to give to you and the sisters."

The matris just nodded and assured him they would all be there. After a short workout with Elaina he went to his room and took the bag of runes out of his dresser. He was going to give them to all the sisters at the meeting. At the appointed time Michael went to the great Hall and found everyone already there and waiting. He went to the altar and spoke to them.

First I want to thank you all. When Evie and I first arrived here we didn't know what to expect. All of you helped us and made us feel welcome, and I can never thank you enough for that. The Council and wizarding orders are getting close I feel to finding the location of the enemy's main base and when they do we will go and destroy that base and send all these dark creatures back where they came from, but it's not going to be easy and I know you are all planning to come and fight alongside us."

Elaina thought she knew where this was going so she interrupted and asked Michael to come aside for a moment.

"Michael please tell me you're not going to tell them they can't come with us."

"No Elaina I've learned enough to know what an insult that would be to them."

He went back to the altar.

"Elaina was concerned that I was going to say it's too dangerous for you to come along with us, but I wouldn't do that. You're all like family and although I fear for your safety I wouldn't try keeping you from doing what I know you must, but in order to help when the battle comes I have a gift for each of you."

He opened the bag and took out one of the runes.

"These runes will help protect you. They're not a shield and you still need to be careful because you could still be hurt, but they will enhance your natural abilities to help you think and react much quicker."

He handed the bag to the matris and asked her to hand them out. The matris stepped up to the altar.

"Thank you Michael, were proud to be with you and not just because you're the Dragon mage because of who you are.

She went and started handing out the runes.

Elaina came over Michael "that was nice Michael, I think that's one of the reasons I love you" and she hugged him.

After the meeting the ladies all thank Michael for their gift. Then he and Elaina went to the library to study. All the while Michael couldn't focus on what they were going over. Elaina noticed that his mind was not on what they were doing and asked "Michael is something wrong your mind doesn't seem to be on our studies."

"No Elaina nothing is wrong just thinking about tomorrow's meeting. Going to be very important that all goes well. Keep feeling I'm forgetting something I'm missing something."

"I'm sure it will go perfectly Michael, you've done everything you can to make it work and we will all be there with you, me, Durell and Dade. Come on we're done studying for today let's just go relax."

They returned to his room and went straight to the balcony they sat beside each other holding hands.

"Now this is what I call relaxing" said Michael.

Elaina just smiled and said, "I know I so look forward to our time here."

Suddenly Dade came running in with six of his wizards.

"Michael, there is another attack going on at what we believe is a munitions factory. It's happening now Richard and his wizards have gone ahead I grabbed some wizards and came for you."

Michael jumped up "let's go, come on Elaina."

They all formed the group and teleported to the location when they arrived the battle was over the factory had exploded and Richard was on the ground. Dade's wizards joined the blue order in case another attack started. Dade Michael and Elaina ran to Richard.

"Richard are you all right" asked Michael

"yeah, I'll be okay when we got here the building was already on fire. It was Henry and his wizards. We didn't see Henry at first. We attacked the wizards and there was a huge explosion in the building went up that's when I was hit from behind. Fortunately I had a shield up but didn't expect an attack from behind. Then Morgan and some of his wizards came to my aide. Henry couldn't take the assault and teleported out. His wizards quickly followed."

Morgan came over and greeted them.

Michael said, "sorry we're late we got here as quickly as we could."

"That's all right Michael we got here to late too. The building was already burning when we arrived. How are you Richard."

"I'm okay Morgan, thanks to you and the others." Michael said,

"Richard if they left in a hurry may be possible to track where they went."

"It's possible Michael, Morgan can you see if they left any residual to where they went. I need to get back to our base."

"Sure thing Richard will see what we can find. We can't stay long I'm sure the authorities will be here soon."

Michael and Dade help Richard up with Elaina close by. They all teleported to Richard's base.

Dade asked, "whether people in the building when it exploded."

"Yes Dade, we don't know how many but we think a lot only a few got out before it went up."

"How did you know the attack was happening."

"It was one of Michael's maps, magic showed up and when the search team arrived they discovered the attack. He immediately signaled for help, the map worked perfectly. If we could've gotten there a little sooner we might have prevented this tragedy. Well I need to go and lay down and rest for now. I'll need my strength for the meeting tomorrow."

"All right Richard will see you there." When they arrived back at Ghostra Durell in the matris were waiting.

Durell said, "Michael we were looking all over for you and Elaina we didn't know you had left."

"I'm sorry Durell we didn't have time to send word we were leaving. There was an attack by Henry and his wizards they struck a munitions factory. It was over when we got there Richard and the Blue order got there before us."

"Oh my, is everyone alright."

"Richard was hurt but he'll be okay. The factory was destroyed and the people inside were killed."

"Oh no" said the matris "how many were killed."

"We don't know, but from what Richard said only a few got out before it exploded."

"How could a mage and his wizards do something like that." Asked Durell

Michael shook his head "I don't know."

Little Herbert came walking in to see the matris, "hello Michael Sir, and lady Elaina and master head wizard. I just came to ask Miss maîtris what she needed me to do next, if that if that's okay."

"Sure Herbert," said Michael "wait a minute Herbert tell me what you remember aboutwhere you were before you were brought here."

"Well sir I don't know where it was."

"That's okay Herbert just tell me what you do remember, what did it look like."

"Well we were in the caves most of the time but our master would take us out when we needed food or water it was a great open area with great stone walls all the way around there was a passage that went all the way out very far where he would take us. It was a passage with stone walls on both sides at the end of the passage was trees and water he would kill things and we had to carry the food and water back to the caves."

"You said stone walls on both sides of the passage like a canyon."

"I'm sorry sir I don't know what that means."

"That's okay Herbert it doesn't matter."

The matris said, "if you're done Michael all show him what to do next."

"Yes of course Emily."

Michael turned to Dade, "maybe we should have one of our teams start looking into canyons in remote areas."

Suddenly Michael had a thought he turned to Elaina.

"A Canyon, Elaina a Canyon."

"What you mean Michael."

"Where we captured Raymond and those wizards that was in a Canyon."

"It can't be Michael. I didn't see any other creatures except those Bogan's, and I didn't see the huge opening he mentioned."

"But he said it was a long way and we were barely into the mouth of the canyon."

"But surely Michael if they were there they would've left after we captured Raymond."

"But they don't know where we captured Raymond and if they knew we were there they would've attacked us rather than let us captured Raymond."

"Could it really be that simple Michael."

Then Dade said, "you think you know where their base is."

"I don't know Dade it's possible, Elaina and I were in the mouth of the canyon when we captured Raymond and his wizards in the canyon went very far in we couldn't see the end where it led. Dade tomorrow before the meeting have a team from the order here. I'll make them invisible and send them to the location where we landed. They are to walk the canyon and find out where it leads they are not to engage any creatures just out and report back what they find." "Okay Michael I'll have them here first thing before the meeting, with that Dade left.

Michael and Elaina put some food on their plates and went to sit on the balcony. The sun was already setting and the scene from the balcony was amazing. After a while they both fell asleep right there in their loungers. The next morning Lena was awakened by Evie who said "did you guys sleep here all night."

"I guess we did Evie."

TheIr talking woke Michael turned to them and said, "it's morning already and I slept on the balcony again. What time is it."

"It's about 630 Mikey"

"good we have plenty of time before the meeting. Has Dade arrived yet."

"No not yet" said Evie

"oh! I have a stiff neck, but a few minutes under the water fall should help. How about you Elaina how about the falls."

"Michael, don't get fresh in front of your sister."

"Elaina, I meant when I'm done."

Elaina turned a deep shade of red and just said "oh"

Evie started laughing and Michael just shook his head.

Still blushing, Elaina said "that sounds like a good idea. I'll get my things and go after you." She then quickly turned and left the room. Michael was getting ready for his bath when Dade arrived with three wizards.

"Oh hi Dade, I see you brought our scouting team."

"Yes Michael, I brought a more experienced team for this mission."

Michael turned to them and said "let me make sure you understand your mission. This is a scouting assignment. If they are there you are not to engage them unless you have no choice. You will arrive at the mouth of the canyon and follow it to the end if it exits the wide open space let us know. But if it opens into a larger area with caves that may be their base. Just exit back to the mouth of the canyon and come back and tell us what you saw."

"We understand Michael, Dade briefed us thoroughly."

"Good, now I,m going to make you invisible you won't be able to see each other so be careful and communicate whenever it's safe to do so."

Michael raised his hand recited the spell and the three of them turned invisible.

Dade said, "I'll send them off and be back in a little while for the Council meeting."

They left just as Elaina arrived.

"Oh I thought you would be in the bath by now."

"No, Dade arrived with a scouting team and I had to brief them before they left. You go first Elaina I'll wait till you're done."

Okay thank you Michael I won't be long."

"Michael went in for his bath as soon as she was done. Time to the meeting was getting short.

"Elaina have you seen Durell."

"No but she'll be here before the meeting. She's very reliable."

"I know, everyone here is very reliable. That's what keeps me on my toes. I don't want to be less reliable than everyone else."

"Moments later Durell came in dressed in the green and white colors of the desert mage.

"Well Durell don't you look spiffy in your mage colors."

"Thank you Michael, I'm a little nervous but I'm as ready as I can be."

"You will do fine Durell. Just to be clear Elaina will stay next to me. You and Miles will stay close to Dade until after the introductions at which time you will assume your place at the table."

24

MICHAEL, ELAINA, DURELL AND EVIE were all sitting at the table when Dade arrived with Miles.

"it's time Michael, is everyone ready."

"We're ready Dade, just waiting for you to get here."

Evie Said "good luck guys"

They formed a group and teleported to the area just outside the meeting hall.

They immediately entered the hall. Everyone was already there waiting.

Julian said, "hello Michael what's with the entourage."

"Hello everyone I'm happy to see you all here. Sorry Julian but this is not an entourage. Everyone's here has a reason for being here which I'll explain shortly. First things first, I would like to introduce you all to Raymond's replacement, the new desert mage and her name is Durell."

"That's impossible" said Julian, "isn't she one of the little priestesses at your temple."

"She was but now she's a mage and she has all the powers of a mage."

Miles the master mage of her order said, "Durell has the powers of a mage and me and my order support her 100%."

Richard stood and said, "if Michael said she has the power of a mage and Miles in his order stands with her then I say welcome to the Council Durell. Please take your place at the table."

Julian said, "how is this possible that one day she's a priestess at the Dragon temple in the next day she's a mage."

Michael replied, "you've all heard rumors that I took away Raymond's power in his memory. While it's true I did. It gave me no pleasure to do that to anyone but it had to be done. The same way I can remove power, I can also restore or give power to those who deserve it. Over the centuries the mage have become less and less powerful, with each generation the power of the mage has diminished. But I can restore the mage to full power just as they were when they were first created by the first Dragon mage."

David the mountain mage spoke, "we were not aware that kind of power insisted to her that there was a spell for it.

But Michael has proven himself to many and if he says it can be done I believe him."

"Thank you David" said Michael "I don't know if you're all aware of the attack yesterday on a munitions dump. Henry and his wizards were responsible for it and many innocent people were killed. We need to double our efforts to find their main base and keep anything like this from happening again."

Suddenly there were voices that seem to come from nowhere. Michael waved his hand in the three-man scout team from the gray order suddenly became visible.

"Dade, Michael we're sorry to interrupt the meeting that we thought you would want to know right away, we scouted the area and found their base you were right they are there."

Dade said, "tell us what you found"

"we got to the mouth of the canyon and very carefully followed it. About 2 miles in it opened up into a much larger area. We carefully approached the caves we saw on the other side and we saw them dozens of creatures and from the sound of it many more inside the caves."

"What about Baylor did you see him" asked Michael

"we saw someone who appeared human and he was talking to Henry and a couple of his wizards. We don't know if it was Baylor we don't know what he looks like."

Michael walked over to the head of the scout team, he touched his forehead and projected the image of Baylor into his mind.

"Is this him" asked Michael

"yes Michael that's the same person we saw talking to Henry."

"Do you think they sensed your presence or had any idea someone was watching."

"No we're sure no one knew we were there, we followed your instructions, we were very careful.

Michael returned to his place at the table and said to everyone "this is very good news we may have found their main base. We need each of you to return home and prepare we will attack the area in two days. Dade and I will work out plans for the attack but we welcome any input any of you may have. Once we have a plan together which indicates what everyone will do we let everyone know prior to the attack. We don't want to be stepping on each other's toes everyone needs to know what their assignment is and where they will concentrate their energies."

As soon as they returned to ghostra they went straight to work. They set up a table and started working on a strategy. Michael, Elaina, Dade, Durell and Miles all huddled around the table and jotted down ideas and thoughts on what the enemy might do and what they should do. The three wizards who had scouted the area went over exactly what they saw and heard. Richard arrived a short while later and was updated on everything they had discussed. The time seemed to fly by. It was getting dark when they decided to break for the evening. Michael handed Dade the notes and suggestions everyone had.

"Dade if you and Richard get together tomorrow and work out the assignments for the other mage, I'll work on how best to deploy Durell's team and the sisters. Then will meet in the afternoon and go over it all. We don't want to be stepping on each other's toes during the battle so everything needs to be coordinated."

"All right Michael" said Dade

Richard said, "Michael you still determined to bring the women of the temple to the fight."

"Of course" Michael said, "I wouldn't insult them by leaving them behind."

"I understand Michael. I just don't want to see any of them get hurt."

"Neither do I Richard. But I can't leave them behind they know the danger will handle themselves with the honor and strength they have shown me the past couple of years. I know they're ready I just hope the wizards are as prepared."

Dade said, "they will be, we'll see to it." Then he and Richard left.

Elaina smiled and Durell said, "thank you Michael for sticking up for my sisters."

"I meant what I said Durell, in fact you're all like my family. Besides I'm sure will need them."

He had a very serious look on his face.

Elaina said "what do you mean Michael."

"Well think about it the wizards have not developed fighting skills. They normally don't need them. They have their magic. So I'm pretty sure that Baylor will try and take advantage of that and will probably have the front line of his assault the creatures that magic has no effect on like Bogan's. The sisters are all skilled fighters and can handle them while the wizards and mage concentrate on the rest of the creatures. Elaina and I will take on Baylor and whoever else he may have with him. Durell you and your order will go after Edward and his wizards and take care of the sisters as much as possible without putting yourself or your wizards in danger and one other thing."

Michael reached into his pocket and took out a crystal.

"What is that said Elaina"

"this is one of the crystals I found in my sanctuary when I first went there. At first I had no idea what they were used for or why they were there. But in my books I found that there are many uses for them depending on the spell that's used. This one I said in case anyone tries sneaking up behind us the way Edward did to Richard. I have a feeling he'll try again. Which one of you want it."

Durell spoke first "I'll take it Michael."

"Are you sure you already have a lot on your plate."

"I'm sure, Edward and his wizards and mine."

Miles spoke, "you're good Michael I never would've thought of that. Sneaking up from behind sounds just like Edward. Don't worry will handle it."

"Good, but enough work let's eat and then go relax on the balcony come on miles join us."

They sat and ate and then went to relax on the balcony.

Miles looked out and said, "the view from here is amazing you do this often."

Elaina said, "yes miles almost every night."

A little while later Evie came in. "Hi guys how you all doing."

"Fine Evie, where have you been."

"Well I peeked in earlier but you seemed busy and I didn't want to interrupt."

"You should've come in we could have used your input."

"Really Mike"

"sure Evie, you have a good head on your shoulders."

She smiled and sat down with them. They all just sat and talked for a while.

Then Miles said, "this is tremendous and I could sit here forever but I need to go I have to brief the wizards on what's happening we need to be prepared."

They said their goodbyes and miles left.

Durell said, "I should go now too. I need to try and get some rest if I can."

After Durell left Michael, Elaina and Evie while relaxing all fell asleep in their lounges.

The next morning it was Michael who woke first. He reached over and woke Elaina. She looked or frowned for a moment and said, "well Michael looks like we did it again"

he laughed "yes it seems like it's becoming a habit"

they went and had some breakfast and Michael said, "before Dade and Richard arrive I need to go see's Cassondra and see what she wants to do before I sealed their realm. I have to give her the choice. I'd like for you to go and brief the matris and the others about our plans. Then if there's time meet me in the Guardian sanctuary, otherwise we'll meet back here."

"Okay Michael, I'll do my best to meet you there."

She left to find the matris while Michael headed to the library. Once there he went straight to the sanctuary. He went to the altar and called her name and she appeared right away.

"Cassondra it's time you need to decide what you're going to do. Will you come here or stay in your realm."

"I've thought about it a lot Michael and at first I was going to stay in my realm out of loyalty to my people. But one of the guardians is missing our leaders have tried locating him but can't he shielded. I can't let you try to take on Baylor and a guardian at the same time. I know you have Elaina and she is very powerful and a skilled fighter. But they won't let her get close enough to use these skills and even with all the power she possesses she still a novice at magical combat compared to them. So I've decided to come through and help you."

"I thank you for that Cassondra but don't make your decision based on that. I still haven't found the spell to unlock your realm once this is overAnd don't know if it even exists."

"I know Michael and I'm still willing to help."

"All right Cassondra come completely through."

She did as you requested. He then took out another of those strange crystals and placed it on the altar. He stepped back and recited the spell. The crystal floated to the circle and formed a door with a strange symbol on it and then vanished.

"Is that it" asked Cassondra

"I don't know that should be it. I've never done this before."

Cassondra walked to the circle close her eyes but nothing happened.

She said, "well I guess it worked I can't go back."

"Come on Cassondra let's get you some regular clothes. Dade and Richard will be here soon and I'd like you there for the meeting."

They left the sanctuary just as Elaina entered the library.

"Cassondra you're here, that's great we can use your help"

"hello Elaina it's nice to be here."

"Elaina would you take Cassondra and get her some clothes of our order. Then meet me back at my room."

When Michael got to his room Evie was sitting at the table.

"Well Mikey, you left me again. I woke up and you and Elaina were gone."

"Sorry Evie but we had things to do and didn't want to wake you."

"Okay Mikey. Mike are we really going to attack the enemy base tomorrow."

"Not you Evie, I need you here."

"Oh come on Mikey you're always leaving me behind. I need to stand with the rest of my sisters."

"It's not like that Evie. I need you and a few of the others to stay here just in case they try to get past our defenses and get into Ghostra. I need you to alert us and hold them off until we arrive, can you do that."

"Oh! Okay Mikey we can do that for you."

"Thanks Evie I know I can count on you."

Just then Elaina and Cassondra came in.

"Michael said "well Cassondra now you fit in with the rest of us." Cassondra smiled.

"A short while later Dade and Richard arrived.

"Michael greeted them, "well you know Elaina and Durell and this is Cassondra. This is what we have so far. Elaina Cassondra and I will be going after Baylor and whoever he has with him. Durell and her team will go after Edward and his wizards and just so that you know there may be a guardian with them."

"A guardian" said Richard "how are we supposed to defend against a guardian and fight the evil minions he has."

"Don't worry, leave the Guardian to us. Also I expect the front of the attack will be creatures that magic won't affect. If I'm correct the sisters of the Dragon order will take the frontline. Just do what you can to keep them from the magical creatures and be sure not to hit them with your spells. You come up with for the rest of the mage and wizards."

"Michael are you sure you want to put the ladies in harm's way."

"I'm sure, they're all skilled fighters and can keep you from having to worry about the Bogan's and others where your magic won't work."

Okay, well Michael the scouts gave us a rundown of the layout of the area we kind of spread all the teams out so the enemy can concentrate all their energy into one area then we've given everyone several possible scenarios depending on how they come out us. But Michael we have no idea how many there are."

"I know Dade, but we have to end this. Failing is not an option. We have to win this and we need to win it decisively. Tell the others we will assemble tomorrow at seven in the Council chambers and leave from there."

"Alright Michael will see you then"

after they left Elaina came over to Michael and said, "Michael what if you make some of us invisible that way they wouldn't see us coming."

"No Elaina, I thought of that but our side wouldn't be able to see us either and some could get killed or seriously injured by our own side."

"You're right, I hadn't thought of that."

"What about you Cassondra any ideas."

"No Michael you seem to have it worked out fine."

They went and sat at the table. Michael's mind was wandering. "What's wrong Michael" asked Elaina.

"Oh nothing Elaina, I'm just going over everything in my mind. I always feel I'm missing something."

Cassondra said, "you've done everything you can Michael you need to relax and you need to be at your best tomorrow. If a guardian is with them tomorrow I'll deal with him."

"Tell me about him Cassondra. Why would a guardian come to such an illogical conclusion about the fate of the world."

"Well Michael he is probably the one who came up with this crazy idea of letting evil rule the world. He once sat on the high Council but was removed because of his radical ideas about our role in the world, none of which conformed to the original rules we live by. At one point he suggested we destroy life on your world and start over with a more active role in its development which is against our main rule that was set down when we were first created."

"Well I guess we'll see tomorrow" said Michael.

As the day closed and night fell they once again found themselves relaxing on the balcony but they broke up early to get well rested. Michael thought he would have hard time falling asleep with everything on his mind, but he barely put his head on his pillow when he fell fast asleep.

25

THE NEXT MORNING MICHAEL ROSE early feeling refreshed. He hurried to the bathroom and got cleaned up and dressed in his armor. He took Dragon's breath from the cupboard and strapped it on his waist. He then rushed to the training area where all the sisters were waiting. He asked the matris if she had selected those who would stay behind.

"Yes Michael I have chosen the younger sisters to stay with Evelyn."

"Okay that's great."

He went over to Evie.

"Evie, you and the others keep a sharp eye out for anything unusual. They may send some creatures to try to get past our defenses while were occupied. If they do send word immediately and do what you can until we arrive, okay."

"Okay Mikey we won't let you down."

"Good, were not expecting trouble but keep your eyes open just in case."

He then turned to the others "all right sisters does everyone know what to do, either any questions?"

The matris said, "no Michael were good we have gone over it several times."

"Good then let's go."

Michael encircled them all in an energy field and they transported to the area just outside the Council chamber. They walked in and the room was full.

"Are we all here" asked Michael

"yes Michael" said Richard last mage in his wizards just arrived moments ago."

"Good has everyone gotten their assignments."

"Yes we've just been waiting for you to arrive, we are ready to go."

Michael addressed everyone "are there any questions."

One of the master wizard spoke, "Michael is it true that there may be a guardian with them."

"Yes, it's possible."

"How are we supposed to take on this Baylor and Henry in his wizards and whatever creatures they have and the Guardian."

"Elaina and I will deal with Baylor and whoever is with him. Cassondra will deal with the Guardian and Durell and her wizards will handle Henry and his wizards."

"No offense but how is one of your priestesses going to deal with a guardian."

"Cassondra is not a priestess, she is a guardian."

The room went silent. Michael looked around everyone was speechless.

"Okay, are there any more questions?"

No one spoke, Dade came over to Michael "well done Michael, that shut them up."

"Yeah Dade you could hear the proverbial pin drop. Okay let's not put this off any longer let's go."

They all separated into the groups that Dade and Richard had arranged for them. Elaina, Cassondra, Durell and her wizards as well as the sisters all grouped with Michael.

Michael yelled "now" and in a flash they were gone.

They arrived within the target area each group was spread out the caves were ahead of them about three dozen creatures were outside the caves. Off to the left was Baylor along with the Guardian and Edwards wizards.

Baylor said, "well Michael, we knew you would find it sooner or later and we've been preparing for it."

Michael responded "send your evil hordes back where they belong and you can go home and will forget this mess ever happened."

Baylor waved his hand in a rift opened and out poured all kinds of creatures. As Michael expected the Bogan's and other creatures which magic won't affect led the way. The ladies of the order got into position waiting for them. Baylor fired at Michael but Michael responded quickly. The Guardian started attacking what was expertly countered by Cassondra. Elaina was also attacking both Baylor and the Guardian. Durell put a shield around the sisters to protect them from magic her and her wizards then countered attacks by Edwards wizards but Durell still saw no sign of Edward. All of the mage and there wizards had already engaged the oncoming assault. The sisters now went beyond Durell's shield and began fighting the oncoming creatures.

Durell yelled to Michael "the sisters are no longer protected what shall we do."

"There is nothing we can do now. Just hope will be all right."

The battle raged on creatures were dropping but more and more came, there was no end in sight. Michael and Baylor were locked in battle. Spell after spell of fire or lightning and powerful energy blasts were flying everywhere. Suddenly Durell felt the crystal telling her an attack was coming from behind. She spun around and saw Edward firing a lightning bolt which hit one of the sisters and dropped her to the ground. Durell screamed "NO" and began a vicious attack on Edward. He fired back but the real blocked and returned fire blast after just blast Edward was backing away with a look of shock on his face. Then it happened three blasts right in a row got through his defenses and hit him dead on and he went down hard. Durell then turned back with a devastating attack on Henry's wizards another of the sisters went down from a lightning blast. Michael saw that three of the wizards were down and not moving into others were hurt.

Richard call to Michael, "Michael we need to get out of here were about to be overwhelmed there's just too many. No matter how many we kill more just keep coming we can hold them off for much longer." Michael looked out at the scene it look like thousands of creatures now. He called to Elaina can you keep Baylor busy for just a moment."

"Yes Michael I'll take care of it."

Michael got behind her and dropped to one knee and called out with his mind. "Malum, Elon we need you."

And then he heard their thoughts, "we hear you young prince and we are on our way." Michael got up and resumed his attack on Baylor. Suddenly the ground shook in a dark cloud formed above them, and out of the clouds to dragons appeared. They swooped down flying low over the attacking creatures with flames incinerating everything in their path.

The creatures turned and ran for what they thought was the protection of the caves. They were climbing over just to get away from the dragons.

Baylor and seeing the dragons quickly opened the portal and jumped in. The Guardian tried to follow but the portal closed behind Baylor. He then tried to open a portal back to his realm but it wouldn't open. Then he opened a portal to another realm. But Michael drew his sword spoke the words in a fireball flew toward the Guardian. The Guardian threw up a shield spell but the fireball passed right through unhindered catching him in the chest and Cassondra cast the spell incinerating him even before he hit the ground. Elon flew past the creatures and blasted the entrances to the caves collapsing them. Michael opened a huge portal back to their realm and they ran into it as fast as they could. The wizards were cheering but the mage were not as excited they gathered around the four wizards that had fallen in battle. When the wizards realized their joy turned to sorrow. The dragons landed in front of Michael and bowed. Michael returned their bow. "Thank you my friends we couldn't have done this without you."

"We will always be there for you young prince. Now we'll return to Ghostra, just call if you need us again."

They flew off and disappeared into the clouds. The sisters were gone down stood back up. Michael looked at Elaina and Durell looked just as surprised as he was.

He said "how is this possible I saw them hit with powerful magic. The matris ran over and hugged the sisters "you're alive it's a miracle."

Cassondra looked at them she noticed the runes they were wearing around their neck.

She asked, where did you get these."

The matris said "Michael gave them to each of us"

"Michael where did you get these, they are stoic crystals."

Michael said "these are crystals that I magically made into protective runes, are you saying these are what save them."

"Yes, I've only seen stoic crystal once it was a gift from the first Dragon mage to his aide."

"Well I knew they would enhance their abilities but how did it save them Cassondra."

The way they work Michael is with the proper spell they absorb energy from the spell, and when a non-magic person puts it on it becomes there's and gives its energy to them. That is how it enhances their abilities. But the crystal is then drained of energy, but the spell stays with the crystal so that when they are hit with energy the crystal absorbed most of that energySo they were not hurt. It makes them almost immune to magical attack."

"What you mean by almost immune."

Well it takes a while for the crystal to drain the energy absorbed. So if they were hit multiple times before it could drain the crystal would break trying to absorb more than he can handle and the wearer could die."

"So the rune does more than just enhance their abilities." "Yes Michael much more."

Michael looked over at the fallen wizards. "I should've made some for the wizards."

"It wouldn't worked on them Michael. The crystal couldn't give its energy to them they already have magic. The crystals would be useless to a wizard or mage."

Michael walked over to the mage and wizards. "We need to take the time to honor those who have fallen. Today we will mourn and bury our comrades and tomorrow we will all meet in the Council chamber and inscribed their names in a place of honor on the chamber walls so all of us and all those who come after us will know of their sacrifice."

Cassondra said I saw their spirits leave them they all went to the good realm. People can go there only spirits and in that realm they will enjoy eternal peace."

Many of those listening had tears well up in their eyes.

The wizards began to gather their wounded and dead. The matris went over to them and said

"we will carry them back is our way to honor them." They made stretchers and the sisters lifted them and carried them through the rift. They reappeared outside the Council chambers where they slowly walked inside and placed the bodies down and gathered around them. They got on their knees and prayed for them.

Michael asked, "what do we normally do with the bodies now."

Richard said, "their order will normally take the bodies back with them and bury or dispose of the body their own way."

"I don't think that's good enough for them" said Michael "I think we should bury them just outside the Council chambers with proper markers for everyone to see. Their heroes and deserve to be remembered."

"That's a nice idea Michael let's put it to a vote."

They put the idea forward to be voted on and the vote was unanimous. Metal coffins were magically made and graves were dug. The bodies were carefully lowered into the graves. The markers were placed over the graves with their names, their order and their colors.

Michael announced, "they are here so that their friends and loved ones can pay their respects whenever they want."

When they returned to Ghostra the sisters turned toward Michael and got down on one knee. Michael looked at them.

"What is this" he said

Elaina said, "they're thanking you for putting your trust in them."

The matris added, "and for saving our sisters lives with your special gift."

Michael said, "please arise is I owe each of you my thanks, you performed with bravery and skill and probably save more lives with your courage. Now get some rest you earned it."

Evie came running over. "How did you go Mikey, nothing happened here."

"That's good Evie. We won the battle. We drove the evil creatures back to their realm, but Baylor got away and four of the wizards were killed. We paid a high price for this victory. We're heading back to my room want to come along."

"I'll be along later Mikey I'm going to talk with the sisters and make sure they're all okay."

Elaina, Cassondra, Dade, Durell and Miles all went back to Michael's room.

Cassondra said, "they have great respect for you Michael."

"It's I who have great respect for them. They were amazing today."

Kathy and Herbert had brought their dinner.

Michael said." And what you guys start eating Elaina and I will be back shortly." They exited the room and Elaina asked, "what's up Michael."

While he waved his hand and they popped up to the roof. Malum in a line bowed to them and they returned the bow.

"My friends, the war is over. Many thanks to you. So now it's time for me to keep my promise. It's time for you to return home to be with your family. They miss you terribly. About"

"Elon said "home, we've been away so long."

Malum said, "if you sure you won't need us any longer we would love to see our family again.

"If I need you my friends I know where to find you. But for now" he waved his hand and opened the portal "go home meet those you left behind and tell them Elaina and I will be home soon."

"We will young Prince." And they flew off into the portal and were gone. Then Michael and Elaina returned to the others. When they got there everyone was eating and talking.

Michael interrupted "tomorrow after the ceremony Elaina and I will be leaving."

"Dade asked what you mean leaving, where are you going."

"We're going home. Cassondra I was wondering if you would be willing to take my place while were gone."

She looked at Michael, she hadn't expected this. She looked around at the others then she said,

"yes Michael I would be honored to help while you're away."

Dade said, "will this be a permanent move, you will be coming back won't do Michael."

"I've thought about it Dade and yes I will come back I have made too many friends not to."

As they broke up for the evening Durell said "Dade if it's okay I'd like to go with you and Miles tonight. I think I should be close to the wizards of my order."

"Of course Durell happy to have you."

Michael said, "Durell give your wizards my thanks, they performed admirably today and Dade please tell the gray order the same. I'm proud of all of them."

"I will Michael, I know they'll appreciate it."

After they left Cassondra said she was going to retire to her room. Michael and Elaina went to the balcony Michael made two glasses of wine and they just sat and enjoyed the view.

"Michael said, "this is one of the things I'll miss the most, our time relaxing here on the balcony."

"I know" said Elaina "Michael just think how beautiful it is where were going. The gardens in the view from the tower. Plus will get to spend time with your Mom and Grandfather."

"You're right Elaina it's going to be great. One thing that you can do for me that would make it better."

"What is that Michael."

"Elaina will you marry me."

Elaina was caught completely off guard, she was speechless.

"Do you need me to ask again" said Michael

Elaina was crying, "yes Michael course I'll marry you." He put his arms around her and kissed her.

"Tomorrow after the Council ceremony, I'll have Evie contact mom I'd like her to be here if possible."

"Michael I'm so happy" she threw her arms around him. Just then Evie came in

"hey none of that you two."

Michael said, "Evie, Elaina and I are getting married."

Evie started screaming, "that's fantastic, I always knew you would. When are you having the wedding. Will I be there. That's crazy of course I will I'm your sister. I know what about mom and grandfather."

"Evie relax, take a breath we want to get married tomorrow before we go home. I need you to contact mom. I want her to be here and grandfather too if possible."

"Okay Mikey, I'm on it. I'll go right now." And she ran out of the room. Michael and Elaina looked at each other and both laughed.

"I'm going to Michael. I need to tell the matris and my sisters, they'll want to prepare."

"Okay Elaina, I'll see you in the morning."

The next morning Michael woke to find Evie, Elaina and the matris all sitting in chairs next to his bed.

"Hello, is something wrong."

Evie jumped in, "no Mikey we were just waiting for you to get up. This is all very exciting. I told mom she said she would be here for the wedding she's very excited too."

"Okay, calm down Evie I'm not even awake yet."

The matris said, "this is a monumentus occasion Michael. For the Dragon Mage to marry one of our sisters doesn't happen every day, in fact it's never happened. So you will forgive us if we were all very excited."

"Yes of course Emily, but let's not forget we have a solemn morning to get through first."

"Yes certainly Michael the sisters are getting ready as we speak."

"Oh I didn't know you were all coming to the ceremony."

"Yes Michael, we feel we need to acknowledge their courage and sacrifice."

"That's nice, I'm sure it will be greatly appreciated."

Evie and the matris left to get ready. Elaina took Michael's hand "you made me very happy Michael."

She kissed him and left to get changed. A Short while later Dade arrived with Durell and her wizards and the gray order.

"Hello Michael, we got here a little early where is everyone?" Asked Dade

"they're all getting ready for both **ceremonies**."

"Both ceremonies, What you mean"

"Elaina and I are getting married this afternoon."

For a moment they were all speechless. Then Dade said "I knew you two cared for each other but WOW this is amazing news."

Durell threw her arms around him and said, "this is incredible Michael, I know you will both be very happy together."

The wizards all came and congratulated Michael and shook his hand.

Michael asked everyone to sit and relax while he went to see if the sisters were ready. When he got to the great hall they were all dressed in black.

"Wow" he said, "you all look amazing."

The matris said, "we honor those brave souls who gave their lives for peace."

Michael went over to Evie. "You look spiffy to Evie."

"Thanks Mike, apparently this is a great honor to attend their memorial dressed like this, and this time I'm going I'm not staying behind."

"There is no need for you to stay behind this time the evil is gone and we don't need anyone to guard the temple, our protective barrier is all the protection we need now."

"He asked Evie to get Dade and the others. Cassondra arrived and said "this ceremony is a nice gesture Michael but their spirits have already passed to the other realm. They won't know what you're doing for them."

"Cassondra, a funeral and the ceremony are more for those who are still here. It's nice to know your friends or loved ones will not be forgotten."

"I see" she said

when the others arrived they all teleported to the area outside the Council chambers and walked in. The sisters walked off to one side and kneeled down and began a soft chant.

Michael walked to the wall.

Richard said, "Michael we'll have to drop the magical barrier or carve the names by hand."

Michael looked at him "that will not be necessary Richard."

He took a list and called out their names and as he spoke the names were etched into the stone.

He spoke slowly "Jack Warren, Tim Hastings, Greg Matthews, and James Perkins. We honor these wizards for their sacrifice but we also honor each and every one of you for your actions against an overwhelming evil that would have destroyed the world as we know it. But our work has just begun. We now have to keep the world from destroying itself through its ignorance and greed. We need to put our people in positions of authority in the governments of the world and slowly work toward peace between all nations."

After the ceremony everyone talked for a while then the wizards left and Michael sent the ladies back to the temple with his thanks. the mage all went to the meeting table.

Michael said, "later today Elaina and I will be leaving and will be gone for a while, in the meantime I've asked Cassondra to take my place if that's agreeable to the Council."

"You're not leaving for good are you Michael" asked Richard

"Dade asked me the same question the answer is no I will be back just not for a while. If I'm needed Dade can get in touch with me."

"Okay Michael, I don't think anyone will object to a guardian leading the counsel for a while. You came up with a great idea to put our people in power to help create peace. Instead of just reacting to prevent catastrophes we can actually move the world in the right direction toward peace. It won't happen overnight but it's our best chance to get more involved."

As the meeting broke up Michael and the others went back to Ghostra. When they got there Cassondra said, "that's a brilliant idea Michael. I can see I was right to trust you, for the first time there really is the hope of peace."

"Yes, you Dade and Richard can work out the details and then get all the others involved. If you get them all working toward the same goal it's much more likely to succeed."

Evie and Noreen came into the room. Michael went to his mother and hugged her. Cassondra came over to them "you're Michael's mother, you must be very proud of him he has come up with a plan to finally bring peace to the world."

"I've always been proud of my son and peace is what Creighton hoped for when he created the mage counsel. You must be the guardian I heard about, it's a pleasure to meet you. Well Michael getting married. I didn't expect that this soon, but I'm very happy for you both." She hugged him again

"Evie where is Elaina she should be here."

"She's getting ready Mikey they said you can't see her now until the wedding."

Noreen said "that's all right Michael I'll go say hello and you stay here."

Evie Noreen and Cassondra left. Michael looked around just shrugged his shoulders and went to sit at the table. Dade arrived with Durell and Miles and they joined Michael at the table

"oh Dade, I forgot to ask earlier, I need a best man would you stand up for me."

"Of course Michael I'd be honored."

A little while later Noreen came to escort Michael to the great Hall. He and the others followed Noreen. When they arrived they were all amazed the hall was decorated in white and a cloud ran along the floor up the walls and across the ceiling and sort of floated all around.

Michael said "wow, this is amazing how did you do this."

"I couldn't let my son have a normal wedding."

The sisters were now dressed in all white Dade and Michael went up to the altar where the matris was waiting. Soft music began playing in the background and Elaina and Evie entered. Elaina also was in white with powder blue accents her hair was done up long and fluffy. She looked like a vision.

Dade whispered to Michael, "she looks really beautiful Michael." Michael without words just shook his head in agreement. She walked to Michael and took his hand. Noreen went to them and gave each a shiny metal ball and whispered to them what to do. They turned to the matris who began to conduct the ceremony.

Then She said "do you have the rings that will bind you to each other for life."

Michael held his hand over Elaina's and said "I give you this ring with all my love." And the ring formed around Elaina's finger. He opened his hand and the ball was gone. Elaina held out her hand and said "I give you this ring with all my love" and the ring formed around Michael's finger then the matris said "with the power placed on me as head of the sisters of the Dragon order I pronounce you husband and wife." Everyone started to cheer.

The matris said, you may kiss your bride Michael."

He took Elaine in his arms and gave her a long passionate kiss, everyone was still cheering.

Evie said, "okay, you two can come up for air anytime now."

They both broke their kiss and laughed, Noreen was crying and hugged them both.

Michael said "I'm looking forward to just relaxing for a while and not worrying about war or evil or most of all Baylor.

Elaina said "but we can't stay away too long some of the sisters may retire from service and leave the temple to make room for others."

"Really" said Michael "I've always wondered what happened to the older sisters."

Noreen interrupted, "I don't think that's going to be a problem. The runes that you gave the sisters should extend their lives by nearly 200 years."

Elaina and Michael looked at each other and Michael said, "what you mean mom, is that true."

"Yes Michael, the runes gather and store energy that it gives to the owner the person that it has become part of. It will constantly revitalize the priestess that owns the rune by giving its energy to them."

"But where does the energy come from" asked Michael

"well just like when you create a mage or wizard by drawing on the forces all around you. Whether it be the light the wind the air or even the ground itself. Once the spell has been placed on it and absorbs the energy all around it."

"Wow this is great news" said Elaina, "we'll have our sisters and friends for a long time. I've got to go tell the matris and the others the wonderful news."

"Thanks mom, I've grown very fond of all of them. It's nice to know they'll be around for a while."

Noreen waved her hand in the clouds disappeared and they could see food and drink on the table along the wall that had been covered by clouds. They all ate and danced and had a good time for the rest of the day. As the sun began to fade Michael said "it's time to go."

He thanked Dade for everything. He hugged Durell and each of the sisters as did Elaina. It was a very emotional time.

Then he said to Evie "are you sure you're going to stay for a while."

"Yes Mike, I'll be sure to let you know when I want to come home."

"All right Evie, Dade will let you know if he needs me for anything important."

Then he hugged her. Noreen also hugged her and then Elaina.

Then he turned to the matris, "we'll see you all soon, but not too soon."

She replied take as much time as you need Michael will all be here when you get back."

He Elaina and Noreen went to the library and straight to the sanctuary. Michael took book number one from its hiding place and said "after all this time I'm still only halfway through the first book."

"We are ready when you are mom."

Noreen waved her hand and opened the portal home. She took Michael's hand he took Elaina's hand and they stepped into the portal and went home.

The end

Even as a child the Author like telling made up Stories to tell both family and friends, but never thought he would actually write a book. As he grew up the story telling became a thing of the past, after the Military he went on to become an electronic and computer technician. But he still love fictional stories. but no matter how many films he saw or books he read he always felt something was missing. So he decided to write stories. He was only expecting to write a short story but once he started writing the words and ideas just seemed to flow and the next thing you know he has the book he always wanted to write.

Lightning Source UK Ltd.
Milton Keynes UK
UKHW011351271220
375924UK00007B/438/J